THE
DIVINEXUS
By
HALLIE MATTHEWS

COPYRIGHT

Table of Contents

Chapter one

As she stood nervously in front of the wooden church doors, Grace felt an ever-familiar rush of loneliness wash over her. She had been alone for almost her entire life, and this moment would be no different. She had no father to walk her down the aisle, no mother to fuss over her hair or her dress. Nobody to tell her how proud they were of the woman she had grown into. Grace had become used to being alone; she had learnt to be self-sufficient, and necessity bred a fierce independence within her. Despite all of this, the ache for someone who was there just for her was ever present and threatened to consume her.

Her earliest memory flashed through her mind. The first time she arrived at a foster home to live with a family that she did not know. Scared and alone, that was the beginning of the endless moving around from one family to another. Love was not something her foster parents readily shared with her.

One wet and windy morning at school, Grace met Charlie. He was the first person who spoke to Grace with any amount of decency. After years of verbal and mental abuse, she had finally found someone to trust. That day changed her life, and things improved for her in other ways. A new couple took her in, and things settled; she liked them, and they liked her. She felt loved. Grace knew in her heart that Charlie loved her. There was no doubt about that. Despite this, she could not stop the loneliness from resurfacing.

As she stood alone, waiting for the heavy oak doors to open, a string of memories played out in her mind. Every first day at a new school, and every parents' evening, when nobody bothered to show up. This time, things were going to be different. This time, she was becoming part of a loving family, one that she had longed for her entire life. A smile spread across her face and her heart felt full.

The church doors creaked open, and Grace spotted Charlie. Her childhood sweetheart stood in front of the large and impressive altar with his best man, Alfie. Both men looked so handsome in their morning suits. Grace's heart swelled as she looked at the man that she was going to spend the rest of her life with.

There had been many discussions about the wedding; Charlie and his family were religious, and they wanted a traditional church service. Grace was not overly comfortable with religion, but she wanted them all to have a memorable day. They had accepted her into their family many years ago and so it felt right that she should honour their family beliefs.

Grace craved love, but never settled long enough to build bonds that resulted in it. Charlie's parents had given her the love and support she needed when things got tough for her. They had been her sanctuary for many years.

There was one thing that Grace had insisted on for the wedding, though. She would not be wearing a traditional white meringue dress. She had decided on something completely different.

Grace's ebony hair tumbled down in soft curls, and her piercing pale blue eyes highlighted with a light touch of make-up. She wore no jewellery and carried no flowers. Grace looked radiant in a beautiful, deep red dress, which accentuated her slender frame. Tiny jewels adorned the bodice, which caught the sunlight and sparkled like diamonds. From the waist down, the lighter material of the skirt flowed to her feet and swished as she walked. As their eyes met, a spellbound Charlie was in awe of the woman in front of him.

As Grace waited for her cue, she noticed the intricately carved stonework that adorned the building. She understood now why this church and all it stood for meant so much to Charlie and his family.

The sun cast an opalescent light through the stained glass, which gave everything and everyone a bright and beautiful glow. As the music played, Grace took a moment to compose herself and settle the incomprehensible nerves that had struck her. She looked at the small congregation; there were only a couple of their friends, and Charlie's parents. It would never be an enormous affair, but both Grace and Charlie were both extremely happy with a small and intimate service.

Grace began her walk towards her husband-to-be, shaking off the nerves and feelings of unease. She could not understand why, but something deep within her was screaming, telling her that this was wrong. Grace shook her head; she would not let self-sabotage ruin her perfect day with Charlie. Taking a deep breath, she continued to walk forward towards her new life.

With the music gently guiding her towards her future husband, Grace suddenly felt an excruciating pain in her head. She stopped walking and tried to compose herself again. The pain had come from nowhere and felt like lightning bolts in her head. Charlie had turned around to look at her again. He could not keep his eyes from her, but this time, his look of love turned to shock when he noticed the pain on Grace's face. A worried Charlie moved towards her, but she gestured to him she was alright.

One foot in front of the other was the only thing she could do. As she walked, she told herself that the pain would pass, that it was just nerves. The uneasiness resurfaced, and her head was throbbing. As she continued to walk unsteadily towards Charlie, Grace stopped to briefly hold onto one pew. The pain eased slightly, allowing her to push forward. It upset her to see the look of concern on Charlie's face, and she saw the same look etched on the faces of those in the congregation. She forced a smile as she walked.

Charlie stepped forward as Grace approached and gently took her hands in his. The half-smile on his face was one of concern, not the goofy one that she loved. He had the most infectious laugh, and he could make her smile without trying. She loved him so much and could never imagine her life without him. As she smiled back at him, happy to be there, the pain intensified and seared across her eyes. She could barely see and became so unsteady that she could barely stand, but Charlie's firm hands stopped her from collapsing to the floor. Grace took a few deep breaths to rid herself of the agony she felt.

"Are you ok?" his face still full of concern. She nodded, smiling as if to ease his worry. He seemed to relax a little as they turned to face the vicar.

"You look beautiful as always, Grace, but today you are absolutely glowing," whispered Charlie as they stood side by side.

Grace squeezed Charlie's hand and tilted her head, resting it on his shoulder for a few moments. The few guests behind them watched the young couple together as they said their vows.

"Grace, you have been the light in my life since the first day we met. I would not be the man I am today without your love and support," began Charlie, "You encourage me to be a better person every day and I promise to show you the same love, support, and respect that you have always shown me. As we grow old together, I will take care of you whenever you need me, even if I am a terrible nurse! I will be by your side through the good and the bad, through the happy and the sad times. This is my oath to you."

Grace was fighting back the tears forming at the corners of her eyes as she heard his words. Looking at Charlie, Grace stared deep into his eyes, ready to pledge her never-ending love to him.

"Charlie," began Grace.

"Divinexus! Abomination! I will destroy you!" bellowed a loud voice from the rear of the church.

It shocked Grace, and she nervously looked around the church, but she could see no one that would shout such words. Had she imagined them? Nobody else seemed to have heard them. Putting it down to nerves, she took a deep breath and looked back at Charlie. He looked confused.

"Charlie, you are my world..."

"Abomination, you will die! You should never have been born!" the disembodied voice shouted once more.

"What is it, Grace? Are you having second thoughts?" questioned a concerned Charlie.

"I am fine, sorry I think it's just nerves," replied Grace, squeezing his hand to reassure him.

"Charlie, you are my world, the centre of my universe..." she stopped again, this time there was no voice.

As she was about to continue her vows, Grace felt a heat rising through her. Her whole-body temperature got hotter and hotter, as if a fire had been lit. It was out of control and raging in every cell of her body. Pain radiated everywhere, and she could not control it. Closing her eyes for a moment, Grace tried to compose herself. She did not understand what was happening.

The heat that engulfed her was so unbearable that she stumbled forward and fell to her knees. Grace heard the voice shouting again, this time louder and more aggressively. Joined by a chorus of other voices, the noise threatened to overwhelm her. Grace closed her eyes and curled up into a ball to stave off the pain. Still, the voices rang in her ears.

"You are an abomination! One day you will seek me out and I will be waiting." Grace's body shivered violently, even though she was burning up.

"Grace, Grace, what is the matter? Look at me, tell me what is wrong!" a worried Charlie urged, crouching over her.

THE DIVINEXUS

As much as she tried, she could not open her eyes. The heat was searing inside her. Feeling dizzy and sick, Grace struggled to get to her feet. She felt off balance. Her legs would not support her, and as each second passed, the heat became increasingly unbearable. Grace fell back to the floor.

Suddenly, something pulled Grace's head back with a violent jerk. She did not know what was happening to her, scared and unable to fight back at the unseen entity taking control of her. Charlie stumbled backwards and watched in horror as her face contorted with the pain. He did not understand what was happening. All he saw was the woman he loved struggling on the floor.

As he watched helplessly, the beautiful woman in front of him appeared to be having some sort of seizure. Stepping forward again, he bent down to hold her, but as he did so, flames shot up from nowhere and surrounded Grace. The shock, coupled with intense heat, instantly forced him backwards again. He could not get near her, nor could he help her. Moments later, before anyone could react and save Grace from the flames, an explosion erupted and shook the entire building and the surrounding area. The force of the explosion caused the church to crumble around them.

White-hot flames spread, melting the stone, metal, and glass. The fire destroyed everyone and everything, to a smouldering pile of ash. At the centre, curled up in a ball, was Grace. Untouched by the fire, she had passed out from the pain just as Charlie tried to put his arms around her. She lay there, eyes closed and feeling nothing.

There had been no time for anyone to help. The fire brigade arrived quickly, but the fire was already out when they got there. Shocked at the scale of the destruction, they walked through the remains of the building, searching as they went for any survivors. It did not take long before one firefighter spotted Grace. He called to his colleagues, who quickly joined him next to her body. They looked at her in disbelief; how could she appear to be completely unburned amongst this catastrophe? Any evidence of the other guests, the priest, and the bridal party were gone. The fire swallowed all of them up.

"Is she still alive?" The Fire Chief asked one paramedic.

"She has a faint pulse, and by the look of her skin, she appears severely dehydrated. We need to get her to the hospital quickly," one paramedic explained.

"How on earth has this woman survived this? There is not a mark on her, no evidence that the flames even touched her," the paramedic asked the Fire Chief.

"I don't know. It is a miracle. I can see no other explanation at the moment," he responded.

The paramedics gently lifted Grace from where she lay in the foetal position and secured her to a stretcher. They placed lines in her veins to rehydrate her and moved her quickly into the ambulance. Grace did not open her eyes, nor did she respond to any attempts to rouse her. She remained unconscious throughout her journey to the hospital and indeed for many days afterward.

Over the next few weeks, and after exhaustive searching, the authorities could find no evidence that anyone apart from Grace had been present at the church during the blaze. Not one bone, tooth, or body part remained. Grace was the only survivor found amongst the ashes.

The investigation progressed slowly as Grace lay unconscious in a hospital. There was no obvious cause to the fire. The latest forensic testing methods available revealed nothing. With Grace unable to tell anyone what had happened, the investigation stalled. The doctors told the investigating officer they did not expect Grace to survive.

Police and fire officers worked together to find anyone who was missing, but they found nothing.

All anyone could do was wait and hope that Grace would wake up.

Chapter two

The investigation stalled. The Police Commissioner, unhappy with the progress, called in a new officer to review the case. Marcus Anderson was a relatively young officer in the force, but he had a reputation for getting results. The son of Simon Anderson, a renowned police detective, he was soon following in his father's footsteps and rising through the ranks. Simon was a legend in the department because of his dogged and unrelenting character, and the results that he achieved. Marcus was very much like his father, which had not gone unnoticed by his superior officers.

With his ability to crack complicated or inexplicable cases, Marcus had quickly become the go-to officer for anything unusual. The Police Commissioner had overseen many cases that Marcus had worked on, and he requested that he take over the investigation of this perplexing case.

Marcus impressed people, or they kept their distance because of his reputation for being a hard taskmaster and not suffering fools gladly. He was not a very sociable person and his entire focus when at work was finding answers. Some of his colleagues did not appreciate that he was so single-minded.

Eager to begin, Marcus spent a few hours reading the reports submitted by the previous team and by the fire investigation office. He was quickly disappointed that there was no evidence to prove that anybody else had been in the church with the young woman. The Fire Chief concluded that the fire started near the woman and quickly engulfed her, causing her to curl up into the foetal position to protect herself as the church burned down around her. The mystery remained how she had escaped uninjured, and nobody understood why she was unconscious. Marcus was told that the young woman had made no progress in her recovery, but despite this, he telephoned the hospital to see if there had been any change in her condition.

He was yet to visit the young woman, and after reading the handover reports, he noted that nobody had been to the hospital for at least a couple of weeks. To Marcus, that was unacceptable, and he resolved to change it. After a quick coffee, he tidied his desk and made his way out of the office.

"I am just off to visit our victim," Marcus announced to no one in particular. A young officer tasked with collating all pertinent documentation for the investigation nodded and continued with what he was doing, without engaging Marcus in conversation.

Marcus made his way to the car park, grabbing the keys to one of the designated pool cars on his way out of the building. The drive was slow; roadworks and accidents thwarted him from getting anywhere quickly. He listened to the news on the radio while he waited in another static queue of traffic.

"The government has come under fire today after the chancellor admitted his failure to implement certain policies that would have eased this latest economic downturn..." he heard a faceless voice announce on the radio. Fed up with bad news everywhere, Marcus leant over slightly to choose a different station. He settled on one that was playing music from the 1980s, which was an era that he loved to listen to. Marcus was soon singing along to the likes of *Madness, U2* and *Adam and the Ants.*

Eventually, the traffic in front of Marcus moved, and he continued his journey towards the facility where the unidentified woman had recently transferred to. Located just outside the city boundary, Velatus House Rehabilitation Centre offered specialist treatment for patients who needed long-term care, as well as care for those who showed no signs of recovery. He made a mental note to investigate who had funded the transfer - treatment centres like this were not cheap, so someone must know who this Jane Doe was.

Marcus put his indicator on and turned left into the driveway. It surprised him how it appeared; far from looking like anything remotely medical, it was more in keeping with being a country manor house. A dark imposing building loomed in front of him. He got a chill looking at it. An old building, it appeared well maintained. The closer Marcus got to the building, the more uneasy he felt. He could not explain it, but this place gave off weird vibes.

As Marcus pulled up to the front of the main entrance, he felt for a second that he may have arrived at the wrong address. If this was a medical facility, why was there no sign of anyone? Why was there no signage? He double checked his notes against his navigation system and found that he was in the right place.

As he got out of the car, Marcus saw a gardener tending to one of the large flower beds on the opposite side of the lawn. He had noticed the heavily scented air and to his left, he spotted a bed filled with roses and dahlias. Marcus smiled; he had known nothing about flowers before he had met Stephen. In fact, he only knew what dahlias were because they were his husband's favourites!

As he looked up from the flowers, he noticed the gardener watching him. The man had stopped what he was doing and was now staring in his direction. Marcus raised a hand to greet him, which prompted the gardener to pack his tools into his wheelbarrow and to swiftly make his way off in the opposite direction. Taken aback slightly by the rudeness of the gardener, Marcus continued his way up the path towards the stone steps that led up to the door of the building.

Moments later, Marcus was standing in front of the large wooden doors that he had assumed were the entrance to the facility. He went to open the door to go in, but found it locked. Marcus looked to his right and found an access panel with an illuminated screen. He pressed the button and heard a bell echoing somewhere in the distance. There was no response, and so he tried the button once more. Again, there was no response to his call, but just as he was about to press the button for a third time, he heard a click on the panel. "Yes, who are you?" snapped a female voice.

"Detective Sergeant Marcus Anderson, I am here to see the woman from the church fire."

"Do you have some identification?"

"I do," an impatient Marcus replied.

"Hold it up to the screen, Detective."

Marcus removed his warrant card from his pocket and held it up to the screen as she had asked. He heard a click, and the door opened. Stood in the doorway was a woman. He assumed it was the one that had asked him for his identification. The stern and unfriendly looking woman looked Marcus up and down before making eye contact.

"Come in. My name is Sister Margaret, and I am one of the nursing staff here."

It shocked Marcus to see that Sister Margaret was a nun. He had been unaware that the rehabilitation facility was a religious place.

"I am tasked with investigating the fire at the church, and to work out who our mystery woman is. Can I see her please?" he replied.

"I will take you to her room. She is still unconscious, and the doctors do not know whether she will ever wake up or recover in any meaningful way." She spoke coldly and her tone was flat, showing not a hint of compassion. Marcus found it very odd, considering her profession.

"I thought it would be highly unlikely that I could speak to her, but I wanted to visit, anyway." Marcus took nothing he was told at face value.

Sister Margaret beckoned for Marcus to follow her. Not one door was open along the maze of corridors that they walked through. Some had little glass windows in them, but all Marcus could see was darkness. He noticed that the building was weirdly quiet and wondered if it was void of other patients. Eventually, Sister Margaret gestured at one door.

"She is in this room," Sister Margaret announced as she opened the door. Marcus looked through into the room and took in the scene in front of him. The décor was very much in keeping with the country manor styling of the building. Heavy curtains hung at the enormous windows; the dusty, worn material had seen better days. A modern plastic venetian blind was down, stopping any sunlight from brightening the room.

In the darkness, Marcus could just make out a bed surrounded by medical monitors in the centre of the room. As his eyes adjusted, Marcus could just about see a woman's dark hair splayed across a white pillow. In the dim light, she appeared to have various wires attached to her, and he could hear that she was on a ventilator. As Marcus stepped further into the room, Sister Margaret told him not to stay too long as she stepped back out into the corridor and left him alone with the woman. He thanked her as she left but got no response as she closed the door behind her.

As soon as she had left, Marcus opened the blinds fully. The light beams from the sun, bathed the young woman in an angelic light; he studied her face and wondered again how she could have survived the fire that had reduced the church to ash with no visible injuries.

There was a big comfortable chair next to the bed, nothing like you would get on a hospital ward. Marcus sat down in it and talked to her.

"Hello, I am Marcus. It is nice to meet you," he began. "I am the detective investigating what happened at the church.

You need to wake up. I need your help to figure out what happened to you."

As he expected, there was no response. Marcus sat quietly, watching her chest rise and fall in time with the noises from the ventilator. He did not know how long he had been sitting there, but the afternoon had seemed to get away from him. The sunlight had faded, and he could see the afternoon had become early evening. The next thing he knew, an angry-looking Sister Margaret had entered the room with another nun. It shocked Marcus that he had sat there for so long; he was not one to stay still for more than a few minutes normally.

"I thought I told you not to stay long!" Sister Margaret snapped, her eyes narrowing as she spoke. "I take it that there was no response or movement from her, as I predicted?"

"No, nothing. Has anyone else been in to visit her?"

"Nobody. You would have thought someone would be missing her. It is incredibly sad - she seems to be completely alone in the world," replied the second nun, much to Sister Margaret's displeasure.

"I would like to speak to one of her doctors, if there is someone available." Marcus said, dissatisfied with Sister Margaret's unhelpful attitude. He wanted more information than she seemed willing to share.

"No, the doctor treating her is not on site. Of course, I could pass a message on if you would like?" Sister Margaret replied, her tone suggesting that she was becoming purposefully obstructive.

"No, that will not be necessary. I will be back tomorrow. Hopefully, there will be someone available then."

"You have all the information we can tell you about her condition. The doctors cannot add more to that, so it would be best that you do not to disturb them."

Marcus handed Sister Margaret his card as he stood up, ready to leave.

"If there is any change, or if she wakes up, please contact me on this number." Sister Margaret regarded the card for a second before passing it to her colleague.

The other nun, who walked slightly in front of him and in complete silence, escorted Marcus to the building entrance. As he walked, he reflected on Sister Margaret's demeanour and looked more closely at the building. There were no religious crosses or artefacts to suggest that the building was one of faith. In fact, the only part of the facility that suggested a religious link was the nuns themselves, and Sister Margaret did not strike him as being a typical woman of the cloth. Marcus was uneasy and felt that the whole place needed looking at; nothing about it felt right. He thanked the nun who had escorted him to the exit and walked out of the building towards his car. There were a lot of unanswered questions, and he found himself even more determined to find out what had happened on that day.

Marcus sank into the driver's seat of his car and telephoned the office. He instructed his colleague to run a complete check on the facility; if they had any hope of progressing this investigation, they needed to know everything about who was running things there. He hung up the call and turned the key in the ignition. Marcus had not realised it until just then, but the day had exhausted him. It was an effort to even shift into reverse and back the car down the driveway.

Distracted by his thoughts as he drove away from the building, Marcus knew that the investigation was going to be long and complex. He hoped the woman would wake up but based on the information he had about her condition; he doubted that she ever would. The thought dragged his mood down even further - nobody deserved to be stuck on a ventilator indefinitely.

Chapter three

G race had heard a voice that she did not recognise in the distance. She could not follow what he was saying, but she heard him say something about a church.

As soon as she heard the word church, Grace was back in the fractured memories of her wedding day. In her dream, it was a beautiful day, and she was wearing the dress that had caught her eye in a local shop. Even before Charlie had proposed to her, she knew she would wear that dress at their wedding.

Feelings of happiness and contentment surrounded her as the memories of the wedding day replayed in her mind. Love and support radiated from Charlie and his parents. Grace felt like she was floating down the aisle towards him, and as she stood by his side, she heard his vows, and her tears flowed with every word. The reality of what had happened at the church did not seep into her memories. She was so happy, and they were looking forward to their lives together. As she said her vows, something had happened. She tried to remember what it was, but the memories were all jumbled and she could not focus. The next thing she knew, flames had taken over, and her memories were gone. What had happened? Why couldn't she remember? All Grace had was an overwhelming sense of loss.

Grace stirred in her bed. Constricted and uncomfortable, she struggled against the medical equipment. There was a tube down her throat that made her want to be sick, her stomach wretched as she tried to pull it out. Confused and scared, she hit out at anything that was within reach. There was not much, but what she could get hold of, she threw. Grace needed help, and the only way to draw attention to herself was to make as much noise as she could.

Sister Margaret heard the racket coming from the room and rushed in with her colleague, Helen, who was following close behind her as usual. The young woman was flailing about on her bed, her eyes wide open and full of terror. Both women rushed over to restrain her and to offer her some comfort.

"It is okay, you are safe. Try to calm yourself down," Sister Margaret told her. It took a lot of effort to hold the young woman down. She was fighting against their efforts with all her strength.

"You need to keep still. I will get a doctor to take out the ventilator tube. It will just take a few minutes. Then you will be more comfortable, I promise."

Sister Margaret instructed Helen to fetch the doctor at once. Grace waited for what felt like a lifetime. She was so uncomfortable and was finding it difficult not to be sick. Minutes later, the doctor arrived and quickly removed the ventilator tube. After a bout of coughing, Grace thanked the doctor in a hoarse voice.

"Where am I?" she asked once she had composed herself a little more.

"You are in a rehabilitation facility. Can you tell me your name?" asked Sister Margaret.

"It is Grace Johnson. What happened? Where is Charlie?" she asked, trying once more to catch her breath between fits of coughing.

"You were in a fire, Grace. We were worried that you would not wake up, but here you are, and we are absolutely thrilled to see you awake," replied the doctor as he gave her a glass of water to sip on.

"Where is Charlie? Where is he?" Grace demanded, almost shouting in her desperation. Sister Margaret took a deep breath and sat on the edge of the bed, taking Grace's hands in her own.

"I am so sorry, Grace. Charlie is not here–he has not been to visit you. Nobody has been to visit you. We did not know who you were, but now we have your name. We can try to contact your family and let them know you are here," she answered.

"Was Charlie at the church with you?" she asked.

"It was our wedding day. Where is he? Is he okay?" Grace's body physically shaking with fear as she waited for the response.

"There was no one else found at the church, Grace. No sign that anyone was with you," the Sister replied, with little emotion, "The obvious conclusion is that he is likely dead."

"No! He can't be dead! We were saying our vows. Please, tell me where he is!" her body wracking with sobs. What little composure that she had was gone.

"Grace, I am so sorry. I know this is hard to take in and I cannot answer all your questions, but you need to calm down." Sister Margaret's dismissal of Charlie's whereabouts only spurred Grace into action.

"I am leaving. Right now. I need to find him! Where are my clothes?" she demanded.

"Grace, you have just woken up. You are not well enough to leave. I am so sorry for your loss, but we cannot allow you to leave," replied Sister Margaret.

"I am not staying here. Now tell me where my clothes are! I need to find Charlie!" she screamed as she got out of bed.

Sister Margaret tried to calm her, but the more she tried, the more hysterical Grace got. Becoming impatient with the young woman in her care, she shot a withering look at the Doctor, who nodded his understanding.

"I will sedate you if you do not calm yourself down. I would rather not, but my job is to protect you from further harm," the doctor told her firmly.

"Calm down? How in the hell do you expect me to do that? You have just told me that the person I love most in this world is most likely dead! We were getting married! We had plans!" she snapped back at him, her breathing ragged and her speech punctuated by sobs.

"Grace, you are the only survivor. They didn't find anyone else in the church." Sister Margaret reiterated.

"Only survivor? What do you mean?" this could not be. She knew Charlie was with her that day. She refused to believe that he was dead!

"There was no sign of anyone else in the church. The fire consumed everyone and everything it touched; it is a miracle that you survived."

Grace was having trouble believing anything this woman was telling her. They could not all be dead. If they were, there would be remains. A fire would not have destroyed everyone who had ever loved her, and not left a trace.

"I need to see; I need to go to the church."

"Not yet, Grace. You need a few days to gain some strength, both physically and mentally. I will release you as soon as I am sure that you are strong enough to cope with the information overload you are bound to get in the coming days," the doctor told her.

"Please, I cannot stay here. I just can't. Don't you understand? I need to see for myself." Grace snapped.

"Of course I understand, but for today, I believe it would be best for you to rest. Let me give you a mild sedative to help you sleep."

"No, I don't need one. Please don't sedate me," she begged.

The doctor asked the two nuns to make Grace comfortable, and he got the sedative ready to inject. Grace was not about to be sedated and physically hit out at them. Sister Margaret fell backwards. She only just stayed on her feet. The younger nun kept hold of Grace. Her grip seemed gentler, as if she did not really want to restrain her.

"I promise I will rest. You do not have to do this," Grace cried as she continued struggling to break free.

"I am sorry, Grace. Your actions so far have not convinced me you will," he replied as he moved forward, syringe in hand.

Grace finally relented; she had no choice as Sister Margaret reinforced her grip on Grace's arms. Grace did not have the strength to fight her again.

After he injected her, both the doctor and Sister Margaret walked away from the bed and left the room. Grace could hear them talking outside as she felt sleepy, but she could not make out what they were saying. Determined to get out of the hospital, Grace knew that as soon as she was awake, she would escape her room and find Charlie.

Grace lay sleeping peacefully in her bed for the next few hours. The nuns came and went, checking her blood pressure and oxygen levels, but also to see that she was asleep. As she was coming around, she did not let on that she was awake, frightened that they would put her back to sleep. Grace played the game, knowing that as soon as she could, she would leave. However, she was unaware that the other nun from earlier had noticed that she was awake while doing her checks.

"I know you are awake, Grace. Would you like something to eat?" she asked her.

Grace continued to pretend to be asleep. The nun moved closer and whispered in her ear, repeating her earlier question. Disappointed, Grace opened her eyes and sat up slowly.

Grace was hungry, though the sedative had made her feel sick. She did not think she could keep any food in her stomach, but she knew that if she was going to escape and find Charlie, she would need her strength. There was a constant ache in Grace's chest caused by the loss of her family. Her heart felt like it had been ripped out, stamped on, and put back again. Only now it was in pieces.

"I'll try," Grace replied. She hoped that the doctor would not sedate her again.

"I will be right back. It is good that you are making the effort. You will soon be better and able to leave."

The nun left, and while Grace was alone, she looked around for something to wear. She could not leave in the gown that she was wearing, and she also needed to find some footwear. Her search was fruitless. She found that the cupboards in her room were empty, and her heart sank.

Grace was standing by the window in her room when the nun returned with her food. She looked out, expecting to see a built-up city, but she saw nature in all its forms. The view in front of her was beautiful; the moon beamed brightly, bathing everything it touched in a beautiful glow. By its light, she could make out that there were flowers in full bloom. She watched as bats flitted in and out of the trees, looking for insects to eat. Was she still in the city? She realised she did not know where she was.

She turned away from the window and saw the nun holding a plate of scrambled eggs on toast. Grace was hungry, but her stomach churned at the smell. She did not feel like eating, but she knew that if she did not show that she was cooperating, she could never get away. Grace needed to find Charlie. She refused to believe that he had died in the fire.

"Thank you. Please excuse my rudeness, I have not asked you your name," said Grace, to appear more amiable.

"My name is Sister Helen. You should get yourself back into bed and eat this. Would you like coffee?"

There was a glass of orange on the tray, so Grace declined the offer. She did as she was told and got back into bed. The nun looked on as she lifted a slice of toast and chewed. She struggled to swallow. Grace was fighting back tears, thinking about Charlie and his parents. Her throat felt closed and sore from the ventilator tube, but she forced the food down.

The scrambled egg was much easier to eat, and she could swallow it without too much of an issue. To Sister Helen's delight, Grace ate most of the food.

"I am glad that you have eaten something. You are going to need your strength for the trials ahead of you. I will be back a little later to see if you need anything, but in the meantime, you must try to remain calm, otherwise Sister Margaret will ask the doctor to sedate you again." She picked up the tray and turned to leave the room.

"I will try, but what trials?" Sister Helen's use of the word confused Grace.

Sister Helen did not answer her but closed the door gently and left Grace with an even greater feeling of unease. She laid back down on the bed, images of Charlie rushing around her head. Grace decided that she would rest for a few minutes, and she lay her head back on the pillow. Even though Grace had every intention of leaving to search for

Charlie, the exhaustion of the day's events won out, and she fell into a fitful sleep.

Chapter four

After Marcus left the facility, he headed to the church. He wanted to see for himself what remained, to check that there were not any missed clues which could explain further what had happened on the day of the fire. Marcus was poking around in the ash when his mobile phone rang; the display showed an unknown number. He pressed the button to answer it, and it took him by surprise when Sister Margaret spoke. He had not been expecting a call from her.

"Good evening, Detective, our young lady is finally awake, although she is, of course, very fragile. I have spoken to the doctor, and he does not think she will be ready to see anyone for a few days," she told him whilst seeming to take great delight in denying the Detective his wishes.

"I would usually agree to any requests a doctor makes, Sister Margaret, but this is a major investigation, and she is the only surviving witness. We need answers so I will be there in the morning, about eleven o'clock." Frustration with the situation rising through him.

"Has she at least been able to tell you her name?" he asked.

"Grace Johnson," she responded, "She has given us a little information. For instance, she told us that the day of the fire was her wedding day. She has also mentioned a man called Charlie."

"Thank you, that is helpful, but I will still need to talk to her directly." his tone was resolute, but Sister Margaret was not about to give him what he wanted.

"Detective, the doctor has expressed his opinion on the situation, and you must give her more time. You can surely work with what I have told you. We will let you know anything else she says that could help with your investigation. Once she is well enough for visitors, I shall contact you again. I will stress to you once again that she is not to be disturbed." She replied curtly, relishing in her non-cooperation.

Marcus would not leave it any longer to question Grace, and he would not accept Sister Margaret's dismissal. The doctor would have to turn him away himself if there was medical reason enough to do so. At least that way, he could find out more from the doctor.

Marcus was determined that he would speak to Grace, and he was not afraid to make enemies during his investigations. It made no difference to him if he upset the staff at the rehabilitation facility.

"I will be there at eleven am. I promise I will tread carefully, but if you insist on barring me from talking to her, I will get a warrant, Sister Margaret." Sister Margaret promptly ended the call, leaving the battle lines drawn between them.

As soon as his call ended with Sister Margaret, his mobile rang again. This time, it was Stephen calling from the office. Marcus hoped he had some information for him.

"Hi, what have you got for me?" he asked.

"Absolutely nothing, apart from the fact that the facility the woman is currently being cared for opened about five years ago. I cannot find anything about the staff, or the trustees of it. It is very odd," Stephen told him.

"Keep at it. There must be something somewhere. The name of the owner would be an immense help if you can manage it. Also, I have the young woman's name now, Grace Johnson. I need you to see what you can dig up about her. She was marrying someone called Charlie. I know that is not much to go on but see what you can find out about him, too."

"As it is a business, I have checked the company details on the government website. There are directors listed, but I cannot find anything out about any of them. I am hitting a dead end at every turn. My next step is to find out who owns the land and buildings. Tomorrow I will contact the Land Registry," Stephen replied. "I will also run a search on Grace's name, see what that produces. Leave it with me."

"Thank you, Stephen. While you are investigating, can you also try to find out if the facility is associated with a religion? Nuns run the place, so I figured we may find out more if we come at it from that angle," he suggested.

"Will do, but now it's time for you to book off shift and spend the evening doing something else, isn't it?"

"Yes Mother! It is a good job we have known each other for such a long time. Nobody else gets to tell me what to do, Stephen." Marcus laughed as he answered him.

"Will you be coming into the office tomorrow?"

"I may pop in for a bit, but first I must go to Velatus House in the morning. I told them I will be there at about eleven. Are you on your way home?"

"Yes, I am. Are you cooking? It is your turn," came the reply that he always dreaded. Marcus was not a cook and never would be. Stephen knew that, but he loved to taunt him occasionally.

"I'll grab a takeaway on my way back and I'll see you at home in about an hour."

"One day you will cook me a meal, but it might be when hell freezes over. I am ever hopeful!" he replied, laughing. "See you at home soon. I love you."

"Ditto," he replied.

Marcus disconnected the call and walked away from the remains of the church; it disappointed him he had found nothing. As he got in his car and started the engine, he found he was still thinking about his visit to Velatus House earlier. He could not get over the feeling that something was wrong there, he just could not pinpoint what. He drove to Stephen's favourite Chinese takeaway, which was on his way home. It was empty when he arrived, so it did not take long for them to get his order ready. Marcus ordered all of Stephen's favourites, and they smelled delicious. He did not realise how hungry he was.

As he pulled his car onto the driveway, Marcus saw Stephen had beaten him home, as usual. He opened the front door to be greeted by their dogs, Beau, and Henry, each of them trying to snatch the bag of food from him. Stephen rescued the food while Marcus knelt and embraced their two excited cocker spaniels, who were soon on their backs waiting for the usual tummy rubs. The dogs were the centre of Marcus and Stephen's world. Marcus always found that when they were there to greet him at the door, it did not matter what the day had thrown at him; they made him feel better.

"I hope you are hungry! We have got all your favourites," he shouted above the barking dogs.

"I am starving. I set the table ready; can you give the boys a biscuit each? Hopefully, it will calm them down a bit," Stephen answered, knowing that it was highly unlikely, but it was always worth a try.

Marcus did as Stephen asked, and although the dogs did not settle completely, it allowed enough respite so that he was at least able to say a proper hello to his husband.

"Happy anniversary, Stephen! Can you believe it has already been a year?" he asked as he kissed and hugged him.

"I thought you had forgotten when you said nothing this morning!" he replied while rolling his eyes in mock anger, "Can you believe it has gone this fast? I couldn't be happier, Marcus. Happy anniversary husband."

"Oh, and there might be a little something on the table for you," he replied with a smile and a wink.

Marcus had never really bothered with presents before he met Stephen, and he was terrible at giving them too, so it was lucky that his husband was so forgiving. There was a box on the table with a purple bow around it. Marcus was excited to find out what was in it. Stephen looked on as Marcus picked it up. Gently undoing the bow, Marcus took his time, the anticipation building. Stephen impatiently stood watching him. He just wanted him to hurry and open it.

"I can't believe it! How did you get this?" Marcus asked, with tears forming in the corner of his eyes.

"I got it when we were on our honeymoon. I snuck back to the shop that you spotted it in while you had a lie in one morning," he replied.

Marcus looked at the beautiful ring in the box, a white gold band with small diamonds set in it. Stephen told him to look at the inside the ring. Marcus could see an inscription that read '*Love and happiness forever, Stephen x*' on the inside of the band. Stephen took the ring from him and slid it on his finger. Marcus did not have a wedding ring yet, as he never quite found one that was exactly right. Stephen had outdone himself - this one was simply perfect. Marcus became emotional. He had never been a sentimental man at all, but Stephen had changed all of that, and he could not have been happier.

"If only they could see you like this at work, that tough reputation of yours would soon be history," Stephen teased.

To Stephen's delight, Marcus stepped forward and handed him a box that he had tucked away in his jacket pocket. Stephen opened it to find a silver heart on a chain. The initial M was in the centre of the heart with an S entwined around it. The engraving was so beautiful it took his breath away. Stephen looked at his husband, unable to find words to express how he felt at that moment. An enormous smile had spread across his face. His love for Marcus was too much for him to bear.

Marcus took hold of Stephen's hands and drew him into his arms, kissing him passionately. Dinner went cold that night as the two men celebrated their first wedding anniversary.

The next morning, both men were up early. The dogs needed a walk before they left for work. It was a lovely sunny morning, and they had a nice, relaxed start to the day. Both men were in a happiness bubble and not eager to start their working day. Unfortunately, they could not ignore the fact that they had a great deal to do for the investigation and chatted about it while they walked.

"So, it is another visit to Velatus House for you today; while you are busy over there, I will continue my background investigation. Hopefully, now that we have a name, we might get a better picture of what happened in that church and who else was there that day," said Stephen.

"Let's hope so," Marcus replied. "It is very odd that nobody is missing in the area, so we need a bit of luck with this case."

"Fingers crossed then!"

"You do not need to call me; unless you find something out that needs my urgent attention. I should not imagine you will find anything that can't wait, but I will leave it to your judgement. I will keep my phone on, and I will call you once I have spoken to Grace." Marcus smiled at him as he spoke, he was one of the few people to really appreciate how tenacious Stephen was when he was getting stuck into a case.

Once they were home, the dogs soon settled in their beds. Their routine was the same each morning. Beau and Henry had a sense that neither man understood. Both always knew when they were leaving and when they were on their way home.

"Bye boys, see you later," they both shouted as the door closed behind them.

Stephen kissed Marcus, and they parted ways, each going to their own car. Marcus waved as he pulled off the driveway first. The contented detective blew a kiss to his husband as he drove off. Marcus had a softness that Stephen adored, one that nobody else ever saw.

Marcus went directly to the rehabilitation facility and not into the office. He did not want to get caught in traffic like the day before. The drive did not take as long as the previous day, and Marcus arrived very early. He caught up with some emails while he waited in his car.

Chapter five

Just before eleven, Marcus climbed out of his car and walked towards Velatus House. As he approached the doors, one of them opened and Sister Margaret stepped outside to greet him. It did not surprise Marcus that she was out of the building so quickly, as While he was waiting in his car, he had a sense that he was being watched. He was right.

"Detective, I believe I made myself quite clear on the telephone yesterday, did I not?" she asked with the same sternness that she had shown the previous day.

"Sister Margaret, you made yourself crystal clear, but didn't I make myself just as clear with my response?" He replied with an equal amount of firmness.

The atmosphere between the two of them was cordial but cold, neither of them willing to give an inch. Sister Margaret stood tall and firm in front of Marcus. He stared at her determined face, not sure what to do next; he was not about to physically move her out of his way.

"Can you get whoever is in charge of the hospital, or the doctor dealing with Grace's care, please?"

"The doctor is not here yet, and I am the key person in charge of the hospital today, and as such, my decision is final. You will not see Grace."

Frustrated by the situation, Marcus snatched his phone out of his jacket pocket and looked through his contacts. Judge Arnold was a friend of his. He called him immediately.

"Judge Arnold, I am sorry to disturb you, but I have an issue that requires an immediate warrant," he said loudly for Sister Margaret to hear.

Marcus explained the situation to the judge, who listened without interruption. Initially, Judge Arnold agreed with his friend that Grace needed to be interviewed. However, when Marcus told him that the doctors had said she was not strong enough, he turned down the request saying that there was nothing he could do at that point. It frustrated and angered Marcus that he would have to give in to Sister Margaret. He tried his best to persuade the judge otherwise, but he would not budge on his decision. Marcus was disappointed.

A smug looking Sister Margaret had listened to Marcus during his telephone call and smiled at him. She had won, and that gave her a great deal of satisfaction. The detective would not be entering the building that day.

"Goodbye, Detective." She said dismissively, an air of superiority radiating from her as she turned and walked back up the stone steps towards the building. She turned and smiled at him again before entering the building and slamming the door behind her.

Marcus was livid. He was not used to being told no during an investigation. He fumed as he walked back to his car. Before he got into the driver's seat, he turned around and took one last look up at the building. As he surveyed the façade of the building, Marcus spotted Grace looking out of one of the upstairs windows. She looked well enough to him from that distance. Marcus decided he would call the judge back once he was back in the office. It was essential that he get in to speak to her, and this time he would let no one stop him.

Sister Margaret watched him closely from a window and noticed something upstairs had caught his attention. She guessed he had spotted Grace. She was relieved when he finally got into his car and drove off. Marcus sped down the driveway at speed, gravel flying up from the ground, displaying his anger through his aggressive driving.

As he drove away, Marcus decided that would he go straight into the office to see what information Stephen had dug up. The drive there was uneventful and by the time he arrived at the office, Marcus had calmed down a bit. Determined to find out even the smallest details about the facility or the staff that worked there, Marcus decided that no stone would remain unturned in his investigation. Sister Margaret had upset the wrong detective. There had to be a legal way to get into the building, but he was not averse to the idea of using other methods should he need to.

Grace was out of bed when Marcus arrived. She was looking out of the window when his car pulled up. She watched as he spoke to Sister Margaret. Unable to hear what they were talking about, she gathered from their demeanour that their relationship was not friendly. The body language between the two of them was far from cordial. The man left quickly after his conversation with the Sister, and from what she could see, he was not happy.

Grace was in was comfortable room, equipped with everything that she could need. Everything, except for the clothes and shoes that she wanted so that she could leave. Even without her clothing, she was determined to leave that day. She planned to sneak out and search nearby rooms to find the things that she needed. She walked over to the door and quietly turned the doorknob. There was no movement. The door was locked. It shocked Grace. After all, she was not in a prison. She was in a hospital, so why was the door locked?

Voices in the corridor caught Grace's attention, so she quickly climbed back into her bed and waited to see if they were coming her way. Moments later there was the noise of a key being put in the lock and a with a click, the door opened.

"Good morning, Grace. How are you feeling today?" Sister Margaret looked more stern than usual, which was impressive, considering that her demeanour was always unfriendly.

"Much stronger, much better today, so could you get me some clothes, please? I want to go to the church. I must find Charlie and his family," replied Grace, trying to convince the woman stood in front of her.

"Sorry, as we told you yesterday, there was no sign of anyone else. You need to fully recover, and the doctor does not want you to overdo things," came the reply, in a tone devoid of compassion.

"Let me get this right. Are you telling me I do not have the right to leave?"

"You will leave when the doctor says you can. Not before."

"You have no right to hold me against my will. I want to leave! I will sign a disclaimer if I need to, but I will leave today," Grace insisted.

"Okay, Grace, let me make this clear for you. You will not be leaving and there is nothing you can do about it. You will remain locked in this room until we say otherwise." The response shocked Grace, but she decided not to push her further. The nun had made her point.

Grace did not understand why she could not leave and questioned if the woman stood in front of her was a nun at all. Sister Margaret stood firm at the foot of the bed, both women staring at each other. Grace did not break eye contact with the nun, anger at her situation taking over from the shock and heartbreak of the previous day. Grace was even more determined to leave. Something was not right, and she needed to get out of there.

Eventually, eye contact broke between them as Sister Margaret turned around and marched out of the room. Slamming and locking the door behind her. Grace slumped back onto the pillow on her bed. She did not know what she could do next, but she needed a plan.

Sister Margaret walked through the building muttering to herself. The situation was not of her making and she was unhappy to be anywhere near Grace. She arrived at the office to talk to James about what should be done with Grace. She knocked on the door and waited for a response.

"Come in," she heard.

"Good morning, Maggie. How are you today?" James Langton asked.

"Honestly, I am fed up with these clothes and that bloody girl! Who decided we should play at being nuns? As if we would ever be saintly enough for these outfits!" she snapped at him.

"That would be me, I thought it rather ironic." he took great delight in winding her up, and the clothing made him laugh.

"Well, it is one step too far. We could have just been nurses!"

"Have you forgotten your place, Margaret?"

"No, I am sorry," she replied, immediately bowing her head in deference as she answered him.

"What is the situation with our guest?"

"That abomination is determined to leave, and I would happily see the back of her!"

"That abomination is our path to wiping out The Celestials, Maggie. You must not get on the wrong side of her," he snapped. "You know she has powers, even if she does not know it yet. We cannot afford to get this wrong. We have been told to gain her trust, and that is what we must do."

"How are we going to do that? She is already asking questions, and I just do not have the patience."

James Langton was becoming frustrated, but he knew he needed Margaret on his side to help keep Grace away from anyone else. She needed to stay isolated and under their control.

"Maggie, we must play this smartly. You know how important this job is. You also know the consequences for us both if we fail, or do I have to remind you what we were told?"

Maggie bowed her head again; she knew she was on her last chance with The Fallen hierarchy. She was just a lowly cog in the grand scheme of things and completely dispensable.

"Now I will talk to Grace myself. Let us try to build some trust with her and see if we can get this finished as soon as possible. You will come with me and play nice. Otherwise, I will have no issues relaying your failures to him!"

Maggie nodded and followed James towards Grace's room. James knocked on the door before unlocking and opening it. He walked in, with Maggie following behind. Grace looked at them both with distrust.

"You cannot keep me here!" she shouted, anger at her situation taking over.

"Grace, you really should be resting. Sister Margaret has told me she does not think you will allow yourself the time to recover until you have seen for yourself what happened at the church," he began, "so we will both go with you there today. Will that be okay with you?"

Grace had been expecting a fight. The offer surprised her. She readily agreed with the plans.

"Thank you, Doctor," she replied politely.

"Please call me James."

Grace nodded. She relaxed a little and was eager to get to the church.

"Please allow us a couple of hours to arrange things. Sister Margaret will get you some clothes and I have my rounds to finish. In the meantime, just rest and we will be back soon," he responded with a tone of reassurance.

Grace nodded and smiled at the nun standing by his side. Trying to make amends for their earlier altercation, she responded in kind. As they turned to leave, the other nun entered with a plate of food for lunch. Grace thanked her and then ate some of it, even though she had no appetite. The hours passed and Grace waited impatiently in her room for them to come back with some clothes. She was eager to get to the church. Grace's thoughts went back to Charlie and their wedding day again. Deep down, she knew that if he and his family were alive, they would be with her, but she would not give up hope of finding them safe.

Chapter six

M arcus stormed into the office; his frustration was obvious to those around him. They gave him a wide berth as he made himself a drink. He sat down at his desk with a cup of coffee, waiting for Stephen to update him on any information that he might have dug up about Grace and the rehabilitation facility. While he was waiting, he did his own search for information on Grace Johnson.

First, he entered her name into the police database to see if there was anything there, but there was no match. No criminal activity, and no convictions, but that did not mean that she was squeaky clean. Marcus had learned this from experience.

"Okay, Google it is then," he said aloud to nobody.

Marcus entered Grace Johnson into the search bar and looked at the results; there were hundreds of Grace Johnsons. He would need to narrow the search parameters, so he added a location to see if that helped. Nothing came back in the area. How could that be? He tried again in case he had something wrong. There were no results.

Marcus thought for a few minutes, then searched for the church and found that they had a website. Looking through the pages, he found a contact number for the church warden.

He dialled the number, hoping to gain some information about the wedding, but the line just continued to ring. Marcus was about to hang up when he heard a voice.

"Hello, this is Graham Walters. How can I help you?"

"Mr Walters, I am Detective Marcus Anderson. I am investigating the fire at the church. Do you have a few minutes to answer a couple of questions?"

"Of course, Detective, but I am not sure that I can help you very much. I have been away for the past few weeks on a retreat in the mountains."

"Do you have any records for the wedding that we think was taking place when the fire happened?"

"What wedding?" he asked, puzzled.

"We have been told that there was a wedding on the day of the fire. Would anyone else know anything about it if you were away on a retreat?"

"The church has been closed for months. It was in the final stages of refurbishment, so the priest attended the retreat with me."

"Did anyone else have access to the church? Could anyone else have presided over the wedding?"

"No, Detective, the only people who had access to the church were the builders. We were due to reopen to the congregation in the next couple of weeks. It is so sad that we cannot now. Can I ask why you think there was a wedding taking place?"

"I cannot go into detail, but it is a line of enquiry that we are following. If I give you my email address, could you send me the details of the builders that were doing the work, please?"

"Of course. I am sorry that I have been little help," Mr. Walters replied.

Marcus gave him his email address and made sure that he had his telephone number in case he remembered anything, thanked him for his help, and ended the call.

Stephen was standing by the door to the office when he looked up from his phone. He could tell from Marcus' demeanour that the day was not going well for him, and he was eager not to make it any worse.

"Please tell me you have found something. Any news at this point would help," Marcus said.

"I have found a few bits. She was in foster care for the entirety of her childhood. She did well at school, she studied English at university, and her best friend was a man called Charlie Morgan. Charlie was the man she was marrying the day of the fire."

"What about him and his family?"

"The only things I can find on Charlie are the school and university records. There is nothing about his family. It is as if they did not exist. I have checked the birth, deaths, and marriages registers and oddly, I cannot find a birth certificate for Grace, nor for Charlie, so I cannot find the names of his parents."

"Maybe there is an error with the records? Can you check again?"

"Of course. What about you? How did the visit go this morning?"

"Not well. I was fucking blocked by an obnoxious jobsworth of a nun who will not let me have access until the doctor agrees that Grace is well enough to answer some questions." His earlier anger reared up again.

"I guess you will have to wait longer. I know you are impatient to get on with this, but if she is not medically fit, there is not much you can do, is there?"

"Well, she looked fine to me when I saw her looking out of the window. That bloody nun is just being a fucking jobsworth!"

Stephen felt frustrated with Marcus. He knew how he got when things did not go his way. Thankfully, it was not very often. Early in their relationship, they had both resolved to keep home as a work free zone. They both agreed to leave their jobs in the office, and that worked most of the time.

Stephen told him he was waiting for some more records to be sent to him, but unfortunately, it could be a few days before they arrived.

"Have any missing persons reports come in that could link to the case?" Marcus asked.

"None. We do not know if anyone apart from Grace was in the building. It is a puzzle, that is for sure!"

"I would have expected many reports to have been made by now! Surely if there was a wedding, there would have been guests?"

"Agreed, unless it was a private family service, but even then, there would be clergy missing, wouldn't there?" Stephen questioned.

Marcus told him about his telephone call with the church warden, both men confounded by the lack of evidence, and questioned whether their first intel had been correct. Perhaps there had not been a wedding at all.

"I am out of avenues here–I must speak to Grace Johnson, and it needs to happen now. No matter what that bloody nun says!"

"How? You have tried for a warrant; I do not think you have a choice but to wait. Unless there is something else you have thought of?" Stephen replied, trying to be as sympathetic as he could be.

"I can set up some surveillance at the facility. There is something very peculiar about that place. I will grab a few things, some food etc. and spend some time there."

Stephen agreed that there was not much else they could do while they were waiting for information to come through. He told his husband to be careful.

"Keep me updated. I will chase up my contacts and see if I can hurry the process up a bit. Again, please be careful. I know how frustrated you get when things do not go your way."

Marcus reassured his husband and left the office, heading towards his car. As he drove back towards Velatus House, the sun broke through the clouds and glared through his windscreen. He found himself suddenly unable to see where he was going because of the glare. He pulled the car over to the side of the road and parked it with two wheels on the grass verge. Other cars passed him, none slowing down or stopping like he had needed to. It was as if the glare was not affecting any of the other drivers at all.

The light got brighter and brighter until he could not see anything at all. He worried that there was something wrong with his eyes. Blinking repeatedly, he tried his best to focus. The light blinded him, it was as if he had looked directly at the sun. Suddenly, a sharp pain coursed through his head; his eyes felt like they were about to explode. The pain was so intense that he passed out in his car.

Marcus remained slumped in his car for hours, and when he finally woke up, it was dark. He was confused and did not know how long he had been there. As far as he was aware, nobody had even stopped to see if he was alright, but that was the world that they lived in, nobody cared about others anymore. Marcus' phone rang, startling him. It took him a few seconds before he could focus on the screen. It was Stephen calling.

"Where are you? Are you okay? I have been trying to get hold of you for hours!" a frantic voice asked when he finally answered.

"I am fine now. Please do not worry. I am not sure what happened. I think it might have been a migraine attack. I could not see anything, so I pulled off the road. It was the worst pain I have ever experienced. It was so bad, I passed out," he replied. His tone was flat, and he knew he was not doing the best job of convincing Stephen that he was okay.

"Tell me where you are. I am coming to get you. You should not drive home."

Marcus tried again to reassure Stephen that he was okay, but that proved to be quite difficult. His husband was not accepting his assurances and continued to insist that he come and collect him. Eventually, Marcus persuaded Stephen that he did not need to be rescued, so they said their goodbyes and he promised he would call if he felt ill again.

Marcus sat quietly for a little while until his eyes could focus completely. He was feeling better, but when he glanced at himself in the car mirror; he noted that he looked pale. As he was studying his own face, it shocked him to see a man sitting in the back of his car. He reached for the gun at his waist.

"Who are you? What are you doing in my car?" he asked the stranger.

"Marcus, we need your help." He replied, giving nothing away.

"How do you know my name? Who are you?" he asked again.

"It is a long story and one you may not believe, but we have no choice but to ask you for your help. We hoped that when you woke up, you would be where we needed you to be, but unfortunately, there was an unforeseen hiccup in transporting you, but not to worry. I can sort that out."

"Transporting me where? If you want my help, then I suggest you contact me at the police station, not by getting into the back seat of my fucking car. Now get out!" he shouted at him.

"I cannot do that. I am sorry about this."

"Sorry about what?"

The man did not answer, instead the car filled with the same bright light Marcus had seen before, but this time, it did not blind him. He closed his eyes against the glare, but the light lasted for only a few seconds. When he opened his eyes again, he was no longer in his car. His surroundings were unfamiliar, and Marcus did not know where the stranger had taken him. The man who had been sitting behind him in the car was now nowhere to be seen; instead, there was a woman dressed entirely in white standing in front of him.

"What the fucking hell is going on?" an incredulous Marcus asked.

"Welcome, Marcus, we need your help," replied the formidable-looking woman.

"Who are you? What in the fuck is going on?" Marcus demanded to know.

"No need for that language, especially not here. My name is Thella, and I am what you would call a Celestial," she replied, "And you are in Elysium."

Marcus did not believe what he was hearing. His immediate thought was that he had developed some sort of brain condition and was still in his car. Either that or he had died.

"Am I dead?" he asked aloud.

"No, Marcus, you are not dead. As you have already been told, we need your help. Allow me to explain."

Chapter seven

Grace sat on the chair in her room, hoping that they would be back soon, eager to find Charlie. The hours passed slowly and there was no sign of the Doctor or Sister Margaret returning to take her to the church. The daylight faded into dusk. It was not long before she was looking out of her window into complete darkness, disheartened and angry that they had not come back to take her to the church. She looked around the room in search of anything that could help her pick the lock, but there was nothing at all. Eventually, Grace lay on her bed and gave up hope of getting out of the room that day.

Just as she was closing her eyes to get some sleep, the door to her room was unlocked and Sister Helen entered. Grace expected her to be bringing some food, but she did not have a tray. Instead, she was carrying a bag.

"Grace, here are some clothes. Get dressed as quickly as you can. You need to follow me," she urged, as she passed them to her.

"What's going on?"

"I do not have time to explain. Just get dressed and follow me!"

Grace hesitated for a moment, weighing up her options before she did as Sister Helen asked. Stay locked up or get out of the room she was a prisoner in? It took her seconds to decide. She quickly got dressed in the jeans and top that were given to her and pulled trainers onto her feet.

"You must be extremely quiet if we are to get you out of here with no one knowing. Your life and mine depend on us escaping unseen," the nun whispered as she opened the door, getting ready to leave the room.

"Why? Who are we avoiding? I don't understand what is going on. Can't you tell me something now?"

"I promise I will explain once we are out of here, but for now, please be quiet and follow me closely."

Grace really did not have a choice if she wanted to find Charlie and his family. She nodded and followed the nun out of the room and down the corridor. Looking at her surroundings as they quickly and silently made their way through the building, she noticed that corridors that they went through were completely empty. It surprised her they did not meet anyone as they made their way through the building. This did not seem like any hospital she had visited before–they were usually bustling places full of staff and patients.

"Keep up!" the nun snapped in a hushed tone as Grace fell behind.

Grace quickened her step, making sure that she was right behind the nun. It was not long before the two of them were standing by the door that would lead them out of the building. Sister Helen took out a bunch of keys and searched for the one she needed. She unlocked the door, and they stepped out into the dark night. It took a few seconds for their eyes to adjust to the dark, but when they did, they hurried across wet grass towards the trees that lined the property. Once they hid in the tree line, Grace grabbed the nun's arm and demanded that she explain what was happening.

"It is a long and extremely complicated story. I cannot go into detail with you here. I just need you to trust me."

"Why should I trust you? You were keeping me prisoner in that room! And how do I know you are not taking me into a worse situation than the one that I have just left?"

"I know it looks like I was collaborating with Margaret, but you do not know the full story. I do not have time to explain everything now. We need to focus on getting out of here."

Grace stared at the woman in front of her. She could not see her properly in the dark, so she could not gauge her intentions. Eventually, though, she decided she had no choice but to do as the nun asked. She would get answers later, and if they did not satisfy her, she would give her the slip.

The nun bent down and retrieved a bag from behind a bush and undressed in front of Grace. Her habit removed and discarded on the ground, leaving her standing in her underwear. The clothing she removed then hidden under the same bush. The nun pulled a pair of jeans and a jumper out of the bag and quickly re-dressed. It shocked Grace to see how different she looked.

"You're not a nun at all, are you?"

"No, Grace, I am not. Now let's get out of here, shall we?"

Suddenly there was a horrendous noise, bellowing loudly from the direction of Velatus House. It reminded Grace of air raid sirens in old war films. The assault on her ears made her jump. She reached to cover them.

"Quick! They know you have gone; we must move now! Run as fast as you can, and do not lose sight of me!" Helen urged.

Grace did as she was told. Her mind racing as she ran. Helen looked back to check that Grace was behind her. Grace had stopped. Frustration rose in Helen. She did not need the complication of this stubborn girl slowing them down.

"Grace, MOVE! I have already told you that you will know more when we are safe. It is my job to get you away from here, but if you insist on slowing me down, I will leave you behind!"

"It's just that I can hear them. We should hide!" Grace replied.

"There is no time to hide! We need to get out of here now before they find you!"

Grace took a deep breath and looked at the woman, ordering her to run. She saw an annoyance that was not there before, but aside from that, she looked frightened too. Grace took a leap of faith, nodded, and they both ran through the woodland, trying their best to keep ahead of those chasing them.

The path through the woods was hazardous, but somehow, both women kept their feet underneath them. It was not long before the two women found themselves at the edge of the trees. Grace could see a car with its engine running parked in a clearing ahead. It appeared to be waiting for them. Grace saw a man sitting behind the wheel, and instantly burst into tears as she recognised his face. It was Charlie! As soon as he saw Grace, he jumped out of the car and ran towards her.

"We have not got time for you two to catch up. They are right behind us! Get back in the car, Charlie!" shouted Helen.

"No! I need to know what is going on. Charlie, why didn't you come to see me? I was so worried! They told me you were dead." Grace's voice punctuated by violent sobs.

"GET IN THE CAR, NOW!" Helen's frustration at the pair now becoming palpable.

"I won't until I have the answers you promised!" Grace's defiance was likely to get them all killed, and Charlie could see that Helen was about to decide on a course that they would all regret. She pushed past him and lowered herself into the driver's seat.

"Grace, Helen is right. Now is not the time. They will be here soon. We can't be here when they arrive. Please, just get in the car!" snapped Charlie, and she knew him well enough to know that she would not get anything else from him then. She would just have to wait.

Charlie and Grace got into the rear of the car. Unable to believe that he was there with her. Grace gripped his hand, refusing to let him go. Not even for a second. As she looked at him, her emotions overwhelmed her, and tears streamed from her eyes. She was cross that he had left her alone for so long, but so happy to see him. Helen sped away just as a group of men ran into the clearing.

"Who are they?" Grace demanded once they had travelled a distance.

Neither Charlie nor Helen answered her. Charlie kept looking out of the rear window. Grace could feel how nervous the pair were. She wondered how they knew each other. Grace certainly had not met Helen, nor had Charlie mentioned her before all of this happened. She knew no answers would come for a while, so instead leaned her head on Charlie's shoulder and tried to calm her breathing.

The three of them had been travelling for about half an hour before Charlie and Helen finally relaxed a little. Suddenly, out of nowhere, bright headlights shone into the back of the car, lighting up the silhouettes of all three occupants. Grace and Charlie looked behind to see a large van gaining on them at speed. Moments later, the van was almost at the rear end of their car.

The headlights were on high beam, making it impossible to see into the van. Charlie checked to see if Grace had on her seatbelt. The van got closer still and within seconds, their car lurched forward as the van struck from behind. Grace and Charlie somehow avoided hitting the headrests in front of them, but Helen banged her head on the steering wheel and lost control of the car.

They swerved across the road and ended up on a grass verge; mud and grass flying up behind them, landing on the windscreen of the pursuing vehicle. Eventually Helen regained control and guided the car back on to the road. Scared, Grace could not comprehend what was happening.

The van hit the car again, but this time Helen kept control of it. The driver was relentless in his assault, time after time hitting the car, each time with more force.

Looking out of the back window once more, Charlie saw the driver veering towards them again and realised that this would be the last time the van would hit them. If they did not get out of the car, they would all die.

Charlie put a hand on Helen's shoulder and one on Grace's. A white light filled the car, and moments later, their vehicle exploded. The van driver could not avoid the flames as he hit the car at high speed. There was no time for him to escape as flames licked around the van, engulfing it in an inescapable inferno.

The bright light eventually faded, and Grace realised she was no longer in the car. Instead, she stood in the centre of a room next to the man she had seen from her window at the hospital. Detective Anderson regarded her curiously, and after a few seconds opened his mouth as if to speak to her. A woman's voice interrupted him.

"Hello, Grace, my name is Thella."

"Where am I? Where is Charlie?" she asked as she looked around the room.

"We will explain everything to you both soon."

Grace looked at the man as if to ask what was happening. Grace recognised him from outside the hospital. His reply was only to shrug his shoulders. He clearly knew as little as she did about what was happening.

"Are you going to at least tell her the same thing you just told me? Are you going to tell her you are a Celestial?" he huffed.

"Of course." Thella snapped back, "But first, let me introduce you. Grace, this is Detective Marcus Anderson. Marcus, this is Grace, as you already know."

Grace could not believe what she was hearing and from his demeanour, she did not think the detective did either.

"A Celestial you say?" she laughed as she said it.

"Yes, Grace, she is a Celestial, as am I," Charlie replied, suddenly appearing behind her.

Lost for words, Grace turned around and stared at Charlie in disbelief.

A Celestial. How could Charlie be a Celestial? How could he have kept that secret from her for the whole time that she had known him? Grace stared directly into his eyes. After a few intense moments, he broke her gaze and looked at his feet, ashamed that he had kept secrets from her. Charlie knew he had a lot of explaining to do.

Grace turned away from him and looked back at Thella. Her head was pounding. She did not know what to believe.

Chapter eight

"Please, sit down both of you," Thella said, gesturing towards a couple of chairs.

Reluctantly, Marcus and Grace did as asked, both eager to get answers, each of them needing to know exactly where they were and why they were there.

"Grace, Marcus, what I am going to tell you will be very difficult for you both to believe, but you need to listen to what I have to say. I will answer questions once I have finished, so please do not interrupt me," Thella told them both.

There was not much either of them could say, so they listened.

"My name is Thella, and I am a Celestial. I am high in the order, so I have knowledge and influence that many do not," she began. "You are now both in Elysium, a place you may not have heard of."

"Of course we haven't heard of it! This is a joke, isn't it?" an indignant Marcus asked.

"Please, I asked you not to interrupt. And no, this is not a joke, Marcus. Many years ago, Elysium was a harmonious place. We lived as one, happily and we watched over the world, and mostly that world was peaceful. Man was in his infancy and naïve to the notion of good and evil."

"Give me strength! You expect us to listen to fairy tales?"

"Again! Please don't interrupt me, Marcus. I understand your impatience, but the more you stop me, the longer it will take for me to explain everything to you."

An exasperated Marcus was not used to being told what to do or when he could or could not talk. He crossed his arms and stared at Thella. As much as things frustrated him, he realised she was right, so he stopped his interruptions and let her continue.

"One Celestial called Berran, bored with his life here, decided that he would liven things up by tempting Humankind. The temptations he offered were too much for them to ignore, and as such, greed, anger, and war broke out on Earth." Thella continued.

Grace and Marcus looked at each other, neither convinced by what they were hearing, but each of them wondering if Thella's outlandish story could have some truth to it.

"Most of us ostracised Berran in Elysium, and he became an outcast as his antics became uncontrollable. He gathered some other like-minded Celestials, and fighting broke out here. Elysium became as violent and volatile as the earth had become. Eventually, the Council of Elders decided that Berran and his followers could not stay in Elysium. That is when the factions were born. The Celestials stayed here in Elysium and the new faction called The Fallen unwillingly left. After all of that, Berran formed the Underworld." She told them.

"Were no other Celestial banished from Elysium before that?" Grace asked.

"No. Berran was the first Celestial ever to be banished. The Elders decided that as a further punishment he should also have his wings forcibly removed, publicly. Berran and his followers were all gathered in the great hall and stripped of their wings. It was a horrific scene and one I can still picture to this day."

Thella stopped for a few moments, lost in her memories, but as Marcus and Grace watched her, she composed herself and carried on.

"Berran swore that The Celestials would pay for the punishments that they had enforced for all of eternity. Everything changed that day for both Elysium and Earth."

Thella looked at Grace and Marcus. They were both surprisingly level with their emotions, but she knew that could change when the rest of her story was told. Charlie remained silent as Thella continued; it would be his turn soon enough to explain himself to Grace.

"War has raged periodically between Celestials and The Fallen for centuries now, but there has been peace, too. In those times of peace, The Fallen would throw something into the mix to change it. You will know the history of your planet, of the wars that have been and gone, of the genocide man has inflicted on his fellow man, so I do not need to cover that with you. But know that Berran and his fellow Fallen were the instigators of all that is bad in your history."

Thella took a breath and continued to explain some facts that she knew they needed to hear.

"Fast forward to the year of your birth, Grace, which is when things pivoted. You, Grace, are the reason that Celestials are walking the earth at the minute. The Fallen have decided that they must have you, and once they get hold of you, they believe that evil will destroy good and Berran will have his revenge. We cannot allow that to happen, and that is why you are here."

Thella paused, knowing that there would be questions after the last statement.

"Why do they want me? I am nothing special," Grace asked.

"Have you ever heard of a Divinexus?" Thella asked.

Marcus shook his head, but Grace remembered the voice she heard on the day of her wedding. Grace remained quiet. Divinexus and abomination were still fresh in her mind from that day.

"I am not surprised. There have been so few, and most of them have not survived the wars between The Celestials and The Fallen," Thella told them.

"What is a Divinexus?" Marcus asked.

"Divinexus is the progeny of a Celestial and a Fallen. Grace, you are the latest one, but also you are the most precious one ever born," replied Thella.

"That cannot be true. I am nothing special, just a baby that was abandoned and left to fend for myself."

"Grace, your mother did not abandon you. Banished from Elysium, her story is sad, and one that we can go into later. Because of circumstances that she could not control, there came a time when she was not able to take care of you. We stepped in and kept you hidden from those who would use you for their own gains. For your safety, we placed you on earth with a human family. It took a great deal of planning, but we made sure that The Fallen did not know where you were."

"Who are my parents?" Grace asked.

"You father was Berran, and your mother, a Celestial called Athena. There is much to explain, but for now all you need to know is that ultimately, she realised she could never stay part of your life. You are the first child of Berran, which is why you are so special."

"Surely you can tell me more about her. What was she like? I deserve to know how I ended up in this situation," Grace questioned.

"It is not my place to go into more details about your mother. Another Celestial will tell you about her, and the circumstances of your birth and how we ended up here," Thella told her.

"What about my father? What happened to him?"

"Berran continues to live in the underworld, where he still rules. I suppose that you have heard tales. You know of him as either Satan or the Devil. Grace, he wants you by his side. If you choose that, it will lead to the destruction of Elysium and the world as you know it."

Marcus sat listening to Thella's story, unsure what any of it had to do with him? He did not believe a word of it.

"Marcus, I know you must be wondering why you are here?" the question took him by surprise, as if Thella had heard his thoughts.

"You could say that. What you have just told us is so unbelievable. Do you expect me to accept it without question?"

"No, Marcus I do not. Let me tell you about your family history. You are the descendant of another Celestial, Theodore The Peacekeeper. As Elysium broke up, Theodore left here to become the broker of peace between Humans, Celestials, and The Fallen. All respected him, and he got the balance exactly right for a time." Thella replied.

"Well, I have never heard of him. Nobody in my family has ever mentioned a Theodore."

"Over time, memories fade and history lost. Other family members have taken on his role over the centuries. Your father Simon was the last of The Peacekeepers. Did he never tell you?" Thella asked.

Marcus's patience was being severely tested. He rolled his eyes, took a deep breath, and responded to the woman who claimed to be an ethereal being.

"If he had told me, I would have thought him completely mad! Just like I think you are!" Marcus snapped, "No, he never told me anything like that before he died! Surely, he would have mentioned something if I was that important in all of this!"

"I would have expected you to know about your role, Marcus. It disappoints me that your father did not share it with you."

"I don't know what to tell you. He never said a word," he told her curtly.

"Marcus, Grace, I know what I have told you is unbelievable, but it is the truth, and I need you both to accept it. Do you have questions?"

"Tell me why a Divinexus is so special, please?" Grace asked.

"A Divinexus has all the attributes of The Celestials and The Fallen. You have the best and worst of us all, Grace," Thella replied.

"And what is that supposed to mean? The best and worst of you both?"

"I would like to hear that explanation. You have been very vague, if I may say so," Marcus said, clearly annoyed by the situation he was in.

"I know, but we do not want to overload you both with too much information. We will tell you both everything in good time, I promise you that. Grace, you are still recovering from the fire, so it would be prudent for you to get some rest."

"Charlie, you will take Grace to the room we have prepared for her; I am sure you both have a lot to talk about. Marcus, I will give you a tour and answer some more of your questions. I am sure that you have many."

"Oh! You are damn right I have questions!"

Not particularly impressed at being told what to do, both Grace and Marcus reluctantly agreed with what Thella had set out for them, at least for the time being. Charlie held out his hand, which Grace took, and he led her out of the room.

THE DIVINEXUS

Marcus watched her leave. He turned to Thella as the door closed behind Grace and Charlie, ready to quiz her for more information.

Chapter nine

Charlie opened the door to a room at the end of a long corridor. It was a plain room, nothing fancy was in it, just a bed, wardrobe, dressing table, and a couple of chairs. It was a light-coloured room but impersonal, and Grace did not like it much. Sunlight filtered in through a large window that brightened it up, but the room reminded her of many of her bedrooms in the different foster houses she lived in. The room was not what she would have imagined in a place like Elysium.

Grace had walked into the room first. After scanning her eyes around, it, she turned and faced Charlie. As soon as they came face-to-face, Charlie saw the steely and determined look in her eyes. It was a look that Charlie had only ever seen once before. Waiting for her to speak, he knew he would not like what was coming his way.

"What the fuck, Charlie? Where do I start?" she raged at him. "You have a lot of explaining to do! You have lied to me every second of every day since we met, haven't you?!" she screamed, "Start talking, Charlie!"

Charlie took a deep breath before he tried explaining. He knew he could lose her, but he could not and would not lie to her anymore.

"As a child, I was born human, but I was extremely ill and suffered. For years, my parents tried all they could to relieve my pain and find a cure for my illnesses. There was none and my time on Earth was short. Nothing they tried could change that. It was not my destiny to live for very long," he began.

"I died incredibly young and as with all children who die, The Elders welcomed me to Elysium, where I stayed. The Celestials protected and looked after me, though emotionally, I missed my parents every day. I struggled; I cried for so long, I wanted to go back to them. Many years went by, and I watched my parents grieve, I saw them age and eventually I watched them die."

Grace listened carefully to what he was telling her. Her heart ached for the pain he had felt while he was alive and as he watched his parents' lives unfold without him, but it did not explain his lies.

"On the days that each of my parents died, they also came to Elysium, much to my delight; we spent lots of our time together and became integral to the community here. One day, The Elders summoned us and informed us about you. The protection you had as an infant had failed, things had gone terribly wrong, and you were in foster care. The Elders asked my parents if they would go back to earth to look out for you. They agreed. Their only stipulation was that I got to live my life as I should have, without pain and suffering," he continued.

Grace waited for him to finish talking. She held out her hand to take his, her demeanour softening as he spoke. Grace could never stay angry with him for long. She loved him.

"We were all sent back to Earth. My parents were as I remembered them as a child, and the Elders restored me to the age that was when I died. We settled into a new life, one where we were close to you. My parents enrolled me in the school that you went to, and as soon as I saw you, you enthralled me. You know everything from there. You know our history together, but you probably doubt now that I love you. That is not the case, Grace. I have loved you from the moment we met."

She looked deep into his eyes; she knew without a shred of doubt that he loved her.

"So, you were not a Celestial on earth then? You were all human?" she asked.

"Yes, we were just there to look out for you. We had to let the others know if there was any danger or anything out of the ordinary," he told her. "I also got to live that fuller life, more than I had before, and I got to share it with you."

"Where are your parents? What happened to them and the priest in the church?"

"They are here, all of them back in their Celestial form just like me. The Elders plucked us from the church just as the fire started."

"Why was I left there in the church?"

"Thella could not get you out of there. She believes that a Fallen took control of you and caused you to burn the way you did. There was a block around you, and nobody could get close to you," he explained.

"How did you know where I was after the fire?" she asked.

"For many years we have had people ensconced with The Fallen. They were undercover if you like. Helen was one of them. She pretended she was a Fallen and infiltrated the Underworld. Helen was the one that told us where you were," he told Grace. "She is very brave. Who knows what would have happened to her if they had found out about her? Thankfully, they did not."

"If that had not happened at the church, would I have ever found out about my heritage? Would we have lived a normal and happy life together, do you think?" she asked.

"Grace, I don't know. There was always going to be a chance that your father would find you. We were lucky that you stayed safe for as long as you did."

"What happens now?" she asked him.

"I am not sure, really; apart from I think you will meet the other high up Celestials soon."

"Are you one of them, Charlie?"

"No, I am an ordinary Celestial. One that loves you very much," he grinned and winked as he replied.

"Do Celestials have wings, because Angels have wings, and you sound very much like them?"

"We do. Would you like to see them?"

"Yes please, of course I would," excited by the thought of seeing them, Grace took a slight step back.

Charlie stood in front of Grace; his eyes fixed on her face. He did not want to miss the expression that would fill it once his wings fully extended behind him. Grace could see slight movements behind him, then suddenly a mass of white feathers dramatically unfurled. His bright white wings were huge and beautiful. They looked so soft but strong too. The sight took her breath away.

"How do you hide them? They are huge!"

"They both tuck away within my body; nobody would ever know that they are there."

"It must be uncomfortable with them tucked away and hidden?" she asked.

"No, it is quite comfortable, and I have been used to them being away for so long. I hid them away until you were ready to see them. All The Celestials here hid their wings until you and Detective Anderson were ready to accept what you were being told. It is a lot for you to take in," he told her.

"I am not sure the Detective has accepted it yet. My mind is racing with all this information. I want to know everything about you all, but the most important thing is, will I have wings?" Grace asked, smiling at Charlie.

"No that is not the most important question I have, Charlie. What I really want to know is if we can still marry and I hope the answer is yes."

"That is something that I am keen to find out too, Grace, and I also hope the answer is yes," he replied, kissing her on the top of her head gently.

"I am so sorry I lied to you, Grace," there was deep sadness on his face. Grace kissed him gently on the lips, happy that she had not lost him.

"You must never do it again, Charlie. I can forgive you this once, even if it is something this massive, but if you break my trust again, then there is no hope for us. I understand why you did it. Even if I do not believe what is going on right now, just give me some time to process everything properly."

"Of course, Grace. I love you so much and I will never let you down again."

As Grace and Charlie talked, Thella took Marcus on a tour of the immediate area. The detective was a curious man on a normal day but faced with the idea that he was in the company of Celestials (which he was finding extremely hard to understand), he made sure that he took in as much information as he could.

Elysium was not what he expected it to be. He expected everything would be white, and surrounded by a mist, just like he had seen in the many movies he had watched. In fact, it was just like home, which made it more difficult to accept what he had been told so far. They spoke as they walked, Marcus making mental notes of everywhere she took him.

"Thella, you tell me that I am a Peacekeeper; what exactly does that entail?" he asked.

"In your role as a law enforcement officer, you have to be firm, compassionate, fair, and able to dish out justice, don't you?"

"Well, I pass the criminals through the system and judges and juries dish out the justice, but yes, I suppose I am a big part of that process," he responded.

"As a Peacekeeper, you will need those attributes; you will weigh up the situations you face and deal with each of them on a case-by-case basis. It will be a tightrope walk for you and you will struggle," which was not helpful in his understanding of the role that she was telling him about.

"Will I have any way to protect myself? As a detective, I have the backup from my colleagues. What will I have to keep me and my family safe from The Fallen who do not like what I do?" he asked, even though not convinced by anything he had been told.

"Do I sense scepticism in your tone, Detective?" she queried.

"You can't tell me that surprises you, can you?"

"To answer your first question, yes, you will have a way to protect yourself, but it will take a lot of work on your part," she answered curtly, ignoring his last question.

"Can you elaborate?"

"There will be time for that. You will be here for a while, but now I need to deal with a few things; I will take you back to the room you arrived in. There you will wait," she told him bluntly.

"Wait for what?"

"All in good time, Marcus. Just do as I have asked, please?"

"I am not a man used to being ordered about, Thella, so tell me exactly what I have to wait for or send me home."

"Here we are, back where we started." Without answering, Thella opened the door and gestured for him to walk in. The tour ended abruptly. That was all that she said. Standing firm in front of him, she had no expression on her face. Marcus also stood firm, neither of them giving way to the other.

Eventually, Marcus had no choice but to walk into the room. Thella closed the door behind him and walked away. She did not like Marcus, and he was not a fan of hers, either.

Chapter ten

Marcus sat down, completely bewildered by what had happened to him that day. He was out of his comfort zone, which took a lot of doing. Taking his phone from his pocket, Marcus scrolled to his husband's number and pressed the button to dial him. Nothing happened, there was no signal, which should not have been a surprise to him. He put it away again.

"Can I help you with anything?" a voice asked from behind him. He turned around and recognised the nun from the hospital.

"I didn't hear you come in. There is one thing you can do for me, you can tell me that I can wake up now, and that this is just a stupid dream," he replied.

"I am sorry, but I cannot. Let me introduce myself properly, I am Helen, and I am a Celestial. You may have seen me at the hospital caring for Grace when you visited," she told him.

"Sorry, Helen, but I am having a real problem accepting all of this. Yes, I remember you. Why were you there?"

"I was undercover," she answered with no further information.

"Undercover? A Celestial you say?"

"Yes, I can show you if you would like?" Helen replied, choosing not to acknowledge the undercover question.

Marcus nodded and said he would like to see exactly what a Celestial was like, not expecting anything to change his mind or ease his doubts about what he was being told. Helen unfurled her wings; Marcus was in awe of the sight in front of him. Speechless, Marcus was certain that he had to be dreaming. Surely it could not be real.

"You can touch them if you want," she told him.

Marcus stepped forward and touched the soft white feathers of her wings. He walked behind her to see how they were attached; he did not trust that it was not some elaborate illusion. Marcus took a detailed look. If he could have, he would have completed a forensic inspection, but he could not. He decided that they did not look fake, but he was still not one hundred percent convinced.

As he stepped back around and stood in front of her, Helen sensed he was not a convert just yet, but there would be time. She knew he was not going anywhere soon.

"You say you were undercover at the hospital? How long were you there for and why?" he asked again.

"I was only at the hospital for the time that Grace was there; but I was undercover with The Fallen for many years. Long ago, we knew it would always be prudent to have someone on the inside," she explained.

"They must have trusted you if you could care for Grace."

"I was. It was hard to gain their trust. I told them I was a fallen Celestial. It took a long time for them to believe me. I had my wings removed before I went to them, which was traumatic but necessary. They would have known I was lying if I hadn't. Trust me, they were very thorough in every aspect of their investigations before they allowed me to stay with them. Thankfully, now that I am home, I have my wings back; I missed them," she told him.

Marcus could only imagine what she meant by being thorough, and what he imagined was difficult to understand.

"Now you have blown your cover by rescuing Grace and bringing her here, I would imagine that they will look for you to enact some sort of retribution, is that the case?" he asked.

"There is a bounty on me already. My capture or death is high on the list for Berran. I knew the risks, but Grace is far too important for The Fallen to have her. It was a necessary risk that I needed to take."

"Can a Celestial die? Could they have killed you had they found out?"

"Yes, they could, but it is not death like you know, but yes, in some circumstances we can cease to exist," she answered. Helen did not give any further details.

Marcus already understood that The Celestials would only give him small amounts of information, as and when needed. He gathered it would only be that which was relevant, and it would be extremely hard for him to accept. As a detective, he was used to getting what he needed. It would be no different in the situation he found himself in. He changed the subject.

"Helen, I need to get to my husband. He will be worried about me. Is there a way to contact him?" he asked.

"Your husband will not know that you are missing. Time works differently here. While you are here, time will pass for you, but when you go back home, it will not have moved on. He will not have missed you for one second. You will not age here no matter how long you are with us," Helen explained.

"How long will I be here?"

"For as long as it takes for you and Grace to be prepared for the battle that is coming. It could be days, weeks, months, or years. Thella will decide when you are ready," she told him.

"You cannot keep me for that amount of time. I have a life, a husband that I love dearly and who I do not want to be apart from. I will not stay here if that is the case," he snapped at her.

"Marcus, may I call you Marcus?" she asked, trying to calm him.

Marcus nodded at her, not happy with the way things were panning out.

"I know how you must be feeling, I was alone and away from everything I knew and loved while I was on earth, it is very hard but sometimes sacrifices need to be made, sometimes we have no choice," she explained as sympathetically as she could.

"But I did not choose this. I was oblivious to my role in this, whatever that may be. Understand that I did not ask for this, and it is unfair for me to be put in this position."

"I know, but you were born for this role. Your father should have prepared you. In a way he has, your choice of career makes perfect sense. Did he guide you into that?" she asked.

"My father was a detective as well, and he always told me stories when I was young. I wanted to have adventures like he had, to be a man that had influence in people's lives. I never thought of doing anything else. It was just natural to follow him into the police force."

"You father died when you were a young man, didn't he? It was before you took up this career, wasn't it?" she asked.

"How do you know that?"

Helen explained that the Elders watched over Marcus and protected him for his whole life.

"We stood by your side when you buried your father. You did not see us, but we were there. We watched your heart break when your mother died. Again, we stood by your side. We were there for the happy times too. We smiled and sent love to you when you married Stephen. You did not see us, but we were there. We have always been there for you, even if you did not know."

"Then how did you not know that my father had not told me about my role in all of this? Surely you should have had some idea?" questioned Marcus.

"We never interfered in family life. We assumed your father was raising you to take over from him. That we were remiss in; we should have questioned Simon about you. I am sorry that this is such a shock to you."

"And what about Grace? Were you there for her too?" he asked.

"Charlie and his family protected Grace. We were with her too, as much as we could be," she answered. "Charlie will explain everything to her now."

"There was extraordinarily little on record about her when I tried to find her family after the fire. Why was that?"

"She needed to stay as invisible as we could make her. Some things were impossible to hide, especially when she ended up in foster care. We did what we could."

"I have so many questions. I will be honest; I am having a challenging time digesting all of this. It is beyond crazy to me."

"I understand, Marcus. Just give it a little time," she said reassuringly. "Is there anything that I can get you?"

"Do you have food here? I am starving. Do Celestials even eat?" He realised that he knew nothing about the lives of anything mythical, supernatural, or whatever they were. Marcus was very much a sceptical man, always questioning what was in front of him. That was what made him a good detective.

"I can get you something to eat and drink. Do you have any preferences?"

"Whatever you have got will be fine with me," Marcus answered, though he really wanted a steak with all the trimmings.

"Marcus, would you like a steak?" Helen asked with a smile.

"Please, but how did you know?" He asked.

"I understand what hunger feels like. I felt it many times on earth, but now I am home, it is unnecessary for me to eat. Give me a few minutes and I will be back with some food for you. Please stay here as Thella asked."

Helen left Marcus alone, wondering how she knew what he wanted to eat. He watched her leave, closing the door behind her. The detective had decided that he was not about to stay put. He was much too inquisitive and wanted to do some investigations of his own.

Opening the door slowly, he checked to make sure that nobody else was around. The corridor was empty. Marcus walked out of the room and began his own tour of Elysium, with a route that he would choose to follow.

Thella watched Marcus leave the room. She silently laughed as she watched him creep along the corridor. She followed him discreetly at a distance; he was unaware of her presence.

Chapter eleven

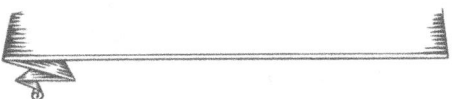

The corridor stretched out in front of Marcus. It seemed to go on forever. Surprised that there was nobody around, Marcus crept along it as stealthily as he could. He passed a few doors as he walked, trying the handles as he went. He soon found the doors locked. That seemed odd to him.

The endless corridor eventually ended, leading him to a huge, ornate wooden door. Carvings of what he assumed were Celestials adorned it; it was the most beautiful door he had ever seen. Marcus tried the handle, turning it as quietly as he could. Unfortunately, it had a heavy metal ring for the handle that screeched as it turned. The noise reverberated along the corridor. Marcus stood still, looking, and waiting for someone to appear and ask him what he was doing. Nobody came.

Opening the door slowly, Marcus peaked around the edge of it once there was a big enough gap for his head to fit. The room was empty. He walked into it. The sight in front of him shocked Marcus.

An enormous room opened before his eyes, lined with floor to ceiling wooden glass-fronted cupboards which were filled with weapons; some Marcus recognised others he did not. Swords, bows, axes, and other weapons filled them all. There was not one cupboard empty.

"Why so many weapons?" It disturbed Marcus to see so many.

In the centre of the room was a large wooden table that was empty apart from a goblet in the centre. The goblet had a gold base leading up to a crystal glass which had some delicate symbols engraved into it. He could not make out what they were. Marcus walked over to the table and lifted the glass to inspect it. It was heavy, heavier than he had expected. He needed both hands to hold it without dropping it.

"PUT THAT DOWN!" a voice bellowed from behind him.

A startled Marcus almost dropped the goblet. He composed himself and then put it on the table. He turned around to see Thella stood by the door. Marcus had not heard her enter the room. Once he saw who it was, Marcus stood his ground, not wanting to appear bothered by her bellowing or stern demeanour, though she must have seen him jump when she shouted. He looked her directly in the eyes and waited for her to speak. She did the same.

The atmosphere in the room was thick, neither of them liked the other. First impressions had not gone well. Their relationship was deteriorating with every meeting. Neither Marcus nor Thella wanted to give in to the other, nor be the first to speak. Time seemed to stop, but eventually Thella backed down and broke the silence, though her impatience and anger were obvious to Marcus.

"You think it is acceptable to enter here?"

"I was not aware that I was a prisoner and unable to look around," he replied curtly, knowing that he had clearly been told to stay where he was.

"And I was not aware that you would be so disrespectful, Detective."

"I am not disrespectful, but you have not given me a choice about being here, so doesn't that make you the one with no respect?"

Thella took a sharp intake of breath. She stared at Marcus before choosing her response.

"I had no choice but to bring you here. You were the one investigating Grace and the fire at the church. You are The Peacekeeper, and that was not my choice, may I add!" replied Thella.

"It was not my bloody choice either! Just send me home, let me go back to my life, and I can forget all about this place."

"I would happily send you back, but I do not have that in my power!"

"Then who the bloody hell does?"

"Marcus, I do, but I am afraid that it will not be happening soon," a voice answered from the doorway.

Marcus had noticed no one else enter the room. His focus had been completely on Thella. He looked over Thella's shoulder to see an old man, all dressed in white, stood by the door.

"I am in charge here. You are my guest, Marcus, and by now you should understand that there are many things that you need to learn; Thella, please leave us." Thella turned, bowed her head, and stormed out of the room, slamming the door behind her.

"I see that you and Thella have got off to a good start."

"She is not my biggest fan, that is for sure. I will be honest; I do not like her much either. She has one hell of an attitude, not one that is very endearing or one that I feel that I can trust. Who are you?"

"I am sorry about that. I will have a word with Thella. She has not given you the best impression of us so far. To answer your question, I am the one in charge here. My name is Adred."

"I am sorry but is that supposed to mean something to me?" he replied, the anger he felt for Thella ebbing away.

"No, Marcus, it is not. Let me explain a few things to you. Once I have, then I hope you will understand the necessity for us all to work together. First, none of us here are trying to ruin your life. Nobody wants to hurt you. You have been told that you are The Peacekeeper, and that is what you were born to do," he replied.

"I don't want to be here; I can't say it any clearer than that."

"Marcus, please just give me a little of your time, and if you still feel like that, then we will, of course, send you home and deal with the consequences ourselves."

Marcus took a deep breath. Although his anger had lessened, he remained frustrated that not one of them was listening to him. He knew nothing about being The Peacekeeper, and he did not want to. Marcus just wanted to go back to his normal life, that he loved and shared with his husband and dogs.

"Okay, I'm listening."

"Thank you. I understand from Helen that you knew nothing about this, nor about what we expect of you?" asked Adred.

"No, honestly, this is just crazy, and I think I am in a nightmare that I can't wake up from."

"I am sorry for that, Marcus; your father should have prepared you. From what I know, he had planned to tell you everything, but he never got the chance because he died. I should have been in touch with you then. That is my mistake. But we are here now, so let us begin again, shall we?" he said.

Marcus nodded, not sure that they could. He was prepared to listen to Adred, but did not believe that he would change his mind.

"Welcome, Marcus. I am the Celestial in charge here in Elysium. I was a close friend of your father's. It is an honour to meet you," he began.

"If you were a close friend, then why have I not met you before?"

"Simon kept his life separate from his duties as The Peacekeeper. He did that to protect you as you grew up. He got in the habit of living two lives, and sadly, the choices that your father made back then have led us to this."

"And this seems like a right mess to me," replied Marcus.

"I believe that you have been told a little information about the war between The Celestials and The Fallen. You are a Peacekeeper. Your role is to keep the balance between Celestials, The Fallen, and Humankind, which Thella has explained briefly. That role is more important than ever now, and that is because of Grace's existence," he told Marcus.

"Has there been anyone like Grace before?"

"There have been other Divinexus, but Grace is the daughter of Berran. He has never had a child before and he wants her with him. Previous Divinexus have not survived, so we are unsure how this will play out. We are going into the unknown, which is a scary prospect, Marcus." Hearing the anxiety in Adred's voice, Marcus softened his stance.

"What is so special about me? Do I have some sort of magical power to keep that balance?" he asked.

"You have no magical powers, Marcus; your ancestor Theodore relinquished the Celestial powers when he left Elysium to become the first Peacekeeper. What you have, though, is the perfect sense of what is wrong and what is right. We will train you to defend yourself and any innocent that needs it. Be that a Celestial, a Human, or even a Fallen, depending on the situation you find yourself in," explained Adred.

"But how will I know? How will you train me? What will that involve?"

"All I can say is that your conscience will guide you. There can be innocence in any of us, as well as evil. I am sure that you have seen that in your work."

"I have, many times."

"You see these weapons, Marcus?" Adred asked, gesturing to the cupboards that lined the room.

"I do."

"Well, these are the weapons that The Peacekeepers have used over the centuries. There are many and they vary in their uses. You will choose your weapon, the one that you feel most comfortable with, the one that connects with your soul," he told him. "It can take a long time to find it, or you could discover it instantly. Your father's weapon was the bow and arrow over there. He was an expert with it; it was very impressive to watch him using it."

Marcus saw a golden bow and arrow glisten as Adred told him. It was as if it was making itself known to him. Marcus walked over to the cupboard and opened the glass door that it sat behind. He bent forward to remove it. There was a spark that made him jump back in pain as he touched it. He immediately realised that it was not his weapon.

"There are so many to choose from. How will I know?" he asked.

"You will know, Marcus, just don't rush the search."

Adred watched on as Marcus looked in each of the cupboards. He already knew the weapon destined for The Peacekeeper, but he could not interfere. Marcus had to discover it for himself.

"I will leave you here to continue your search. I will know when you have found your weapon, Marcus. Take your time," Adred told him and then left him alone.

There was something about Adred. Marcus felt drawn to him. He felt like he could trust him. Adred was certainly much more amiable than Thella. Marcus did as asked and continued his search of the cupboards for a weapon. Although he was still unconvinced by everything he had been told, it could not hurt to be prepared. Marcus sat down on the only chair in the room and thought of Stephen. He wondered what he would make of all of this.

Chapter twelve

Grace and Charlie talked for hours about their history; about the good times they had shared; they also talked about the secrets that Charlie had been keeping. Grace, like Marcus, was still very sceptical about what Thella had told them. She needed something more than the appearance of Charlie's wings as proof that all she had learnt was true. As they continued to chat, there was a knock on the door. Charlie opened it and bowed his head to the man stood in the doorway. The two of them spoke for a few moments. Charlie turned back to Grace and told her he would see her later.

"Hello, Grace, let me introduce myself. My name is Adred, and I am the Celestial in charge of Elysium. It is a pleasure to meet you. I have watched you for many years."

Grace found his last sentence a little creepy and did not know how she should respond to it.

"It is nice to meet you as well," she tentatively replied

"Are you ready to hear a little more about yourself?" he asked.

Grace nodded. Adred gestured for her to sit down. She sat on the edge of the bed and Adred pulled the chair up closer to it.

"As you have been told, your mother was a Celestial, and that her name was Athena; what you don't know is that she was my sister, Grace, so as you would understand it, that means that you are my niece," he began.

Grace's mind was ready to explode, and her heart skipped a few beats, causing her to feel feint. Adred saw her response and paused for a few moments while Grace composed herself. He checked to see if she was ready to hear more. Grace told him she was.

"Your mother and Berran were so close when they were here together. We believed they loved each other deeply; at the time that he betrayed The Celestials, she was heartbroken. Athena struggled for a long while, but eventually she seemed to get over losing him," he told her.

"It was not until centuries later when Athena was on Earth after some disaster or other that he contacted her again. They had an affair resulting in a pregnancy. When she could not hide it any longer, she admitted to me what had been going on."

"Did she leave to be with my father?"

"Not immediately. She stayed with us for a while, and you were born here. It was a tough time for Athena. She struggled, even though we never judged her. We welcomed you with love. Eventually, however, she decided she would leave here and go to him, and she was taking you with her. When she made that decision, there was no choice but for her to give up her wings, and she left Elysium. My heart broke on the day she left with you; my sister gave up everything for him."

Grace was shocked to find out that she was born in Elysium.

Although it had been hard on Adred, Grace understood the choice her mother had made. She could not bear to be apart from Charlie for a moment. It devastated her when she was told that he was dead. She asked Adred to continue.

"What you must understand is that Berran was power hungry and determined to rule the Earth. He had easily persuaded more Celestials to follow him with the promise of unconditional power over Humankind, and ultimately, the destruction of Elysium. The underworld was born out of his ambition. We tried our best to protect Humankind as much as we could, but we could not guard against his actions. Wars began, evil was prevalent and still is to this day. His first act of violence against Humankind turned him in to The Fallen, we know. Word got to us that my sister and Berran were happy. Though, unfortunately for Athena, that happiness did not last long," he explained.

"What happened?" Grace asked.

"Athena contacted me when you were still quite small and told me that Berran was using your powers. We strongly believe that it was likely that he used my sister to produce you. He knew a Divinexus would be the most powerful being in Elysium. Once he had you both with him, it became obvious to Athena that he no longer loved her how he had before," he explained.

"My sister told me what was happening, and that she was frightened of what he might do; she asked us to help protect you from Berran. We agreed we would take you and put you somewhere he would not find you. Once my sister left you here and returned to him, she suffered at his hands. He was brutal to her. Berran did all he could to break her spirit. He killed the wonderful soul that she was. Athena took her own life and every day I regret not fighting to keep her here with us. I should never have allowed her to go back to him once she had left you here," he told her with a tear in his eye.

Grace's emotions welled up inside her. She felt grief for the mother that she could not remember. For the first time in her life, she understood why she was alone as a child. Her father sounded as evil as she expected him to be.

"Why didn't she stay here in Elysium?" Grace asked.

"I asked her so many times. I told her she could, but what you have to understand was that she could not forgive herself for turning her back on all she knew and loved; my sister could not live with the guilt she felt for those who had suffered at the hands of Berran, she felt responsible for him and his actions," he explained, "I tried so hard, Grace, but I could not persuade her, I failed to save my sister."

Grace took hold of Adred's hand, both sharing a moment of silence while he gathered his thoughts.

"You say that my father was using my powers? What powers are they? I am sure that I don't have any."

"There are so many, Grace, and you will be told about each of them in time. It has been a lot for you to take in today. Do you have questions you want answering?" he asked her.

"How do I access these powers?"

"They are part of you. They are there whenever you need them, Grace. I must warn you they can come at a cost, so you should be incredibly careful. I will guide you as much as I can, but that must be something for another day," he told her.

Overwhelmed by all the information Grace needed to rest. Adred sensed Grace was struggling. He could see the strain on her face and told her he would give her some time alone to absorb everything.

"Once you have rested, we can meet again. I will answer any further questions that you have. When you are stronger, you will also train with some of The Celestials that have experience in defending against The Fallen. We will show you how your powers work and how you can access them. So, for now, rest and I will see you soon. Please make yourself comfortable," he said and then he left her alone.

Grace's mind was racing. She wanted to know what her mother was like. She had finally buried her feelings about her after being angry for so long. Adred's story had made her feel sorry for the things that her mother had gone through to keep her safe, and now she wanted to know everything about her. Her father, not so much.

She laid on the bed looking up at what should be a ceiling; instead, she saw a clear blue sky, still and bright. She soon found herself lost in its vastness; as her mind matched its stillness, her body floated upwards, embraced by a white, cotton-like cloud. Grace felt like she was on the softest bed she had ever experienced; she could not keep her eyes open. For many hours she slept, something she had always struggled with her whole life. She felt safe and warm. Grace felt like she was home, a feeling that until now, she had only ever had when she was with Charlie. Her sleep was deep and restful, and when she woke up, it was with a strength that she had never experienced before. Grace understood many things that she had not fully grasped during her life. She felt whole.

She floated back down to the bed in her room and sat up. At the bottom of the bed, she was surprised to find a white dress, along with some shoes. As she picked up the dress and inspected it, she could see that it was made of a delicate silk. Grace rubbed it against her cheek and found that it was one of the softest materials she had ever felt. The design seemed odd to Grace, though. There were two large holes in the back of it, which confused her. She put it back down on the bed. A knock on the door startled her. She was not expecting anyone.

"Come in," she answered.

Helen opened the door and walked into the room. She bowed her head to Grace, which made her feel uncomfortable, but she responded by bowing to her.

"Grace, you need to get changed into the dress provided for you. There is a ceremony being held soon. It is a blessing of sorts," Helen told her.

"What do you mean *a blessing of sorts?*"

"A simple ceremony to welcome you to Elysium. It will not take long, and we hope it makes you feel like this is your home," Helen explained.

"The dress has large holes in it. I can't wear that. Is there something else I can put on instead?" she asked.

"You will need to wear that one; I cannot tell you any more than that. Please let me help you?"

Grace reluctantly nodded, though not at all comfortable at what she was being asked to wear. With Helen's help,

Grace was soon wearing the beautiful white dress. Sensing how uncomfortable she was, Helen secured the material, reducing the size of the holes.

"You look beautiful. Now, follow me, please."

A nervous Grace followed Helen out of her room and down the corridor, not knowing where they were heading to or what she was about to experience.

Chapter thirteen

When Adred left Grace, he walked back to the weapons room to see how Marcus was getting on choosing the weapon that he would need to help him in his role as The Peacekeeper. As he opened the door, he could see that he was studying the weapons in the cupboards. Adred watched in silence for a few moments. Marcus was struggling with his decision.

Marcus had not heard Adred enter the room and jumped when he gently tapped him on the shoulder.

"No luck yet?" Adred asked.

"Do you always creep up on people like that?" a startled Marcus asked.

"Not very often," he replied, laughing.

"I know you said that the weapon would show itself, but everyone I have picked up has either shocked me or I felt nothing. I think you must be wrong about me."

"First, we are not wrong about you. Second, let me just say that your father took six months to find his weapon of choice. You cannot rush these things. In time, you will find it."

"I can tell you now that I am not staying here for six months! I have a life, and this was not part of the plan," he replied defiantly.

"You have had it explained to you about the way time works here, haven't you?"

"I have, and I am still not living through all of that time without my husband, and it is out of order for you to expect me to," he snapped back.

Adred had hoped that he might have been more accepting of the future he needed to be a part of, but it was becoming clear from what he had been told and from his own experiences with him, that they would need to have a lot of patience with Marcus.

"Marcus, let us leave this for now. You need to be elsewhere. Please follow me," he told him flatly.

Marcus looked up; his frustration was obvious for Adred to see. He could tell that he was not feeling cooperative. Whilst he could understand the Peacekeeper's perspective of the situation as it was, Adred knew that he would have his work cut out while dealing with him.

There was not the time for arguing backwards and forwards. A war was looming, there would be bloodshed, and he needed Marcus on board as soon as possible, and for him to accept his role as The Peacekeeper that he would need to become, even if he did not like it.

"Marcus, I understand your feelings. I promise we will talk more about this later to see if we can come to some sort of compromise, but for now, we have more pressing things to deal with. Will you come with me, please?"

Marcus rolled his eyes and reluctantly followed Adred. What else could he do? Adred led Marcus out of the weapons room, and they walked in silence along the corridor and into another room. As they entered through the door, the vastness of the hall shocked Marcus. It was empty apart from a few chairs and an altar at the end. The altar made it feel very much like a church to him. Marcus looked around and he spotted the goblet he had seen earlier.

"Please take a seat at the front of the room. There is a space there for you," Adred informed him.

He sat in the chair that Adred had pointed to and watched as others made their way into the hall. Marcus assumed them to be Celestials, he was surprised that there were so many.

His speculation about them being Celestials was soon answered; everyone in the room unfurled their wings, leaving Marcus as the only one without them. In that moment, he felt tiny compared to the Celestials surrounding him.

Helen led Grace down the corridor to a large wooden door and opened it. The room was full and the sight in front of her took her breath away. Large, beautiful wings were the first thing that she saw. Grace stood motionless; she was nervous about walking into the room. Looking around, Grace eventually spotted Charlie and his parents; she relaxed a little, but not much.

As she continued to look around the room, Grace saw Adred standing at the end of the hall behind a large altar. He beckoned her forward. Grace slowly walked towards him, memories of her wedding day flashing through her consciousness; walking down the aisle before the fire that ruined everything. She did not know what to expect.

Grace felt the eyes of everyone in the room on her as she slowly made her way towards Adred. She felt exposed. The room was full, and every person that she looked at had wings. It was breath-taking. She focused on Charlie to help steady her nerves. He had turned to look at her, his reassuring smile guiding her towards Adred.

"Welcome, Grace. Today is the day that we welcome you here in Elysium, the place where you should have lived, since the day you were born," Adred began.

Grace nodded at him; she was just beginning to understand why she had not spent her entire life there, and her heart ached for the life that she had not had.

"Are you willing to accept your destiny, your future and your past, Grace?" he asked.

Grace was not sure what he meant by that; she did not know about a destiny. She stood silently, not reacting to his question until he asked her again. Helen was standing by her side and whispered to her that she needed to answer for the ceremony to continue. Grace told him that she was, even if she did not fully understand what was being asked of her.

Adred lifted an ornate goblet from the centre of the altar. As he offered it to her in outstretched hands, Grace saw up close just how beautiful it was.

"Grace, please take the goblet and drink from it," he told her.

Grace nervously took the goblet; it was much heavier than it looked. Pausing, she held the cup for a few moments before she lifted the goblet to her mouth, though she was a little reluctant, as she did not know what she was drinking. Why was she so trusting of these people? She lowered it without taking a drink and looked over at Charlie, who encouraged her with a nod and a smile.

Adred could see that she was hesitating. He needed her to drink. The future of all depended on it.

"Grace, the liquid is just water. It is from here and it forms part of the blessing. There is nothing to worry about," he told her.

She hesitated for a further moment or two. What could water do to harm her? Grace lifted the goblet once more and took a sip. The liquid did not taste like any water she had drunk before. The chill of the liquid took her by surprise, almost causing her to choke on it. She swallowed it quickly and felt the cold spreading through her, all the way to her stomach. Grace looked at Adred, puzzled. It was not water.

As she gazed at Adred, an intense pain gripped her, first in her head, just like on her wedding day, but this time there was no voice. Her head felt like it was about to explode, her ears were thumping to the beat of her quickening pulse. The pain quickly spread throughout her body, every nerve and fibre of her screamed in agony.

Grace fell to the floor, unable to stand any longer. She writhed in agony, her eyes wide open. She expected someone to help her, but no one came. Just as she thought the pain could get no worse, it continued to build in intensity, and did not abate. She screamed a blood-curdling scream, but still nobody came to her aid.

Marcus watched on in horror as Grace writhed about on the floor. He was also waiting for someone to help her, but nobody did. He stepped forward to help her, but one of The Celestials standing behind him held him back. Marcus struggled but could not get free to comfort Grace.

"What are you playing at? What have you done to her?" he shouted at Adred.

"We have triggered her destiny," he replied. There was no further explanation from him.

"You are killing her! Can't you see she is in agony?" he shouted, still struggling to get free from the grasp of the Celestial who held him in place.

"You will stay where you are and you will not interfere, Marcus. All will become clear soon."

Marcus was helpless. He watched as Grace screamed in pain for what seemed like a lifetime. He could only imagine what she was feeling. It was a horrific sight, and he wanted no part in it, but he could not physically do anything about what was happening only a few feet away from him.

On and on it went. Grace fought with every ounce of energy she had to get through the pain, but it was relentless. She opened her eyes and looked at Charlie, pleading for his help, but he was just standing, watching her with a smile of encouragement on his face. At that moment, all the love she had for him evaporated. Any man that could watch her suffer how she was, was not the man for her. Celestial or not.

Finally, the pain settled in most of her body; but it stayed in Grace's back. She felt the skin on her back rip open from her shoulder blades down to her coccyx, and in her head, she thought that she could hear her skin tearing. A warm liquid dripped from the wounds. Grace assumed it was blood. As she felt it flow down her back, the pain intensified, reaching an unbearable crescendo. Blood flowed freely, pooling on the floor and spreading around her. Marcus watched on in horror. He knew she was going to die and there was nothing he could do to help. They were murdering a young woman in front of him.

Then, in an instant, the pain rescinded. Grace lay on the floor, exhausted and confused by what had happened to her. She felt the blood flowing back into her body, every inch of her feeling whole again. Energy sparked in every single cell, and she felt revitalised.

Marcus watched on, not believing what was happening in front of him. The pool of blood that had spread over the floor slowly disappearing back into Grace.

Grace stood up. It was not relief on her face but anger and hatred that was directed towards Charlie, and all the Celestial's who had watched her suffer. As Marcus watched, he saw the exposed skin on Grace's back. Something was appearing from her. Moments later, two huge feather wings unfurled behind her, each one brilliant white but with bright red tips. It was as if her blood had stained them.

Grace stood defiantly in front of the altar. Her demeanour was not what Adred had expected. She should be grateful, happy almost, but what he saw in front of him was an angry and vengeful woman. A scared Adred regretted that he had not told her what to expect. He should have taken the time to prepare her, but now it was too late. His hopes for their help were in tatters.

Introducing Marcus and Grace to the Elysium had not gone as planned. Adred realised in that moment that they may have made enemies of them both and not the allies they needed for the coming war.

The red tips on Grace's wings were a warning to them all. They showed her Fallen blood. A reminder of her lineage.

Moments later, all hell broke loose in Elysium.

Chapter fourteen

The hall lit up with a flash of light which momentarily blinded everyone. As they struggled to see; the light gave way to flames erupting in the hall, the searing heat from them touching everyone in proximity. The flames raged for a few minutes before dying out. When they dispersed, Berran was standing in the centre of the room. A handful of The Fallen surrounded him, others formed a barrier around The Celestials. Every member of The Fallen was heavily armed. They had appeared so quickly that nobody had time to react.

The Fallen blocked all ways out of the hall. The Celestials, Grace, and Marcus were all trapped, with no way to escape.

"Are you ready to go home, daughter?" a triumphant and sneering Berran asked.

Grace was still in shock at what had happened to her during the ceremony, and she found herself unable to answer him. Adred stepped in front of her, as if trying to protect her from her father.

"How did you get here? You should not be able to enter Elysium!" he shouted.

"You know who I am, Adred, and you know my abilities. Did you think that your little banishment and the magic you have in place would keep me away? You are not a match for me anymore; I grow stronger with every evil thing Humankind does, and I must say that they certainly do like to inflict pain on each other," he smirked.

"You know what to do!" he shouted to his companions.

Each of The Fallen grabbed a Celestial. With their weapons drawn and their intimidating demeanour, they soon had control of the room. Thella stepped out of the shadows behind Adred with a small ornate silver dagger in her hand. Unaware of her presence, Adred stood firm, protecting Grace from Berran. He did not see the attack coming. Thella pushed Grace out of the way and thrust the dagger into Adred's back, turning the blade, as she did, it hit the bone. A blood curdling sound filled the hall. Adred was in agony. Thella took delight in her actions, the wild look in her eyes and the self-satisfied expression on her face said all that anyone needed to know about how she felt. She removed the dagger from his back and then tore at his flesh with it until blood flowed freely from his wounds.

Adred fell to the floor. Marcus, Grace, and The Celestials watched in horror. None of them could help him. Not content with causing Adred harm, Thella knelt beside him, smirking at what she was about to do. Holding the dagger above her head with pride, Thella slowly lowered it towards his wings. She hacked at him, cutting through skin and bone. Excruciating pain etched on Adred's face, and his tormented cries reverberated around the room. Thella severed Adred's majestic wings at the base of his back and held them up triumphantly to the cheers of the other Fallen in the room.

A tortured Adred lay motionless, blood from his wounds pooling around his body.

Thella looked over at Berran for his approval, her clothing covered in Adred's blood. She lowered Adred's wings, letting them fall to the floor. He nodded. She had done well. Thella knew he was pleased, and she grew in stature with that knowledge. The Fallen cheered and laughed. Berran raised his hand above his head, then quickly lowered his arm, a signal to The Fallen. Screams of agony filled the room as The Fallen did the same thing to The Celestials that they had hold of. One by one, they fell, some dead and others maimed. Adred was powerless to defend them.

Grace received her wings that day, Adred and many of The Celestials lost theirs.

Marcus and Grace looked on in horror as the scene in front of them continued to play out, unable to help.

Grace's eyes frantically searched the room. Eventually, she saw Charlie and his parents. The Fallen were ripping at their wings, hacking at them all relentlessly. They did not stop there, though. The group intensified their attack on the three of them. Knives and swords thrust repeatedly into Charlie and his parents, the pain clear for everyone to see on their faces. Tears flowed from their eyes. They were helpless. Grace screamed in vain for them to stop the attack. She watched the agony of their last moments helplessly as the life disappeared from their eyes. The people that she loved most in the world were dead, slaughtered by The Fallen. The beautiful souls that she adored were gone. Only their tortured dead bodies remained on the floor in front of her.

More deaths followed at the hands of The Fallen. The anger that Grace had felt towards Charlie was gone, replaced with fear and loss.

Grace felt the unimaginable pain of losing him and his parents at once. Grief overtook her, her heart broken. She knew they had died because of her. Grace felt guilty that she could not stop what was happening. Charlie died knowing that she was angry with him. Tears of anger mixed with that grief formed in the corner of her eyes and streamed down her face.

"Why kill them?" she screamed at Berran.

"Because they were your protectors, they helped to hide you from me. They deserved a much more painful death than this. I regret they are not coming with us. I had some ideas of how to make them pay, but..."

"You are a fucking bastard!!! What kind of evil fuck does that? How can you be my father?" she screamed, her whole body shaking in anger.

Berran ignored her outburst and calmly looked at his daughter and smiled.

"Grace, you will come with me, or I will make sure more of them die," Berran ordered.

Grace looked around at the carnage in the hall. She spotted Marcus, who shook his head. Grace composed herself and turned back to her father.

"I do not think so. You have just proven yourself to be every bit as evil as I expected you to be," she shouted.

"I can do a lot worse than this, I promise you that. If you do not want to see that side of me, then I suggest you come with me willingly."

Grace looked at Marcus again, frozen where he stood, his face ashen. She knew he would not be any help to her. Grace's eyes met those of Adred. He was in so much pain, but he held her gaze. They kept their connection for a few moments. She did not know how, but she understood what he was trying to communicate to her. They both knew that she had no choice. She nodded to him, tears falling and her heart aching for the pain they were all in.

Grace walked over to Berran, defeated and heartbroken. Her wings hung limply behind her; her sadness clear for all to see. The Fallen around her laughing and congratulating each other, proud of the carnage that they had inflicted on The Celestials surrounding them.

As she got close to him, he grabbed her hand. Flames engulfed them both and a bright light flashed.

When the light faded, The Fallen were all gone, leaving the hall strewn with dead or injured and wingless Celestials writhing in pain.

The flash of light that had filled the room jolted Marcus out of his inability to move. Once Berran had left, the destruction by him and his followers was clear to see. The realisation of what had happened had not fully dawned on him. The Celestials that were not too severely injured tended to those that needed it. Marcus saw Helen helping Adred to his feet. He was unsteady and took a few moments to find his balance. Blood was still dripping from his wounds and pooling on the floor. Marcus wondered how he had survived the attack, let alone being able to stand.

As Adred struggled to stand, everywhere he looked, he saw wings lying strewn on the floor, so many pools of blood and lifeless bodies. Everyone had lost their glow; the beautiful bright white feathers were now a dull grey; lifeless and lost to their owners. Shock and horror had rocked Elysium. The Fallen had taken the lives of many of his fellow Celestials.

Celestials that had not died were wailing in pain, a heart-breaking sound that Marcus had never heard before that day. All he could compare it to was that of a wounded animal; they were helpless, and he did not know what to do.

"Marcus, you must choose your weapon today. We need you now more than we have ever needed a Peacekeeper," Adred told him as Helen supported him.

"How will me choosing a weapon help with this? Surely, I could help the injured, or to bury the dead?" he asked.

"We do not bury our dead. Watch closely, Marcus," Adred told him.

Marcus looked at the dead Celestials on the floor. He watched as the blood returned to their lifeless bodies, just as Grace's blood had returned to hers when she got her wings. As it did, he saw tiny lights leaving them; they reminded him of the stars dancing in the night sky. Marcus assumed it was their spirits, all rising above him and joining as one. As the lights merged, the room lit up so brightly that it was hard for him to keep his eyes open. What he saw was beautiful. He watched in awe, lost in it all, but moments later, it was gone. The light had disappeared and as he looked back down at the bodies; he watched as they all crumbled to pure white ash, which floated away as if on a summer's breeze. There was nothing left of them, nothing to mark the horror of their death. Only the injured remained.

"What just happened?" he asked Adred.

"Our fellow Celestials have transcended to the next part of their journey. They will not be in pain, but they can never come back to us. We will see them again when our time is done, but for now we must leave our goodbyes for them and hold our pain within. The war has now begun," he replied.

The Celestials that survived the attack bowed their heads to Adred. Marcus followed Helen as she took Adred to his room to have his wounds tended to, and for him to recover from his injuries. As they walked out of the room, Adred passed out. Helen could not hold him, and he fell to the floor. Marcus helped Helen to pick him up, and they both carried him to his bed.

"Will he survive?" he quietly asked Helen as they lay him down.

"I hope so, Marcus, but I just do not know. Only time will tell, but unfortunately, we do not have a lot of that now that Berran has made the first move," she replied.

"I will stay with him, I will tend his wounds, you go back to the weapons room. You need to do as he asked; do not underestimate the importance of choosing your weapon," she told him.

Marcus nodded. He reluctantly left Helen to tend to Adred, and he walked towards the room holding the Celestial weapons. He opened the door and stepped inside. This time, though, he felt like he should be there. He understood why he was there. He believed the unimaginable now.

Marcus surveyed the room. The weapons that had stayed silent when he first visited the room seemed to light up with anticipation as he inspected them.

One stood out for him, one that glowed. He opened the cabinet door and picked it up. Immediately, he felt its power. He had his weapon; he knew for certain there was no doubt. The sword that he held in his hand immediately felt a part of him, as if it always had been.

Marcus looked at the label on the cabinet that the sword had been in. It shocked him to see it was called *The Sword of Berran.*

Marcus had a lot of questions about that, but nobody to ask. He held the sword above his head. Marcus was surprised at how light it felt. As the sword pointed towards the ceiling, the same bright light, he saw as The Celestials died coursed from the sword, through the blade and handle, then into his body. He felt every soul within him. He heard their voices as the light spread through him. Marcus was whole. He was The Peacekeeper, even if he did not believe it himself.

Chapter fifteen

The flames that surrounded Berran, Grace, and the other Fallen immediately disappeared upon their arrival at their destination. As she looked around, the view in front of her surprised Grace; they were standing in an opulent library, with solid wooden bookcases with more books filling them than she had ever seen before. There were two leather sofas, each adorned with large, neatly placed cushions. Brightly covered rugs covered some of the highly polished hardwood floor. This place was far from the fire and flames she had expected the underworld to look like.

"What were you expecting, dear daughter?" Berran asked her while watching her closely.

Grace did not respond; she was determined that he would get nothing from her. He was evil incarnate; responsible for the murder of the man she loved, as well as the mutilation and torture of The Celestials.

"Answer me, child!" he bellowed, "and put those disgusting wings away before I have them removed from you."

Grace did not know how to put her wings away; she had only just got them. She looked defiantly at Berran and did not move a feather.

"You do not know how to do you? Or are you just being a brat?" he asked her.

Berran looked impatiently at his daughter, who did not utter a word in response. "It is easy. Just think of it being like moving an arm. Now put them away!" he ordered.

Grace looked directly at Berran, their eyes locked. She said nothing. The silence was almost deafening. Grace could see his anger raging at her attitude. Although she looked defiant, Grace was a mess inside. She was frightened and, most of all, shocked at the way her fiancé had died. The plans they had made together only a brief time ago would never come to fruition. The life that she longed for with Charlie was gone, and she could not imagine that she would ever get over it.

Berran snapped at her again, reminding her what had happened to The Celestials and their wings. Eventually, preservation of her own life won out. She did as he said and imagined her wings hidden. As she did, they folded and disappeared, though she was not exactly sure where they went.

Berran continued to stare at her. He had missed many years with her; years that he could have used to mould her into what he wanted, but he did not have that opportunity, and now his daughter was a grown woman. It had not taken him long to find her defiance endearing and infuriating, but he knew he would break her spirit, and she would do his bidding. He was in no doubt about that.

"Thella, take her away. You know what to do," he ordered.

Thella stepped forward and grabbed Grace by the arm. Grace pulled it away sharply, her feet planted firmly so it would not be easy for Thella to move her. She stared at Thella, goading her to try again. Grace did not know where her strength was coming from, but she would do nothing they wanted her to do or make it easy for them. She was sure about that.

Thella lunged for her arm again, Grace continued to stand her ground. Berran's minion raised her arm again, this time forming a fist. She hit Grace hard on the side of the head. Surprised by the force of the punch, Grace fell to the floor in a dazed heap, blood dripping from the corner of her eye where the punch had landed. Still, she refused to show any weakness, and she was soon standing again staring steely eyed at Thella.

"You bitch! You will fucking pay for that!" Grace shouted, not a person to just give in. She was a fighter. She had to be when she was growing up and the instinct was still there, even if it had been dormant for a while.

Thella laughed and raised her fist again, but this time Grace was ready for it. Forming her own fist, her punch landed hard in the centre of Thella's chest, taking her breath away at once. Her father's lackey now floundering on the floor, trying to recover from the attack. This time, she was the one in pain.

"Never lay your hands on me again, or next time you will not get up!" Grace's voice came out cold and emotionless.

Thella looked over at Berran, ashamed of her predicament. She could see the anger and disappointment on his face. She feared the punishment she would receive for her failure. Her master would forget her help, and their earlier victory. It would now be overshadowed by his outrage.

Grace turned and faced her father again, more determined than ever not to give in to his wishes. She would never help him in his war. The pair held each other's gaze, neither wanting to be the first to turn away until a young man stepped forward and spoke to Berran. He looked a similar age to her and had the same ebony black hair. His eyes were the bluest she had ever seen, apart from her own. She realised she had turned her attention towards him, and when she looked back towards Berran, she saw his cold eyes intently fixed on hers.

She could not hear what the young man was saying, but her father nodded in agreement at whatever he had suggested. He moved towards her and again, her eyes met his. For a moment, she felt a familiarity that felt comfortable, but somewhere deep inside herself, she also felt fear.

"Grace, my name is Cali. I am your twin brother," he announced.

"I haven't got a bloody brother, let alone a twin," she spat, knowing in her heart that she could feel that there was something connecting them.

"Our mother had two children. She did not know about me. Your birth was traumatic, and she was unconscious when I was born. Father did not trust her loyalty. She was a weak soul, so he arranged for me to be taken from her the moment I arrived. Our father hid me away and raised me, so she would never find out. She died never knowing I existed," he continued.

Grace felt a sense of loss for the mother she did not remember, and pity for the things she had been through and the life she had lost. Now she was being told that her mother never knew about her other child. Would it have had an influence on her taking her own life had she known? Her head was spinning. She only recently found out about her heritage, and now she had a twin brother.

"But I was born in Elysium. Someone there would know about you," she replied.

"You were not born there. That is a lie, Grace. You were born in the presence of our father. You spent no time in Elysium."

Grace did not know who to believe, Adred or Cali?

"Are you like me?" she asked.

"Am I a Divinexus? No Grace, I am not," he looked angry. "I do not know why and nor does our father."

"Then how do you know I am one?" she asked, looking at her father.

"You showed powers from the moment you could crawl. I saw them early on. Your mother tried to hide them from me. Unfortunately, one day she saw me trying to get you to do something for me. That is when she left and took you to Elysium and I never saw you again, but I had Cali. I knew that there would be a day that you would return to me and here you are," he gestured with his arms outstretched, smirking.

"You must know already that I will never help you, don't you? Everyone here shares responsibility for the murder of the man I loved. You are all animals, and I will put you down, one by one. I will never forget what you have done today. NEVER!" she snapped at him.

Berran lost patience with her. He had made plans for her arrival, but realised now that he would need to take some time to bend her to his will.

"Cali, take her to her room," he ordered.

"Grace, follow me."

Unsure what she should do next and with no obvious way to escape, Grace decided that she would bide her time and followed the man, that said he was her brother. Exhausted by the emotions of the day, she needed to regroup and regain her strength before she could plan on how to get back to Elysium. She knew in her heart that Charlie was dead, but she wanted to be near him, even in death. Grace followed Cali out of the library and into a large hallway. An enormous staircase was at the centre. She could see that she was in a large country house, and not the underworld as she had expected.

As she continued following Cali, her surroundings looked familiar. She realised she was back in the hospital building. That obviously was not a hospital.

"Why are we in this building and not in the underworld?" she asked Cali.

"Father has a plan. He thought you would be more amiable to us here in surroundings that are a little familiar to you, rather than in our world. Do not worry, sister, you will be there with us very soon. Father just needs to take care of something, or should I say someone, before we leave."

"What is he doing? Who does he need to take care of, and what exactly does that mean?"

"All I shall say is that The Peacekeeper will not be an issue once Father has taken everything and everyone that he loves."

A chill spread throughout Grace's body. She could not let anyone else suffer, but how could she stop them? She was a prisoner, with no idea what she could do.

"You will not stop him, Grace. In fact, I guarantee you are the sole person responsible for The Peacekeepers' loss. If you would have been more accommodating ..." his voice trailed off, she supposed for dramatic effect.

"And before you ask, the answer is yes. I can tell what you are thinking. After all, we are twins, and now that we are back in proximity to one another, we are linked once again," he said with a sinister smile on his face.

They both arrived at the door to the room she had recognised from before. Cali opened it and pushed her inside. Nothing had changed. It still looked like a hospital room.

"Escape is not possible, my dear sister, so just accept what is happening. You have no actual choice," he gloated, then he left her alone.

The door closed and Cali locked it, trapping her in her room once more. Furious and frightened, Grace thumped on it, shouting after him.

"You bastards will not get away with this. I will get away and you will fucking regret holding me here!"

Cali knew what was in store for her and smiled smugly as he walked away from his sister. Eventually, Grace stopped banging on the door and sat on the bed, defeated. Memories of the day flooded into her mind, the emotions that came with them were overwhelming, and tears flowed freely down her cheeks. Her defiance and strength had deserted her once again.

Chapter sixteen

S tephen was worried after his telephone call with Marcus; he sat for a little while wondering whether to check for himself, but finally decided that he would rather avoid being chastised by Marcus for worrying too much. Turning to his computer to distract himself, he searched for more about the hospital. He had learned to trust Marcus and his gut feelings, so did as he had asked. Stephen understood why Marcus needed to watch the hospital and he wanted to gather as much evidence for him as he could. The distraction was minimal though, as his searches proved fruitless, and his mind kept wandering back to his husband.

The office was completely empty; there was a huge operation going on in the city. As a civilian worker with the police, Stephen could not go, which meant that he could continue uninterrupted with his search.

"A strong cup of coffee before I carry on, I think," he said aloud to nobody.

Stephen got up and wandered out of the office and into the kitchen where the coffee machine was found. He put his mug under the nozzle and pressed for his usual drink. Nothing came out. The machine was empty, as usual, so he spent the next few minutes filling up the dispensers and cleaning it. Finally, once he finished that, he could get the coffee that he was craving. A piping hot cappuccino filled his mug, the smell wafting up to his nose, teasing his senses with the wonderful aroma. He took a sip, endeavouring not to burn his mouth, and walked back towards the office.

A noise caught his attention. He had a look around but could not pinpoint where it had come from, thinking nothing more about it. He walked back into the office and put his coffee on his desk. Stephen heard the noise again, but this time it was in the office. His eyes scanned the area, but he could not find the source. The room was completely empty. There was not a soul in sight. Stephen decided he must have imagined the noises and went back to his desk to continue his research.

The computer screen was blank when he sat back down at his desk, which was not how he had left it. He wiggled his mouse to wake the screen back up. Nothing happened, not a flicker. The screen remained blank. Stephen pressed and held the power button to reboot the computer. As he did, all the lights went off. A power outage was his first guess as he sat in the half-light from the sun that streamed in through the only window in the office. Stephen got up from his desk and walked towards the door. As he got there, an enormous man was standing in the doorway, blocking it completely. He did not recognise him, and he did not know why he was there.

"Can I help you?" he asked.

The man in front of him said nothing, the uncomfortable silence punctuated by the blankness of his eyes. Dark and empty, there was no hint of emotion radiating from them. His eyes penetrated deep into

Stephen's soul. A coldness spread through Stephen; fear gripped him. His body was rigid, and he could not move. He did not understand his fear.

"Why are you here? Is there something you need?" he asked, trying to sound confident and not flustered at all.

Without warning, the man lunged at him, giving Stephen no time to react. Instantly, he felt a pain in his abdomen as a knife was plunged deep into him. In shock, Stephens' stare fixed on the man in front of him, his mind unable to process what had happened and what it meant. The man pushed the knife further into Stephen's body. He twisted it around, causing more pain. Then, he dragged it vertically from his stomach to his chest, cutting the skin and muscle as he pulled it up.

Stephen felt every movement of the blade as it moved upward. The only thing breaking the silence in the room was the squelching and tearing noises of the knife as it did its work. Blood spilled onto the floor. As he stood, frozen to the spot, the realisation that he was going to die spread across Stephen's face and tears trickled down his cheeks as every movement of the blade sent bolts of pain through him. Finally, his attacker removed the knife from Stephen's body. He took his last breath as the blade left. His body fell to the floor as his assailant discarded the knife beside him. There had been no life flashing before his eyes, no comforting pictures of his husband and dogs in his mind, just horror and the realisation that he was going to die alone, here in this office. No white light greeted him, just a nothingness, his soul lost.

Not content with taking Stephen's life, the man pulled at the deep wound with his bare hands. He ripped it wide open, his hands slipping into the cavity until they were deep inside Stephen's lifeless body. His fingers curled around the organs, and one by one, each of them pulled from him and spread across the floor. Blood pooled around his knees as he continued to defile the body in any way that he could.

Eventually, the horror stopped, and Stephen's body and entrails were left strewn across the floor. He lay alone and abandoned, and without thought, the murderer disappeared without a trace, leaving no clue that he was ever there.

"Is it done?" Berran asked.

"Yes, Berran, the husband of The Peacekeeper is dead," the man replied.

"And you left clues?"

"I left the knife, and the red tipped feather near his body. The Peacekeeper cannot miss it. He will blame your daughter for his death."

"You have done well. I will release you back to your family. Your work for me is done," Berran told him.

The man who had carried out Berran's dirty work left the room and scurried out of the building, relieved that he could go back to his wife. He had not wanted to kill anyone, but he could not say no to Berran. His wife and children would have died if he had. He had known of Berran and his demands for a long time. Nobody refused him. If they did, they did not live for long and nor did their families. What worried him was how much he had relished in the killing ...

"I have found my weapon, but I am confused," Marcus announced as he walked through the door to Adred's room.

It did not surprise Marcus to see that Adred looked troubled as well as in pain, but he had hoped that the news of his weapon of choice would cheer him a little.

"Why are you confused?" he asked. "What weapon has chosen you?"

"When I looked at the label, it said that it was the Sword of Berran. Why is there a sword named after him?"

"Berran was one of the Celestial Guards when he was here. He made that sword and used it when he took up his role as the head of guards," Adred replied.

"When we banished him, we removed the sword from him. It would have been folly to allow him to keep it in his possession. It holds far too much power."

"I know about the power; I could feel it as soon as I held it. Adred, I can hear the voices of the dead, The Celestials that were lost earlier. I can hear them; I can feel them within me. How is that possible?" Marcus asked.

"It is an incredibly special sword. It chose you to carry their souls with you, for when you need them, they will help you with the fight to come. I am glad that you have it," Adred struggled to reply.

"But, Marcus, there is something else we must talk about; I am afraid that we have received word that your husband is in danger. It is only right that we send you back to protect him. You can bring him here," Adred told him.

"Why is Stephen in danger? He has nothing to do with any of this. He is not of this world, is he?"

"No, he has no connection with anything that is happening here. His only link to us is the bond you both share. With that said, we will protect him the best we can. I propose to send you back to where we picked you up from. You will remember everything, but nobody will know that you left, as we explained before. You must drive back to your office as soon as you arrive," he told him.

Marcus could not bear that Stephen was being caught up in all of this. He had to get him to safety and if that meant bringing him to Elysium, then that is where they would be.

"You cannot take the sword just yet, Marcus, but you will continue to feel The Celestials as a part of your psyche for a little while. You should be able to protect yourself and your husband," Adred explained.

Adred got to his feet. It was an effort, and Marcus could clearly see the pain on his face. He asked Marcus if he was ready to go, and he nodded to him that he was. Moments later, he was sitting back in his car with no idea how he got there. He started the car as soon as he arrived and drove at speed towards the office, as suggested by Adred.

On the way, he tried calling Stephen's mobile phone, but there was no answer. He kept trying the line, but each one of his attempts failed. He pushed the car harder, not caring what the speed limit was–he switched on his lights and sirens and sped past the traffic. Racing to save his husband.

As he parked his car, he could see that the station car park was empty. He had heard over the police radio that there was a major incident on his way there, so the lack of vehicles did not surprise him. He dashed into the building;

all the lights were out. It did not take him long to get to the office that he shared with Stephen and his team. He opened the door, but the horrific sight in front of him did not immediately register. It was grotesque, like something out of a slasher movie.

As the scene permeated into his brain, he rushed over to the mutilated body on the floor. The smell that filled the air caused his stomach to lurch. Blood pooled around the body, and it took Marcus a few moments to register who it was on the floor.

Taking a deep breath, Marcus looked closely at the scene in front of him, and the shock hit him like a ton of bricks. As Marcus fell to his knees, the sound of blood squelching under him broke the silence. He lifted the remains of his husband into his arms and let out the most heart wrenching sound. Marcus sobbed as he tried to wake Stephen up, all the while knowing deep down that nothing he could do would ever wake him again. He shouted and screamed at him. Marcus shook him, but eventually, all he could do was to hold him tight. As the cold blood seeped into his clothing, he knew that he never wanted to let him go. The Celestial spirits that had connected themselves to him through the sword tried to comfort him, but nothing could get through to Marcus. The shock and loss were too much for him to bear.

Word had got to Elysium, and Helen appeared in the office. She already knew what had happened, she was unprepared for the sight of Stephen's mutilated body.

Marcus looked up at her, the pain clear for her to see. As well as the pain, she detected the anger rising within Marcus.

There was a darkness that was threatening to take hold of him, a darkness that was not present before, and she knew she needed to get him back to Elysium as soon as possible.

Suddenly, something caught his eye. Marcus gently lowered Stephen to the floor. He picked up a large red tipped feather close to where Stephen lay. He knew who that belonged to. Anger erupted in him; gut wrenching screams reverberated through the building. Marcus was going to destroy Grace. She would suffer for what she had done to his husband.

Helen put her hands on Marcus and on Stephen's body. She took them both back to Elysium.

Chapter seventeen

Marcus was back in Elysium with Helen by his side. Stephen's body lay on the floor, the fatal wounds clear for anyone to see. He knelt beside his husband. Tears streamed down his face as he lifted and cradled Stephen's broken body once more, careful not to damage the organs that were laid out around him. Marcus could not comprehend fully what had happened or why it had. The feather lay on the floor next to them, its presence in the room an unpleasant reminder of who had been involved in the orchestration of this atrocity. Helen was distraught at the thought that Grace could be responsible for the brutal murder of an innocent man.

"Why have you brought me back here?" he snapped at her.

"I had no choice. We must keep you safe, and here is the only place I know it can be done," Helen replied.

"Look what she did! How could she do this to him?"

"We don't know that it was Grace, not for certain," Helen did not know what else to say to Marcus.

"Then what is this? It is from her fucking wings! I am going to kill her, that bitch will pay for this!" a shaking and broken Marcus screamed at Helen.

Helen knelt next to Marcus, trying to offer comfort, but he was in no mood to receive any. He pushed her away. His life had changed forever, and she was not sure what to do next. Eventually he looked up, slightly more subdued now, but nothing that she could say would change anything.

"I have to get our dogs; they won't survive on their own, and I don't want to be here."

"We will bring them here. For now, though, you need to let me take Stephen," Helen told him.

Marcus refused. Unable to bear the thought of his husband not being whole, he lifted and gently replaced the organs back into Stephen's butchered body. The last one to go in was Stephen's heart. Marcus held it for a few moments, wishing that he could turn back the clock and for it to be beating once more in his husband's body. He placed it back to where it belonged. The last organ returned. Marcus had no idea if any of them were in the right position, but he needed to do it for his husband. He could not bear the thought of him missing any part of his body. Eventually the floor was clear, and the only evidence of the tortuous murder was the gaping wound from Stephen's stomach to his chest, and the blood on his clothing.

The door opened and a shocked Adred walked into the room; the noise causing Marcus to look up. He studied Adred, who looked completely healed. Marcus did not want to see him, and even if Adred could find the words to say, he knew they would not help.

"Marcus, I am so sorry. I had hoped that you would get to your husband in time," Adred said, grasping for anything to say to fill the void in the room.

"Leave us alone, this is all your fault! If you had not bought me here, this would never have happened! I swear I will make you all pay for this!" a distraught Marcus shouted.

The room was silent. Neither Helen nor Adred knew how to console Marcus and so instead, they watched on as he cradled the dead body of his husband.

"Send me back to before this happened. Let me save him!" Marcus suddenly shouted, making them both jump.

"I cannot, Marcus. It does not work like that. We could only send you back to where we took you from. I wish I could send you back earlier. It just is not possible. I am so sorry, Marcus," Adred explained.

"You are a Celestial, aren't you? Surely you can do anything! I cannot do this without Stephen. He is my rock, my heart, and my reason for living. You must help me!" Marcus pleaded.

Adred did not know what else to say to him. It was impossible to do what Marcus was asking. He had empathy for him, but there was nothing he could say to Marcus that would help. Marcus was still on the floor, his head bowed so that it touched Stephen's. The love and torment were obvious to the onlookers.

"Can't you give him his life back? Can't you give me back my husband?" he begged.

"Marcus, we have never done that before. A Fallen killed Stephen and as far as I know that dark force is not one that we can reverse." Adred explained.

"Please, tell me you will try?"

"I can consult with The Elders, but I cannot promise you that there is anything to be done. For now, you need to let Helen take his body, please."

After a few minutes, a reluctant acceptance spread through Marcus, and he looked up, his eyes full of tears. He nodded at her, and slowly let go of his husband, gently placing his head back on to the floor. He moved the hair from Stephen's eyes and wiped the blood from his face with his hand, and then he kissed him for the last time. Marcus could not bear it, but he knew that the man he loved was gone. Memories of the wonderful human being that Stephen was were all that remained for him.

Marcus stood up, his husband's blood covering his clothes and hands, and he watched as Helen gently lifted his husband from the floor. Helen surrounded Stephen with her wings, encompassing him completely, and she left the room. Marcus watched her leave and then fell to the floor. Heartbreak and exhaustion had taken every ounce of energy from him. Adred called for some Celestials to take him to a quiet room to rest, they cleaned him up and changed his clothes. Marcus was completely unaware of their actions in his grief-stricken state. Adred knew Marcus would need time, but unfortunately, that was one thing that they did not have.

Adred sat by Marcus's bed for hours, watching him closely as he slept. He saw the nightmares that he was living through and watched as pain spread across his face and tears trickled down his cheeks. Adred knew that this pain could drive Marcus towards his potential, he just wished that it did not have to be that way. He also knew that it could end the hopes that he would become The Peacekeeper that they needed.

There was nothing he could do but wait for him to wake up and hope that he would stay in Elysium. The door opened and Helen led in Marcus and Stephen's beloved dogs. They both jumped onto the bed and curled up around their dad, snuggling into his body to protect him. Adred could see in their eyes that they knew something was wrong, it always amazed him the how animals understood what was happening. Adred stroked them both on their heads and told them that everything would be alright. They settled down to sleep next to Marcus, and he left the room.

Marcus slept for many more hours with his dogs by his side. They snuggled in closer as he had nightmares, offering comfort to him, even if he did not know they were there.

Eventually Marcus woke to the noise of wagging tails, and the slobbering kisses of the dogs on his face. They were happy to see him, and he was relieved and happy to see them both safe in Elysium. He held them to his chest and cried until there were no tears left. Adred knocked on the door and walked in. He saw the dogs by Marcus. Their love for him was clear to see, and he was glad that Helen had got them to Elysium. He knew Marcus needed them to hold on to, that he needed them to give him some stability.

"Thank you, Adred. I am so grateful that you got our boys here. It means such a lot to know that they are safe," he flatly said, his mood clear to read.

"Marcus, would you like to see Stephen?" he asked.

"I am not sure I can face it. I do not want to see him like that again."

"You will not remember him like that. Please come with me. I promise it will be alright," he replied reassuringly.

"Follow me, the boys can come as well," he told him.

Marcus reluctantly got off the bed, the dogs followed closely by his side.

Marcus, Beau, and Henry followed Adred out of the room and down the corridor towards the weapons room. Adred opened the door and stood in the centre of the room was Stephen supported by Helen. The dogs ran to him; Marcus fell to his knees in disbelief.

"How?" he asked.

"I visited The Elders. We all knew that we could not bring Stephen back as a human, but after a lot of debate The Elders decided Stephen should live and become a Celestial. We will leave you both and your boys alone for a little while. It is a lot to take in for both of you. Come and find us when you are ready. We will be in the main hall," Adred replied.

Marcus ran towards his husband and took him in his arms. As they held each other, the dogs ran excitedly around their feet. Both men were crying with a mixture of relief and happiness.

"How are you?" Marcus asked.

"I am okay now, but Marcus, it was horrific. The pain was indescribable until there was no pain. I tried to stay but I could not. I did not want to leave you." He replied, crying as he spoke.

"What happened and why? I do not understand any of this," he asked Marcus.

"Sit down. I will tell you all that I know. I am still finding it hard to believe everything. Together, we can make sense of it all."

"It is a long and unbelievable story, and one I do not fully understand it myself. I just know that I am The Peacekeeper. A sort of mediator between Humankind, The Celestials, and The Fallen. A member of The Fallen murdered you, and I will make her pay for that."

"Her? It was not a woman, Marcus, it was an enormous man. He took me by surprise, and I could not defend myself. I had no chance to fight back," Stephen explained.

"A man?"

"Yes, a man." Stephen replied.

Marcus continued to tell Stephen all that he had been told. Stephen listened, taking in every word. Less than an hour later, Stephen knew everything that his husband did. Both men caught up in a world that they never imagined and, in a situation, so far removed from their own lives.

"Well, that's everything, but most importantly, Stephen, no matter what the future holds for us, never ever forget how much I love you."

"I love you too, more than you will ever truly know," Stephen replied.

"Not possible."

Stephen smiled lovingly at his husband; they held each other, neither one of them wanting to let go. Although Marcus was the strong one in their relationship, Stephen that knew his husband would never have survived emotionally had The Celestials had not saved him. He promised himself that he would make sure that Marcus never felt that way ever again.

Chapter Eighteen

Grace was not sure what she should do next. The past few days had been such a rollercoaster of emotions that she did not know where to start. Her mind filled with so many questions and there was nobody to answer them. She was alone.

Exhaustion overtook her. She gave in to it and laid on the bed in her room. With no thought from Grace, her wings surrounded her in a warm embrace. She did not know how or why they did, but she was grateful to have that feeling of security around her body.

Sleep came easily, but the dreams that went with it were far from easy to deal with. Her dreams filled with visions of a mother she did not know, mixed with the brutality of Charlie and his parents' murders; a sight that haunted her, even during her waking hours. The pain of getting her wings and the guilt she felt doubting Charlie's love meant that throughout her sleep she cried, sobbing so hard that her wings tightened around her body even more, holding her as she experienced everything again in her nightmares. Her wings became her strength and support. They were now part of her and even in sleep; she felt it. Hours passed, nightmares continued, and dreams were lost as Grace's subconscious processed her recent experiences.

A loud knock on the door pulled her from her sleep. Her wings unfurled from around her and tucked themselves away out of sight. She did not want to see anyone, so she ignored the knock, but whoever it was relentless and continued until she had no choice but to answer.

Grace got off the bed and stood in the centre of the room as the door opened and a young woman entered. Grace guessed that she could not have been over eighteen years old. The young woman bowed her head, which made Grace feel uncomfortable.

"Berran sent me to see if you would like some food," her voice trembled as she spoke.

Grace was hungry, though she was not sure that she would keep anything down if she ate. She could not remember when she had last eaten a meal, so she nodded at the young woman.

"What would you like?"

"Just something light, please," she replied.

The young woman bowed her head again and scurried out of the room. Grace wondered why somebody so young was with The Fallen and her father. It was a question she would ask when the girl came back.

After she had gone, Grace looked around the familiar room that she was in, hoping to find something that would help her escape. There was nothing. Grace walked into the bathroom to freshen up a bit. As she went in, she spotted herself in a mirror above the sink and she saw the blood of The Celestials on her face and splattered all over her white dress. At once, she found herself on her knees with her head over the toilet, her empty stomach reaching for contents that were not there. Grace retched and retched, but nothing came up. Her emotions were manifesting themselves physically.

The door opened, and the smell of food soon filtered into the bathroom. She retched again... The young woman put the tray of food down on the bed and entered the bathroom to see Grace kneeling on the floor.

"Can I help you?" she asked nervously.

As she shook her head to reply, Grace's stomach went into spasm once more. The young woman knelt next to her and gently took her hand in her own. Grace looked at her, she saw that her eyes were full of compassion, and not the nervousness she had seen earlier. The young woman pushed the hair from Grace's sweat-soaked face.

"Please let me help you," she pleaded.

Grace nodded her reply to the young woman, who helped her to her feet. Silently the young woman turned on the shower, gave Grace some shampoo, soap, and a couple of soft white cotton towels, and then left her alone to shower.

Grace slowly undressed; the blood-stained white dress she wore in Elysium falling to the floor and she stepped into the warm shower. The hot water cascaded over her body, warming her skin. She lathered the soap and washed all traces of the blood from her body, and she hoped some of the nightmarish sights that went with it. Grace turned the shower off and stepped out of it. She wrapped the towel around her naked body and used the second to cover her wet hair. Grace was glad to see the steam covering the mirror.

She didn't want to see herself again. It was her fault that Charlie was dead. If only she had been normal and not a Divinexus, they would all still be alive. As she walked out of the bathroom, the young woman greeted her with a smile.

"Has that helped?" she asked.

"It did, thank you," she replied.

"I have some food for you."

"Thank you. Can I ask your name?" Grace asked.

"I am Cayla."

"What are you doing here, Cayla?"

"I am here to serve you," Cayla replied with no further explanation.

"Where are your parents? Do they know you are here?"

"Our father knows exactly where I am. He told me to look after you," Cayla told her.

"Our father? You are my sister?"

"I am your half-sister."

Grace was in complete shock; she had been alone for her whole life and now she had a twin brother and a younger sister. Grace had longed for a family of her own as she was growing up, to feel like she belonged somewhere, but never in a million years could she have imagined all of this. She was the daughter of the most evil being in existence, sister to Cali and Cayla. What else she would discover? Not forgetting that she was supposed to be a powerful being herself.

Cayla pitied her sister; she knew what was in store for Grace. There was nothing she could do but watch how everything played out. She was a little unsettled by how calm Grace had become. She studied her older sister, weighing her up, hoping she could gain her trust.

Grace looked deep into Cayla's eyes, and deep into her soul. She could see defiance, fear, and hope within her sister. Grace was at once overwhelmed by the need to protect her. She felt a responsibility, one that she hoped she could rise to.

"I will not be like him," she told her younger sister, not knowing exactly why she needed to say it aloud.

Cayla did not respond. The two women continued to study one another, each of them unsure how their relationship would progress. Grace broke the silence that filled the room.

"Now let me have that food, and then I have a lot of questions. Will you answer some of them?" Grace said, exuding a strength from somewhere within herself.

"You must understand, Grace, I am just a blip on our father's radar, just a servant that he can order around. I will help where I can, but we must be careful. He would destroy me if he found out that I was telling you anything." Grace noted how scared Cayla appeared as she spoke.

"I will try my best to protect you, I promise."

Cayla nodded and smiled at Grace, but Grace could tell that her younger sister was keeping her guard up.

"First, will you help me understand the layout and hierarchy here?" she asked.

Tentatively, Cayla said yes.

As the young women talked and gradually got to know each other, the door opened, and Cali stormed in.

"Leave us!" he barked at Cayla.

Grace watched as Cayla seemed to become invisible before her eyes. She immediately scurried towards the door, only momentarily looking back at Grace with the look of a scared and frightened child. Grace was angry at how her brother had spoken to Cayla. She could feel hate and bitterness building within her.

"Did you have to be so rude?" she snapped at Cali as soon as Cayla closed the door.

"She is insignificant, you unfortunately are not. Are you rested because Berran has requested your presence?" Cali asked.

"She is our sister; how can you call her that? Don't you have any compassion for her?"

"That girl is just the result of a dalliance that our father had with a human. She is the lowest form of life. Even humans have more use than her. Of course she is insignificant, she is useless and a huge mistake," Cali took delight in telling her.

"No, life is insignificant, except maybe yours, you arrogant prick," she snapped back at him.

"Prick? Nice, I see that you have some spirit, you are going to need that," he laughed. "Now you will do as you are told. Berran will soon put you in your place if you do not. Get yourself ready now!"

"Berran, and you can bloody wait! I need to eat and get dressed, so get out of my room. I will be ready when I am ready," she snapped back at him.

Grace saw the anger flash across her brother's face, his hands formed fists by his side. She could tell that he was fighting the urge to hit her. Grace had made an enemy of him already and it did not bother her in the slightest. She was determined that she would put him in his place. His attitude only confirmed that she was not in the right place and that she needed to get to Elysium as soon as she could. He did not move and instead, stood defiantly in her room. Grace opened her wings and stepped towards him. She was a formidable sight. He turned and walked towards the door, muttering under his breath. Grace did not catch what he said, but she did not care.

Just before he slammed the door, he screamed, "abomination, it's time for your destruction, and I will be the one to do it!"

"Go for it, you pathetic excuse for a man!"

Chapter nineteen

Stephen and Marcus spent some time together and Marcus tried his best to explain the situation to his husband, but what he was telling him just sounded so unbelievable. Had Stephen not died, he may never have believed the story he was being told.

"If I understand this right, Grace is a Divinexus and that makes her the most powerful being ever to exist?"

"Apparently," Marcus shrugged, "though I did not see her use any powers when The Fallen attacked. I am still very sceptical, Stephen. The only thing that makes me believe a semblance of all this is that Grace's wings appeared from nowhere, right in front of me. Also, *you are* here, and not dead. You know me. I need absolute proof before I believe anything I have been told," Marcus replied.

"I have to ask; did you get wings when they made you a Celestial?"

Stephen smiled at the question; he had been waiting for Marcus to ask. Of course, he could not wait to show him, and so his answer came without words; he only smiled as he unfurled the wings. The majesty of them took Marcus's breath away. He was a remarkable sight. He was already the most handsome man in the world to Marcus, but now he had wings! Marcus could not describe how he felt about him now. The dogs were unsure though and spent the next few minutes barking incessantly at him. He bent down and stroked both boys to reassure them as Henry and Beau sniffed at every single feather of the wings before settling back down in their new beds.

"Were you in pain when you got them? Grace was in agony with hers," he asked, recalling the horrific sight he witnessed when she got hers.

"No, when I woke up from my death sleep, I was told what had happened and who I was now, they also told me I had wings and how to unfurl them, and how to hide them, no pain at all," Stephen replied.

Marcus was relieved. He could only imagine the immense pain Stephen must have felt when he died and could not bear the thought of him going through more.

"Now come here," Stephen said, beckoning his husband closer.

As Marcus moved towards him, Stephen wrapped his wings around them. Marcus noticed how soft they were, and as the wings tightened and cocooned them both, Marcus felt safe. For a brief time, the nightmares of the past few days washed away into the distant parts of his brain. He rested his head on Stephen's chest and listened to the rhythm of his heartbeat, which soothed his soul. Marcus had not realised just how exhausted he was. His husband's touch was enough to help him relax. He soon drifted to sleep whilst being held in Stephen's embrace.

Stephen gently lifted Marcus onto the bed. He had a strength that he had never had before. He liked that. As they lay together, he watched his husband sleeping, the worry lines vanishing from his face. Stephen was glad that as a Celestial, he no longer needed to sleep. He knew that the way he died would play repeatedly in his dreams if he did. The hours passed and Stephen cherished every moment; he thought he would never see his husband again or feel his embrace during the attack. His life was different now, but at least he had a life, one that he could share with his husband. Stephen was ready to support Marcus completely, in whatever form that would take.

Marcus woke up, he saw Stephen was watching him. He asked him if he slept too. Stephen explained that he no longer needed sleep as a Celestial. Marcus kissed his husband tenderly on the lips and he responded by drawing his wings around them both. Gently, his wings caressed them, encompassing both men in their own safe cocoon. Stephen groaned as Marcus slowly and gently explored his husband's new body. Marcus wondered if it was even possible to make love to his Celestial husband and if it would be the same as before? He soon found the answers to his questions as they both gave into their desires.

Adred sat waiting to meet with Helen to discuss how the other Celestials were healing. He had never seen such horror from The Fallen; they were like feral animals unleashed on their prey. Berran had gone too far this time. War had always been on the cards after the birth of the Divinexus. He did not expect it to be this brutal, though it should not have been a surprise. Of course, there had been violence over the centuries, but never this extreme; earlier encounters had never resulted in so much death. Berran will not be easy to pacify if his daughter chooses The Celestials over The Fallen. He hoped above everything that she would not join with The Fallen. If she did, Berran would have so much power at his disposal that Adred feared that neither Humankind nor The Celestials would ever recover from the brutality that would surely follow.

Helen entered the room, and she could tell instantly that Adred was struggling. He sat alone, lost in his thoughts; she watched him for a few moments, not wanting to interrupt his thoughts. Patiently, she waited for him to notice that she was there.

"I am sorry, Helen; have you been standing there for long?" he asked.

"No, Adred, I have just arrived. You look tortured by your thoughts. What can I do to help?" Helen asked, trying to keep the worry from her voice.

"There is nothing we can do just yet; we need Marcus to embrace his responsibilities before we can even make this right. Hopefully, with Stephen as a Celestial, he will do just that."

"I hope so. We have taken an enormous risk. He is the first human to have the honour of becoming one of us," Helen mused.

"How are the injured? Have we lost anymore?"

"Sadly, yes. Many others lost their wings, and they feel like they have no purpose without them. I will not lie. We are going to struggle to put up any sort of defence against The Fallen right now," she told him.

"I will see Marcus. I must make him understand the urgency of all of this. He has had enough time with Stephen to repair his own psychological wounds," Adred responded impatiently.

"Be gentle, we need him to be balanced in his approach to The Fallen. He cannot take on your anger along with his own. You know as well as I do, he is key to resolving this without more violence, Adred."

Adred had not felt this much anger before; the attack unbalanced him. He had lost so many friends, and there were many more wounded who would never be the same. Helen was right, he needed to bury that anger for now. He nodded to reassure her.

"Should I come with you? The two of us could make him see how imperative it is that he steps up and embraces his role as The Peacekeeper." she asked.

"I think that would be a good idea. Thank you, Helen, for reminding me of my role here. I lost my way and focused only on my anger. You are right, my feelings are my own and I must deal with them quietly. I will not push them onto Marcus."

Helen embraced Adred, and he felt her calmness flood through him. She had always been a calming influence upon him.

"Thank you, I needed that," Adred told her as they parted.

"Ready?" she asked, studying his face closely.

He nodded and turned towards the door. Minutes later, the pair were standing in front of the chambers where Marcus and Stephen were living. Helen knocked on the door.

"Come in," Stephen responded.

Adred opened the door to see the two men walking towards him, their dogs by their sides.

"Marcus, we need to talk," Adred told him, but before he could add anything else, Marcus interrupted him.

"Yes, Adred. We were just coming to see you. I have finally grasped the severity of this situation. If Berran could kill Stephen, seemingly to get to me, no one is safe. I will try my best to accept my role as Peacekeeper, but you need to give me space to work through the implications," he replied.

Both Helen and Adred were relieved; they had not expected this to be a straightforward conversation.

"That is exactly what I was hoping to hear from you, though I will say that I was expecting to have to do some serious persuasion to get you fully on board. I am relieved, Marcus. Thank you."

"I will try. That is all I can promise you now. So, what is the next step, Adred?" he asked.

"You need to become proficient with the Sword of Berran, and then we need to get Grace," he replied.

"So, an easy ask then?" he cheekily replied.

Although he was happy that Marcus was more understanding of the situation, he seemed a little too flippant for Adred's liking. He was glad that Marcus had begun to accept his place in the grand scheme of things.

Adred hoped Stephen would ground him and keep him focused on the task ahead.

Chapter twenty

Grace purposefully took her time eating and getting dressed. She was determined not to show any weakness to her brother or her father. Grace felt Cali's presence just outside the door to her room, and she sensed his frustration growing more each moment she made him wait. Like a stubborn child, Grace took small morsels of her food and chewed them slowly. She knew it would feed her brother's impatience. Finally, as she finished, Cali stormed back into the room.

"Fuck you! How dare you make me wait like your little pet dog? GET FUCKING DRESSED!" he bellowed.

Grace stared at him for a moment or two, raising her eyebrows and then smiling at him. She pondered how she could wind him up some more.

"You'd better leave then Cali. You will not watch me dress."

Cali looked hard at his sister. He hated every part of her, and she was the abomination he had always believed that she would be. Her attitude to him only fuelled that hate, and just her presence was enough to fill him with rage. He turned and stormed out of the room, snapping at her. Grace smiled in triumph. She had gotten under Cali's skin, and she decided she would continue to annoy him for as long as she was there. Though she did not plan on that being for long at all.

Grace turned her attention from the door and looked to see what clothes there were for her to wear. She could not put on the dress she had arrived in; she could not bear to look at it. Covered in the blood of The Celestials, it was a physical reminder of the horror inflicted by Berran. Grace found a couple of dresses hanging in the wardrobe; they were not her style at all, but there were no other options that she could see. The choice was between a loose-fitting, plain scarlet dress or a flowery version. She chose the red one and found that underwear and shoes were provided for her as well. Grace took her time getting dressed and sorting her wet hair out. There was no hairdryer, so it would have to stay wet. Eventually she walked towards the door and opened it to find Cali standing guard, waiting for her. His face looked like he had chewed on a wasp. It made Grace laugh. He threw a glance at her that told her she was winning in the minor war of their own, though that did not last long.

"You found the clothes I got for you. Don't you look pretty," he smirked, making Grace feel extremely uncomfortable, and knocking her confidence a little.

"I did well with the sizes then," he said.

Grace did not respond. She felt a sense of repulsion bubbling up inside her and tried to hide her disgust at his obvious delight.

"Follow me. Father will not be happy that you took so long to get ready, Grace." He snapped. "One piece of advice

I have for you, do not piss him off any more than you already have. I can promise that you will regret it."

In silence, she followed Cali to her father. As she walked into the room, she saw Berran was standing waiting, anger clear on his face. The atmosphere was far from good.

"Berran," she acknowledged.

"How dare you keep me waiting? Who do you think you are?" he snapped at her.

"Apparently, I am your daughter, but my treatment suggests that I'm more like your fucking prisoner!" she snapped back.

"Yes, you are my fucking daughter, and you will do well to remember that. You will learn you have no protectors here and you will do as I bid. There will be no arguments about that. You will regret crossing me. So, my question to your dear daughter is, would you like an easy life doing my bidding or to be kept as my prisoner?"

Grace did not answer him.

"You have no choice really, do you?" Berran asked, breaking the silence.

"Don't I? I have powers too, so how will you contain me?" she replied with more strength and power than she felt.

"You wish to test me, girl? You know nothing of your powers, and that makes it easy for me to contain you. I have no qualms in showing you just how powerful this Fallen is girl!"

Grace stood firm, defiance written all over her face, though inside she was shaking with fear. She hoped that nobody saw her trembling. He was right. Grace knew nothing of her powers, nor how to use them. How could she go up against him without that knowledge?

Berran stepped forward, he was nose to nose with her. Their eyes locked, she felt his breath on her face, his stared seemed to burn into her soul, she tried her best to resist him. Grace faltered and as she did, her wings tore through the dress she was wearing, the sound of the material ripping breaking Berran's invasion of her soul. The white feathered wings spread quickly out behind her. Shocked at their sudden appearance, Grace wondered if they had appeared because of her emotional state. Could her powers work with her emotions?

"Put those fucking monstrosities away! You will not show them here. I WILL NOT HAVE IT!" Berran bellowed. "May I remind you that it would not take much to remove them from you?"

Defiantly, Grace stood her ground. Her wings did not move, not one feather ruffled. She did not flinch or do as Berran had ordered. Cali stepped towards them both with a large knife in his hands.

"Then you give me no choice."

Berran smiled at his son and nodded. As he got closer, his hand raised high, Grace noticed the glint of the steel as it caught the sun shining through the large windows behind her father. Grace refused to give in to them and stood firm. Inwardly, she felt like her heart was about to explode. She could hear it pounding in her ears and her chest felt tight.

Cali was only a couple of steps away from her when Grace's wings took on a life of their own, flapping hard. Cali lunged towards her wings. He did not have a chance to do any damage as one of them struck him hard and sent him flying across the room; the knife falling from his hand. With a loud thud, her brother hit a bookcase on the other side of the room and landed in a heap on the floor. Books tumbled from the shelves, hitting her brother on the head. Grace tried to hide a smirk as a look of shock spread across her twin's face. He got back on his feet quickly, kicking the books away from him. He looked at his father nervously. Berran stared at him with a clear look of disappointment in his son. Cali lowered his head in shame. Berran soon turned his attention back to Grace.

"You may have outdone your half-wit brother this time, but you will not triumph over Thella, you know what she is capable of." his tone was even more threatening than before.

"Get Thella!" he shouted at Cali.

As Cali left the room, fear rose in every cell of Grace's body. Berran was right, and that scared her. She knew exactly what Thella was capable of, and she did not want to be on the receiving end of it. Grace folded her wings and tucked them away from view. Berran smiled at her, knowing that he had won.

Disappointed by herself and the way she backed down, she lowered her head and looked at her feet in shame. A knock on the door made her look back up. Thella locked eyes with Grace as she walked into the room. Grace smiled at her, their earlier encounter still fresh in her mind. Thella blushed and broke her stare. Beaten during that first encounter, Thella knew that she had felled her before, and that she could do it again.

"Cali said that you needed me, Berran," she said, while bowing her head in deference to him.

"You will arrange for Grace to receive some attitude training. I do not care how you do it, but you will break her. If you fail me, Thella, then you will be...well, I will let you think about what will happen to you, but you know it will not be a pleasant experience," he told her.

"I will get on it right away, Berran. I will not fail," she answered, looking directly at Grace.

Thella grabbed Grace by the arm and dragged her from the room, not uttering a single word, as she marched her along the corridor and down to the basement. Grace struggled, but Thella had a firm grip which she could not break free from.

As Thella dragged her down the steps, an overwhelming stench hit Grace. She could not be sure what it was. A mixture of excrement, sick and something else?

As Thella dragged Grace further into the basement rooms, she saw death all around. Bodies littered the floors. Everyone that she saw had suffered horrific injuries. There were many with missing limbs, some corpses had no heads, and the smell of rotting flesh filled her senses.

A young woman about the same age as her caught Grace's eye. She struggled free from Thella's grasp and looked closely at the body. The young woman was sitting upright against a damp and mould covered wall with chains hanging around her frail body. Water trickled down the dank brickwork and onto her, soaking the remnants of the clothes that she was wearing. As she took in the view in front of her Grace focused in on the woman's eyes, or rather the lack of them. Where her eyes should have been, there were only black empty spaces. There was no light left of what must have been a happy and loved woman. A darkness filled Grace, and anger rose in her, but she knew she would need to pick her time for retaliation. Was someone missing the young woman? Was someone grieving her loss? Were they searching for her?

As Grace continued to study the poor soul in front of her, Thella delighted in the look of horror on her face. Grace saw blood-stained trails on her cheeks, she assumed from tears, which had dried on her face. She could not move or look away from the lifeless body. She could barely imagine the pain and torture which was inflicted on her. Grace's stomach lurched and the overwhelming feeling of wanting to be sick rose through her body. She composed herself and eventually looked over at Thella, who was taking great delight in what Grace was seeing.

"Why?" was all she could say to Thella.

"Because we can," she replied as she grabbed hold of Grace and dragged her further into the death filled basement.

Chapter twenty-one

Adred was relieved that Marcus was finally trying to embrace his destiny and that he was now ready to begin the work needed to give them a semblance of hope in the coming war. He only hoped that Grace could remain strong in the face of her father's demands. He knew it would not be easy for her to go against Berran. For now, though, there was nothing he could do about that; all he could do was to get Marcus ready.

"Follow me, Marcus. There is no time like the present to get started. Stephen, I would like you to stay with Helen. There are teachings she must share with you, and I am sure you have many questions about your new life."

"Of course, I definitely have a lot of questions," Stephen responded.

Marcus kissed his husband and patted both dogs before following Adred from the room.

"Adred, if I am The Peacekeeper, then why is it only The Celestials who are training me? Why are The Fallen not involved in this?" he asked.

Adred stopped in the corridor. He turned and faced Marcus. He knew he needed to answer his questions.

"We have always prepared The Peacekeeper for their role because, unlike The Fallen, we strive to be good and to keep everything in balance. Berran must not corrupt you. You must remain neutral, although with the attack on Stephen, I know this will be difficult for you," he replied.

"You think? That is an understatement, Adred. If it was him who killed Stephen, then he needs to pay. I cannot and will not forget the pain and loss he has inflicted upon us."

"I will ask you one question, Marcus, and you tell me your answer. If you had a choice between saving one life or many lives, what would the answer be?"

"That is an almost impossible question to answer. Surely it would depend on the circumstances?" Marcus questioned.

"Okay, if it was a choice between the life of Stephen and the life of every child born on earth, what would you choose?"

"That is not fair. You know how much I love him and how broken I was when he died."

"This is something you may need to decide. We are going to war, and you must be the one to make peace and keep the balance, otherwise countless innocents will die. I am sorry to be so blunt, but that is how it is. You must always remain neutral and do what is right for all. Can you do that, Marcus?" Adred asked.

Marcus was not sure that he could, and that made him further doubt whether he was ready to step up and do what he was being asked to do. Adred turned from him and continued along the corridor, confirming Marcus' guess that they were heading towards the weapons room.

"Waiting for us in the weapons room are some of the Celestial Guards. They are ready to guide you. They will test you. Marcus, I can guarantee that you will want to give up, but please don't," Adred pleaded.

"Honestly, Adred, I cannot promise that, not yet," he replied.

Adred's heart sunk. He knew he had gone too far by putting Stephen in his scenario with Marcus, but regrets would not help the situation.

"All that I ask is that you take time to think about what the world would be like if Berran seized power, given his loathing for Humankind. Consider whether that is a legacy you would be proud of, Marcus? Whether you could live with yourself if you allowed it to happen."

Marcus could not answer him. He was so used to being sure of his decisions, but he could tie himself up in knots thinking like that. After seeing Stephen lying on the floor with the injuries inflicted on him before his death, he doubted everything he thought he knew.

As Adred opened the door to the weapons room, Marcus saw six Celestial Guards stand to attention and bow their heads once they spotted Adred. Each of the guards dressed in military looking uniform with their wings out at full stretch. Marcus found himself momentarily distracted by their white uniforms, every part of them adorned with symbols sewn in golden thread. He decided he would ask them later what the symbols meant.

"Marcus, these Celestial Guards are your own personal guard. They will go with you, and protect you if you need it," Adred informed him.

"Okay, now I am confused. Surely if I am The Peacekeeper, wouldn't it be confrontational for me to have a personal guard with me?" he asked.

"Until you are up to speed with everything, it would be prudent to make sure that you do not meet the same fate as Stephen. Do you not agree?" he answered.

Marcus could not really argue with that, and so instead, he nodded at Adred in agreement.

"I would like to introduce you to Orin," Adred continued, and one guard stepped forward. "He will be the one training with you. I must warn you, he is not one to be trifled with. He has a short fuse and will not tolerate failure. He will guide you and make sure you are ready for what is coming."

Orin's size shocked Marcus: he towered above the rest of the guards and made him feel insignificant. Marcus extended his hand towards Orin, who took it and shook it with such a grip that Marcus had to stifle his reaction to the pain.

"Peacekeeper, it is good to meet you," said Orin in a booming voice that echoed around the room.

"Please call me Marcus, I am far from a Peacekeeper yet. Hopefully, you will help me change that," he replied.

"It will be my honour, Marcus." Orin nodded as he stepped back to join his rank.

"I will leave you here with Orin and his men. Come and find me when you have finished your first training session, Marcus."

Adred left the room without looking back at Marcus or the Celestial Guard, he had an uneasy feeling that he could not shake. He hoped Marcus would surprise him, but for now, he did not have complete faith that he was strong enough for what was to come.

"I understand that you have chosen your weapon, Marcus, and that it is the Sword of Berran." Orin said.

"Yes, I have, but really, the sword chose me."

One of the other Celestial Guards handed the sword to Marcus. As before, once he took hold of the sword, a power coursed through it and into his body. The Celestial voices made themselves known to him immediately.

"You hear the voices?" Orin asked him.

"Yes, I do. It is very distracting and overwhelming," he replied. "Do your weapons have the same powers?"

"No, Marcus, only the Sword of Berran channels our ancestors. Those who fought before us are the original Celestials. You have access to their wisdom and their strength, which is a good thing," he replied.

"Did Berran have that power when he had the sword?"

"Berran forged the sword for himself. He did the unthinkable when he made it, which is one reason the Elders banished him from here," Orin said without elaborating further.

"Why was he banished when he made the sword? It seems a little extreme."

"Berran imprisoned the souls of our ancestors within the sword. He wanted to use them to take over Elysium and the Earth. We have tried everything to release them, but without success. You are the conduit for them now. The only way we can communicate with them is through you," he replied.

"How have you communicated with them before?"

"We have not been able to, but we know that as Celestials, they will only want peace. We just hope that Berran did not corrupt any of them before he imprisoned them."

"That is a big hope, isn't it?"

"It is one that we all share, Marcus," Orin replied.

"Can you hear what they are saying? Does anything make sense to you?"

"All I can hear is noise, a gentle but relentless noise. I cannot make out a singular voice," he told Orin.

"It may take some time, but I am sure that once you are ready, they will make themselves clear to you."

"So where do we start, Orin?" Marcus asked nervously, looking at the big man in front of him.

"Combat training," he answered with a knowing and disconcerting smile, "but first put the sword away, please."

"Wonderful," Marcus muttered under his breath as he put the sword away. He was not ecstatic about physical training and hoped he would finish his first lesson in one piece.

Chapter twenty-two

Thella continued to drag Grace through the basement, away from the bodies strewn across the floor. Grace kept looking back at the poor wretch that had caught her eye, her heart breaking for the soul lost to violence and torture. She hoped that her spirit had ended up in a peaceful place with no more pain.

Eventually, the bodies gave way to a large space, but the stench remained entrenched in Grace's senses. In the centre of the dingy, dark, and soulless space was a single chair, and Thella was dragging Grace towards it.

It was Thella's silence that unnerved Grace more than anything; she was afraid of what was to come. Thella smiled, shoving Grace towards the chair with a great deal of force. She was looking forward to torturing the abomination. Grace resisted the shove and kept her feet beneath her. She stood defiantly next to the chair; she would not make it easy for Thella.

Grace did not see Thella's clenched fist and did not have time to react when she suddenly punched her in the side of her head again. The shock rendered Grace immobile, and unable to put out her hands to break her fall, as she landed face first on the floor, her nose took the full force; she heard it crack and break. Intense pain spread through her head, causing her eyes to tear up. She lay still, trying to regain her composure. The blood flowed freely from her nose, spreading across the floor and pooling around her face. Once the pain eased a little, she tried to get up. Thella put her foot heavily in the centre of her back and pushed her back down, causing Grace to wince as her face hit the floor again.

In this position and with Thella's weight on her back, breathing was almost impossible; Grace began to cough and choke until Thella eventually removed her foot. She grabbed Grace by the hair, lifting her slightly before smashing her face back down into the puddle of blood on the floor, smearing it across her cheeks. Thella knelt, pushing her knee into the centre of Grace's back, causing immense pain along her spine. Grace struggled beneath her captor. Thella was intent on causing as much pain as possible to Grace. The blood flowing from Grace's broken nose almost completely blocking her airway. She could feel it congealing, and every breath was a struggle. Her head spun, and the room became dark as she lost consciousness.

"Thella!" Grace heard shouted, bringing her back from the darkness. "Get off her. You were told to give her attitude training, not to fucking kill her!"

Thella reluctantly removed her knee and stood up, looking defiantly over to Cali who had just arrived in the basement area.

"She needs to learn who is in charge. You are too soft, which is why your father chose me. Now go back to your comfy rooms and leave me to get on with this!" she shouted at him.

"Have you forgotten your place, Thella? You are the lowest of the low here and he only gave you the task because he knows you will do anything to climb the ranks. That will not happen. You will always be at the bottom of the pile here," Cali snarled back. "I will make sure of that!"

"You!" she laughed in response. "You are just his toy, the spare with no power. He has no use for you. Berran has only ever been interested in her! Why would you want her to stay alive?"

Cali took a sharp intake of breath. He knew what Thella had said was in spite, but she was correct in her description of him. Cali was the spare that his father had never really wanted. He had nowhere near the power that his sister had, but his father had plans and Cali knew he was integral to them. He had decided early on that if he ever met Grace, he would make sure that she did their father's bidding. It would be best for everyone if she did.

"Torture, not death, Thella, which is what you need to be doing. We both need her to stay alive, think on it for a moment. What do you think will happen to you if she dies in your company?"

Thella was a tempestuous soul. She had not thought about the consequences when she lost her temper with Grace. Cali had a point. Resigned to her role, she grabbed Grace by her clothes. She lifted her up from the floor and pushed her onto the chair. Cali reminded her once more and then left them to it. He would normally stay and watch. He had been witness to Thella's special form of re-education before. It was certainly something to admire. Cali had his own way of doing things. If there was someone else capable of carrying out torture, he would happily step aside and keep his hands clean. He was very selective about when he got involved, and he savoured the times when he intervened.

"Now where shall we begin, Grace?" Thella taunted once Cali was out of sight.

The question had been pointless. Thella knew exactly where she would begin.

Grace took a deep breath, as much as her broken nose would allow, and replied,

"Do your worst."

"Your defiance is admirable. Or at least, it would be if you were someone that I cared for. But I do not care, and so I *will* do my worst, as you asked."

Thella moved towards Grace, certain of how she would break the abomination. She walked behind her and put her hands on the chair. Grace sat motionless; not prepared to show any form of weakness. The battle of wills had begun.

Neither of them moved for a few moments. The silence seemed to echo around the basement and the air was still. The stench of death mixing with the metallic scent of her own blood every time Grace took a breath. Time seemed to stop; Thella was determined to make Grace as uncomfortable as possible. Finally, she made her move. With one swift movement, she pushed Grace forward and slashed the clothing covering her back. Grace saw no weapon, the skin on her back now exposed to Thella.

"Time to get started," Thella snarled.

Grace felt a sharp point dig into her back between her shoulder blades. She did not know what it was. Slowly, Thella dragged an unseen weapon from between Grace's shoulder blades down to the base of her spine, scratching the skin as she did. Grace did not flinch; she would not give Thella the satisfaction of seeing any more pain. Grace straightened and pushed her back into the chair. Thella shoved her hard, forcing Grace to reveal her back once more, then she pulled the sharp object back up again. Shallow grooves marked Grace's back, droplets of blood breaking through the broken skin.

"Enough of playing nicely, I think," Thella snarled at her prisoner.

Grace did not react and sat motionless, waiting for the next attack from Thella. Anger was building, but she was not sure how to channel it. She wished she knew how to use her powers. Hate for Thella was at the forefront of her mind. She wanted her to suffer an unimaginable pain, but that was not in Grace's nature anymore. Her younger self would not have been as calm as she was. Grace dug deep. She wanted to find the fighter that she was during her childhood, but she struggled.

"Nothing? Not one word from you? You are pathetic. I do not know what Berran is thinking. You are not what you are supposed to be," Thella taunted.

Thella walked from behind Grace and stood looking at her, waiting for a reaction, disappointed when there was none. Grace spotted what Thella was using on her back. It was not a weapon at all, but claw-like nails protruding from the end of her fingers. Although Grace had accepted most of what she was told in Elysium, the sight of Thella shocked her.

Gone was the Celestial she had first met in Elysium. What Grace saw in front of her was a wild, unkempt, and vicious looking creature that did not resemble a being of pure heart. Her true nature was on show, and it was horrific. Grace was more frightened than she had ever been in her entire life. She took a deep breath and braced herself for what was next.

Thella walked back behind Grace. Immediately, she dug her claw deep into the base of her back, at the point that she knew her wings began. Grace screamed out in pain as Thella pushed deeper and deeper through the skin and then through the dense muscle protecting her organs and her wings.

With the pain of her ordeal fixed on Grace's face, the fighter in her surfaced, anger and fear built up instantly and a fire ignited within her. Heat spread through her body, an almost unbearable heat. She recognised that feeling; her memories took her back to the church where all of this began.

Thella had no time to react. Her claw was deep inside the body of the abomination, and she could not pull it out. A force erupted from the base of Grace's spine; her wings forced themselves out, Thella's claw repelled from her back with force. The wings unfurled and then wrapped around Grace's body, protecting her from the flames which engulfed Thella; Grace knew what was happening and embraced the power. She welcomed it. Screaming filled the room. It was pitiful, but Grace did not have any compassion for the animal that had been inflicting pain on her. Cocooned in her protection, Grace could just about see the skin melting away from Thella. Her muscles and organs were cooking in the flames and the stench of the burning flesh and bone replaced the smell of decomposition in the basement. The immense pain did not relent. Thella screamed in agony right until the moment that she died; her senses were the last to go.

Grace relaxed her wings. Not one ounce of guilt or pity wasted on Thella or how she died. She was relieved that the charred body on the floor could hurt no one else.

Chapter twenty-three

M arcus was apprehensive. The guards were so much bigger than he was. He felt intimidated by their size, but as he stood in front of them, he knew he was ready.

"I will be your first adversary, Marcus. I want to see what you are capable of, so come at me with all you have," Orin announced.

Marcus was not used to attacking others, he was much more used to defending himself; he was not entirely sure where to start. As a detective, he had always been more cerebral in his dealings with others. He usually left the physical stuff to his colleagues. As Orin studied Marcus, he realised that he had asked him to do something that he was not comfortable with. Disappointed at his student's apparent lack of natural aggression, he decided that he would have to force him to become a fighter.

"What are you waiting for, Marcus? A written invitation?"

"Honestly attacking someone for no reason is not in my nature. I resolve issues and find the perpetrators of crime. You are asking me to go against my own instincts. You have not harmed me, so why would I attack you?" Marcus replied.

Orin clenched his fists and lunged at Marcus, causing him to step back quickly, though he was not quick enough to avoid the attack. Orin landed a punch in the centre of Marcus's chest, knocking the wind out of him and sending him to the floor with a thud. The Peacekeeper gasped and flailed around for a few moments before he got any oxygen into his lungs. Eventually, his lungs regained their rhythm; Marcus' composure took a while longer.

"Well, that went well!" Orin laughed. "Now, will you do what I ask, or do I have to punch you again?"

"Point taken." Marcus sniped.

Orin waited in silence while Marcus found his feet. He did not believe that he could attack him without provocation, so he tried a different angle.

"Have you ever done any boxing or martial arts, Marcus?"

"I did self-defence at the police academy, just the usual stuff to help us disarm criminals or to protect ourselves, nothing too aggressive."

"With the violence going on with the humans on Earth, I would think something more aggressive would make for more of a deterrent," Orin saw.

Marcus did not answer him, but he could agree; violence was prevalent and seemed to get worse each day.

"No matter. Let us start from scratch, shall we?"

Marcus nodded; he knew that there were going to be times where he would have to fight. He could not rely on mediation and talking to solve the problems between The Celestials and The Fallen after what he had witnessed so far.

"Let us start with a bit of sparring, hand to hand combat. I want to see what you can do," Orin told him.

They stood in the centre of the room, the other Celestials moved to form a loose circle around them. For the next half hour, Orin and Marcus danced around each other. Orin directed slaps at Marcus, just trying to gauge his speed and reactions. To begin with, they were slow, but eventually Marcus avoided a few of them, his self-defence training beginning to kick in.

As Orin continued to hit his target, Marcus got increasingly frustrated. It did not take long for his aggression to surface, and he began returning the slaps. Orin seemed pleased that some of them found their mark. Sweat was pouring from Marcus. This was more physical work than he had done for a long time. Orin, however, did not have a single bead of sweat on him.

"You did well, Marcus, eventually," Orin laughed.

Marcus did not see the humour. He felt like he was the butt of Orin's jokes. It felt good that he had landed some slaps, but Marcus knew it would take a lot more than landing a slap or two to defend himself and anyone else that needed it. He now wished he had taken up boxing or martial arts when he was younger instead of always doing his best to avoid confrontation.

Orin watched Marcus closely. He could see that he was struggling and regretted laughing at him. He needed to change tact with him, Orin knew he needed to build up his confidence.

"Would you feel more comfortable training with the sword to begin with rather than close contact fighting?" Orin asked.

"I think I would, and I also think that getting to grips with the sword would be more beneficial," he replied.

"Have you ever done any form of sword fighting or seen any?"

"I did a bit of fencing when I was at college, well I had two lessons and found it quite boring, so I quit," he replied, now wishing that he had not.

Orin rolled his eyes. This peacekeeper would soon perish if he did not learn some lessons. His life was about to become more violent and dangerous, and it frustrated him that Marcus did not seem to fully understand that.

"Ok. Let us begin with some simple exercises with the sword, just to get you accustomed to its weight and feel," Orin told him.

"One of you step forward and show him," he said to the other Celestial Guards.

A guard stepped forward, introduced himself as Phelan, and drew his own sword from its scabbard. Phelan stood firm with his feet planted on the ground and his arms bent slightly, holding his sword out in front of him. He showed how to wield it by cutting through the air between them. Marcus heard the sharp blade cut through the space and imagined how effective it would be in battle. He was anxious and quite excited to try for himself.

"Now it is your turn. Get your sword," Orin ordered.

Marcus got his sword from the cabinet. As soon as he touched it, the familiar sounds filled his head, and he felt the souls of The Celestials fill his body. Marcus turned and faced Orin.

Once he was back in the centre of the room, he began the exercises. The sword seemed to join with him and together they put on quite a show. The man and sword were as one. Marcus moved with ease and vigour. Orin gestured to Phelan to hand him his own sword. He stepped forward and provoked Marcus into fighting.

As their swords clashed, the sound of metal on metal reverberated around the room, the two advancing and parrying as if they had duelled together for many years. As the battle continued, the voices inside Marcus became stronger, and one became clearer to him. The gentle voice guided his moves. Eventually, Marcus had the upper hand and pinned Orin against a wall. With the sharp edge of the steel pressing firmly into his opponent's flesh. For a moment, Marcus almost forgot where he was.

"Enough, Marcus, you can stop now," the voice inside told him.

Marcus stepped back. Orin was unnerved, but he tried his best not to show that to The Peacekeeper.

"I think that you just might have found the right weapon Peacekeeper, you are a natural with the sword," he complimented his opponent as he rubbed where the blade had dug into the skin of his throat.

His own abilities shocked Marcus: he had not expected to do the exercises well, let alone hold his own in a sword fight with Orin.

"Thank you, Orin, but I do not think that I reacted the way I did because I am a natural. I had help from the souls within the sword. One of them guided me. They are the reason I did well," Marcus replied.

"Well then, Marcus, may you never be without the sword when you are in trouble? Those who have gone before, those who fought and died by Berran's hand, have truly blessed you."

"We will continue your training with the sword, but it is imperative that we concentrate on how you will defend yourself if you don't have it with you," Orin said. "You must be ready for all eventualities, Peacekeeper."

Marcus nodded in agreement. "Now place your sword in the cabinet and return to your husband. We will continue this tomorrow. I will catch up with Adred and tell him how you have done today."

"Thank you, Orin. I appreciate your help, all of you. I hope I do not let any of you down," Marcus replied.

"You will not Peacekeeper." He replied firmly.

Marcus left the room, leaving Orin alone with his thoughts. Marcus was like a young child learning to take his first steps, yet he was already a talented swordsman. Orin needed to turn him into the complete package, so that he could honour his role as The Peacekeeper. It was going to be a laborious task, but everyone was relying on Marcus to make a stand and reinstate peace.

Orin watched on as the other guards continued to train without the Peacekeeper. One day maybe Marcus would be as good as them, he hoped.

Chapter twenty-four

Grace turned and walked away from the burning body and made her way through the basement, leaving a trail of flames in her wake. She felt nothing for Thella; she deserved to die a painful death.

As she walked, the bodies of tormented and tortured bodies of the innocents seemed to reach out to her; their faces twisted in silent cries for help. She knew they were beyond any help that she could give.

The flames surrounding Grace skirted around the bodies, each one of them left untouched by the fire. Grace wanted them found. She needed the world to know just how evil The Fallen and her father were.

She ascended the stairs and made her way through the building; her wings outstretched in all their glory, brightly coloured flames catching every surface ablaze as she searched for a way to escape. Grace turned a corner and spotted two of The Fallen. Both men reacted immediately, readying themselves in an attack position. Grace smiled at them knowingly, as if she had already decided how this would play out.

Without realising what she was doing, Grace raised her arms from her side, and with a sweeping movement summoned the flames from behind her. For a moment, she caressed the flames between the palms of her hands and whispered something. The flames turned from fire to tiny lightning bolts; one in each hand. They erupted suddenly, as if supercharged with energy, and flew from her hands towards The Fallen. Everything happened so quickly that they had no chance to react.

The lightning hit them both directly in the centre of their chests. At first glance, their wounds seemed insignificant and barely visible, a small scorch mark. There was nothing more to suggest that the lightning had struck them. They appeared to be unhurt, and they moved towards Grace once again. Five ... Six steps closer, and Grace felt panic rising within her. Perhaps she had misjudged her own power? Her situation had shifted, there was fire burning in the surrounding building, and now she had Fallen coming her way.

Both men stopped suddenly, their expressions turning from aggression to looks of extreme pain. The lightning bolts spread from their chests to the rest of their bodies. The white energy coursed through every cell, and as it did, each cell exploded one by one. Slowly they were being destroyed and their screams filled the air; tortured and animal like, intensifying with every cell explosion. Grace watched as they both exploded completely, shards of light floating into the ether, leaving no trace of the men.

Grace was uneasy to discover that she found joy in their deaths, experiencing emotions she had never felt before, not even in her darkest days in foster care. Was she becoming evil like her father? Was that her destiny? She did not want to become like him. After all, she had to defend herself to get out of there, didn't she? Grace tried to rationalise what she had done, but even with all the evil she had seen so far, she felt some guilt for taking the lives of the two Fallen.

There was no time to dwell on what she had done, though; regret would only slow her down. Grace needed to escape and so continued to move through the building. It surprised Grace that nobody else had challenged her. She saw no other Fallen and thought that she could get away. Just as she made it to the door leading out of the building, Cali stepped out in front of her, accompanied by Berran and a few others. Flames continued to rage behind her, meaning that there was no going back the way she came. Grace was not sure what to do. Maybe she could deal with them the same way she had dealt with the other two, but doubt crept in, rendering her momentarily immobile.

"Going somewhere?" Berran sneered.

Grace did not answer. Her thoughts had turned to the intense fire burning behind her. She stood firm, staring at her father and trying to figure out how she could get away from him and her brother.

"I ASKED YOU A QUESTION GIRL!" Berran shouted.

Grace jumped at his sudden aggressiveness, but still did not respond. She stared at Berran, waiting to see what he would do.

"I strongly suggest that you put out those flames," he told Grace. "Cali, take her wings from her. I do not care how painful it is, she will pay for what she has done here," Berran ordered.

Cali removed a large knife from the back of his trouser waistband. The long silver blade lit up with the reflection of the flames that filled the hallway. Grace did not stop them as she was told, and she did not move. Cali walked towards his sister; she stood firm; he looked back at his father for confirmation. Berran nodded his head at his son.

With the blade firmly in his hand, Cali looked at his sister, almost hypnotised by the flames surrounding her. He caught her gaze; she did not flinch or break eye contact. Grace was not sure how she would get out of the situation. Cali was imagining with great delight the pain he would soon inflict on his sister.

"Are you waiting for an invitation, boy? GET ON WITH IT!" Berran shouted impatiently.

His shout caused the twins to break eye contact; Cali lunged towards Grace and tried to knock her from her feet. Grace stumbled momentarily, enough for two of the other Fallen to grab her. As soon as they touched her, an immense heat burned their hands, causing them to release her. Cali thrust the blade at Grace and caught one of her wings. She felt the knife slice through the shaft in it. The pain of the injury to her wing spread through her body at once. Every cell was screaming. The flames surrounding her extinguished, leaving only the building alight.

Cali lunged again at his sister, but this time she reacted instinctively, tucking her wings away from him. She would not offer him any further chance to cause her more pain. Grace fell to the floor and exhaustion filled her body; the fight and defiance she felt had left her. A single wound to her wing had defeated her.

"Bind her!" Berran barked at his minions.

Grace did not fight The Fallen as they bound her with chains.

"Time to take you home, Grace," Berran spat, "Get her out of my sight and into the cell in the underworld."

Cali bowed his head to his father as he grabbed Grace by the arm. She did not know how, but as soon as he did, they were no longer in the burning building anymore. Grace tried to pull away from her brother, but he had a firm grip on her.

Grace looked around. She was in a room, but it was not a normal room. The walls were solid stone, as was the floor. It felt cold and damp, and not at all what she expected; after all, wasn't hell supposed to be all fire and brimstone? There were no windows and just one solid looking door. The room was sparse, an enormous bed dominated its centre, along one side of the room there was a bath, sink, and toilet. In the far corner was a small table and a chair.

Next to the bed was a large solid metal pole with a long chain and a cuff at the end. Cali picked it up from the floor and put it around Grace's wrist. It was tight. The cuff dug in, causing her to flinch. Once Cali finished securing the chains, he removed the binding chains from his sister.

"You asked for this, Grace, enjoy the rest of eternity in this hovel!" he laughed loudly as he walked out of the room, slamming the heavy door behind him.

Grace sat down on the bed, deflated. She did not know what she could do. Her options were now zero. She was a prisoner. She hoped The Celestials would find and rescue her.

As she tried to come to terms with her situation, her wings unfurled and surrounded her body, giving her a semblance of comfort. She could still feel pain from the wound throughout her body. Grace could barely imagine the pain The Celestials felt as The Fallen hacked the wings from their bodies. She would never forget the sight of Adred and the others being butchered as The Fallen removed a part of their identity.

"I have to work out what I can do with my powers," she said aloud for nobody to hear.

Even in the darkest days of her childhood, Grace had never felt so alone. She longed for Charlie, but she knew she would never see him again. She lay on the bed and cried, experiencing every emotion possible all at once. Grace was lost and alone again.

Chapter twenty-five

As he slowly wandered towards his room, Marcus reflected on everything that had happened to him and Stephen. He longed to go home and get back to his normal life, but he had to accept that would not be the case while the threat of war was looming. Marcus finally realised that he had no choice but to accept the destiny that was his future, but it did not mean that he liked it for one moment. His performance with the Sword of Berran pleasantly surprised him, but there were things that troubled him.

Visions of Stephen's death still filled his head; Marcus knew they would haunt him for his whole life. How could they not? Nobody should see someone they love in that state. He could not shake off the sight of his husband's mutilated body lying on the floor, nor could he erase from his memory the smell of his blood. He had relived those scenes more times than he could count and found himself once again lost in the horrific memories.

"Are you okay?" a familiar voice asked, pulling Marcus out of his thoughts. A smile spread across his face upon hearing his husband's voice, but the sight of him took his breath away as it always had.

Stephen was the most handsome man he had ever met, and he felt lucky to be married to him. Just his presence alone made the dark thoughts disappear. Marcus pulled him close and kissed him.

"I am now," he answered.

"How did it go with the training?"

"Better than I thought. Apparently, I appear to be a natural swordsman, though hand to hand combat is going to need more attention."

"Marcus, you can't be perfect at everything all the time," Stephen teased.

"I should have been there for you. I should have protected you," Marcus blurted out, the darkness overwhelming him once more.

"Marcus, what could you have done? If you had been there, we would both be dead. You cannot change what happened. We need to deal with it, move on, and find our new normal," Stephen told him.

"I have not asked you how it feels to be a Celestial yet? Does it feel different?"

"I feel calm and content, confident even. It is hard to describe. And these wings! They are just so...I do not know how to tell you what they feel like. They are a part of me already, I suppose," Stephen replied.

"Shall we take the dogs for a walk? You need a distraction and what better one than that?" Stephen suggested, changing the subject.

Marcus nodded. Walking with Stephen and their dogs in the countryside always cleared his head. It gave them time to talk and put the world to rights.

"Where can we walk them? It is not like we can magically take them home and on our normal walks."

"Have you not been outside this building yet? Marcus, Elysium is beautiful and there are plenty of places here to walk the boys. Wait here, I will get them, and we will take them now," Stephen told him.

Stephen opened the door to their room and called the dogs. They darted towards their dad excitedly. Marcus watched as they bounded about. The dogs were always full of energy and unconditional love. They had not noticed him standing at the door, and so when Marcus called for them, they almost knocked him over in their hurry to get to him.

"Time for a walk, boys?" Marcus asked.

The dogs responded by barking loudly and running between him and Stephen; they loved the walks as much as Marcus did.

"Follow me, I will show you to the gardens and woodlands, you will love it. Best of all, the boys do not need leads; they have the freedom to run here," Stephen said.

Once they were outside, the sun felt unexpectedly warm on Marcus' face. Elysium looked just like earth to him. The blue sky peppered with white fluffy clouds, and the bright sunlight gave everything a wonderful glow. He was not sure what he had expected, but this was not it.

Stephen watched his husband taking in the view. He could tell that it slightly confused him.

"Elysium is different for everyone. For you and me, The Celestials have made the surroundings quite familiar. They want us to feel comfortable here so that you can concentrate on what you need to do," Stephen explained.

"So, what is it like when we aren't here?" Marcus questioned.

"I do not know yet. They are giving me time to get used to my new situation. Helen explained a few things to me while you were sword fighting."

"Are you going to tell me?"

"As a Celestial, I have powers. She did not explain what yet, but she is going to give me a bit of a crash course when you are next doing your training."

"You are excited about this, aren't you?"

"I am a bit I will be honest. It is cool, isn't it?" He answered with a huge smile on his face.

Marcus was a little surprised by Stephen, he had always been the reserved and sensible one in their relationship and now he embraced the changes in their lives without question.

"How can you be happy about this? Our whole lives have changed. We cannot go back."

Stephen stopped walking. He took hold of Marcus' hands and cradled them.

"Marcus, I died in excruciating pain. The brutality of it will haunt me. How can I not be happy that I have a second chance with you, in whatever form that is?" he told him tearfully.

Marcus had not been able to get past what they had both lost. He did not think about what they had gained. Stephen was right. They had a second chance, and that was what mattered.

The men continued their walk with the dogs through the beautiful gardens until they reached a woodland. The trees danced in the sunlight, different hues of green adorned each of them. A gentle warm breeze guided them further into the woods. Birds flew in and out of the trees, singing their glorious songs. The dogs ran in and out of the undergrowth, sniffing everything in their path. They chased the birds, not understanding that anything with wings would not hang around and play with them. Marcus relaxed a little. He reached out and held Stephen's hand, squeezing it gently, and decided then that they needed to make the most of every moment.

They spent a couple of hours walking the dogs and playing with them. By the time they arrived back at the building, a more accepting Marcus had appeared. He was a man grateful that he still had something worth fighting for. His husband and dogs were the centre of that. Marcus knew he would not give that up without a fight. His life, their lives, would differ from now on. But he still hoped that one day they would all be able to go home.

"I am starving. Where do I get some food from for us and the boys?" Marcus asked Stephen.

"I do not need to eat anymore, but I am sure that I can find something for you all. I will meet you back in our room, get a bit of rest," he replied, kissing Marcus on the end of the nose.

Marcus and the dogs made their way back. Once they were there, the dogs quickly settled in their beds, worn out by the walk. Marcus smiled as he watched them both fall into a deep sleep. He lay on the bed and listened to the sound of gentle snores filling the room. As he waited for Stephen, his eyes became heavy, and he was soon asleep, too.

Marcus woke up as the door opened, Stephen was back, his arms laden with a variety of foods for Marcus and for the dogs. Beau and Henry instantly woke. They seemed to know that there was food for them, and both sat patiently waiting for it. Stephen dished some food out for them, which they wolfed down immediately, and then they settled back in their beds again to sleep.

Marcus ate while Stephen watched him. He knew he did not need to eat, but Marcus still asked him to join him. Stephen did. Stephen enjoyed food so much and although he did not need the sustenance; he savoured every mouthful.

"Time for you to rest. You need all your strength for your time with the Celestial Guards,"

"I had a nap while you were getting the food, anyway I don't want to sleep when you can't," an exhausted Marcus replied.

"Who said anything about sleep?" Stephen responded.

Marcus put his plate down and moved closer to his husband. It did not take long for him to dismiss his fatigue, their hunger for each other expelling all thoughts of sleep from his mind.

A while later, a contented Marcus lay cocooned in the softness of Stephen's wings. Stephen held him close, listening to the sound of his breathing, the only thing that could appease his own fears. He was thankful that he did not need to sleep. He realised he would never find peace if he did.

Chapter twenty-six

G race woke from a nightmare filled sleep, determined that her father would not keep her prisoner. Fear was her biggest enemy and right at that moment, her fear was overpowering her. Adred had told her she was a powerful being, so she decided she would try to channel her power into overcoming her fears. It was time for her to discover what else she could do; fire and lightning were a start, but she would need more than that to defeat her father and escape.

Orin loved the physicality of hand-to-hand combat; he relished in it and felt enormous pride when he overcame an enemy. That drove him. There was no other feeling like it for him. As he mulled over the details of the first training session with Marcus and contemplated how best to help him develop his skills, Adred walked back into the room. Orin dismissed the other guards, who were sparring or discussing their protégé. Each of them bowed their heads to Adred in deference and left the room as asked.

"How did Marcus do?" enquired Adred.

"Do you want an honest answer?"

"Always," Adred replied.

"Hand-to-hand combat for him is an issue. He has no real aptitude for it. I genuinely do not think I have ever seen anyone as reluctant to fight. I will need to understand what is holding him back so that I can help him progress."

"And what about how he handles the sword?"

"I have to say he shocked me. Marcus is one of the best swordsmen I think that I have ever seen. I am not sure if it was his own ability with the sword, or the guidance of the Celestial souls within. He troubles me, however. There was a point when it felt like I could have joined those souls," Orin explained. "He had me pinned against the wall, sword to my throat. I am not sure what stopped him; I really do not think that he was in complete control."

"That is disturbing. I will speak to him. Unfortunately, we have no choice but to continue the training. It is crucial that he is up to speed as soon as possible."

"I agree. I will summon him again tomorrow, and we will concentrate on physical combat. That is where we need to do the most work," Orin assured Adred.

"Thank you, Orin. That will be all for today. Can you do me a small favour on your way back to the barracks? Would you ask Helen to join me here?"

"Of course." Orin bowed his head and left the room.

Adred strode over to the cabinet, opened the door, and picked up the sword. He studied the blade. It glowed in the light. He noticed that there was a new mark on it. A new symbol that was glinting radiantly. A confused Adred wondered where it had come from, and he questioned if it was to do with the sword's new owner. He heard Helen enter the room and decided that he would inspect the sword further when he was alone. He replaced it in the cabinet and turned back to the centre of the room.

"Orin said that you wanted to see me," she said.

"Yes, thank you for coming. I wondered, did you feel the disturbance earlier?" he asked her.

"Yes, I did. I am not entirely sure what it was, though."

"It is my belief that it is likely that Berran and The Fallen have travelled back to the underworld. I have felt nothing since they took Grace from us, so I can only assume that they did not go straight there. Can you try to find out?" he asked.

"Of course. If they have Grace there, then we should be able to get to her with the contacts we have, but you know that if we set one foot in the underworld, then we cannot avoid war."

"We are already at war, Helen! Berran declared war the very moment The Fallen took my wings and murdered our fellow Celestials. There is no coming back now," Adred snapped back.

"Sorry, of course I will reach out today, unless..." she began and stopped herself, not wanting to anger Adred unnecessarily.

"Unless what?" Adred asked, his tone gentler.

"Unless you try to contact Grace by joining her powers with yours, you could do that, couldn't you?"

"Grace does not know what she is doing. She has no comprehension of what she is capable of. I do not know if she will be receptive to my attempts to contact her."

"Isn't it a worth try? Surely, we cannot lose anything by trying?" Helen questioned.

Adred was unconvinced, but he trusted Helen's judgement. He had learned long ago that she had great instincts.

"Okay, let me get seated and make sure that nobody disturbs me. I hope this works for all our sakes."

Helen stood by the door to ensure that nobody entered the room while Adred moved one of the few chairs into the centre. The rigid and uncomfortable looking chair did not seem to be the perfect place to be sat when trying to concentrate on forming a bond with Grace, but it was all that there was in the room. Adred sat upright, wincing as his wounds touched the wood. He closed his eyes, his face softening a little as he tried to contact Grace.

Adred searched through the ether, through the memories in his mind, his soul gently reaching out, trying to find Grace's essence. His spirit circled the earth several times. His search for her was extensive, and he yearned for the smallest of connections. There was nothing, not even a glimmer. He continued to search, almost giving up hope of ever finding her.

Eventually, though, Adred felt a force pulling at him; small at first, but it quickly grew stronger and began reaching back to him.

"Grace, is that you?" he whispered. He felt overwhelmed. A cacophony of emotions hit him. Fear, failure, pain, grief, loss, and loneliness filled his mind. Strongest of all, though, was hopelessness. He hoped it was not Grace that he had found in such despair, but something deep inside him told him it was.

Knowing all that he knew about Grace's life, Adred regretted that he had abandoned her to Humankind as an infant. He wished that things could have been different, that he could have helped her prepare for all of this. His regret was useless now, though. He could not alter his past choices.

"Grace, please help me find you," Adred said aloud. Helen watched him closely; she could see that he was visibly upset.

"Grace, I am here. Find me."

Adred became exhausted by the traumatic emotions he was feeling, and after many failed attempts to get a response from Grace, he opened his eyes and looked at Helen. His eyes were full of despair and disappointment.

"I know she is there. Helen, I can feel her. She is so lonely, her spirit broken. This is my fault. I did this to her. We should never have left Grace on earth to go through their system. The Elders could and should have placed her with a Celestial family and hidden her away. Helen, we need to reach her soon, otherwise Berran could offer her what she wants, and then it will be too late to stop the war."

Helen shared in his fear. When The Elders decided Grace should live amongst humans, she argued that Grace would never be safe. As much as she pleaded, nobody would consider letting her raise the child. Now, though, was not the time to say, "*I told you so.*" It was time for her to step in and see what she could do. Hindsight and blame would not change the situation that they were in.

"Let me try?" she asked. "We have nothing to lose."

Adred reluctantly nodded and got up from the seat, wincing. It was Helen's time to save her best friend's daughter, and she would let no one get in her way this time. Like Adred, Helen closed her eyes, but she did not search the ether. She focused in on Grace, on her face and the good heart that she knew was inside her. Helen was not prepared to give up. She could not let Grace become evil incarnate. Helen knew she had the wonderful heart of her mother. She only needed to convince Grace of the fact. Helen was going to save Grace and give her the love that she deserved. She would tell her every detail that she knew about her mother. Grace would know her as well as Helen did once she had finished sharing her stories. She would finally feel loved and wanted.

Chapter twenty-seven

"Grace, it is Helen. Let me help you," she began, "I am here, Grace. All you need to do is to reach out to me. Please help me find you. Are you there?" she asked.

There was nothing. Helen felt extreme sympathy and love for Grace. She hoped that one day they would be close. Helen tried again.

Eventually, Helen's gentle voice permeated through the darkness surrounding Grace. She had heard her, and her heart skipped a beat. At first, she thought she must have imagined the voice. The second time she heard it, she dared to hope that it was real. Was it really Helen? She was not sure what she needed to do.

"Helen, is that really you?" she quietly whispered.

"Yes, Grace, it is. You do not know how relieved I am that we have contacted you. Are you okay? Are you hurt?" she asked.

"I am not badly hurt, just a wound to one of my wings, but I am chained in a cave-like room. I do not know exactly where, but I assume I am at Berran's place," she answered, "I thought I heard Adred before, did I? I did not answer because I was not sure if *they* were trying to trick me."

"You heard Adred. We have both been trying to connect with you. Have you tried to break the chains yet?"

"How am I supposed to break them? There is nothing in the room apart from a bed and a couple of other things."

"You have powers, Grace. It is time for you to use them," replied Helen.

"Do I? How am I supposed to know what I can do when nobody explained it to me? I am like a helpless fucking baby here!" She snapped back at Helen, her words full of frustration and fear.

As Adred had done before, Helen was becoming overwhelmed by Grace's emotions. She knew she would need to resist if she had any hope of helping Grace to escape from her prison. Helen took a deep breath and focused on blocking the feelings out as best as she could.

"Grace, you can do anything that you set your mind to; you are not limited by your thoughts. I know it is a lot to take in, but we will have time to go through everything when you get back home to us. For now, though, the only thing stopping you is fear. Will you trust me to guide you?"

"I do trust you, Helen. Please help me."

"Right, you need to turn your fear into anger and direct that towards the chains that are holding you here," Helen told her.

"How do I do that?"

"It is hard to explain, but every emotion that is causing you pain needs to be harnessed and focused on the chains, like a laser beam. Can you do that?"

"I can try."

Grace did not need to search for long to find the emotions that she needed; her thoughts went immediately to the poor souls killed by The Fallen and she felt the anger building. Alongside those feelings were many others that she had buried most of her life. She felt every built-up emotion running through every cell in her body, and suddenly, power and light exploded from her body and filled the room. Grace tried her best to take control of it, but it was almost impossible.

With Helen's guidance, Grace eventually regained some control and tried to guide the power towards her chains, taking care not to hurt herself. Moments later; the cuffs exploded and dropped from her wrists. The light vanished and she relaxed a little, and then she looked around her prison. She could see the energy burst had destroyed it. A fountain of water erupted from where the bathroom once stood. The door remained firmly shut however, but at least Grace was no longer bound by the chains.

"I did it!" she exclaimed.

"Now we must get you out of there and somewhere safe so that we can rescue you. Are you ready, Grace?" Helen asked.

"I am. What should I do?"

Helen took a moment to think of the best solution and then told Grace to concentrate on producing another energy burst. She told her to aim it directly at the door. Grace took a few deep breaths and then let her emotions guide her. Standing in the middle of the room, surrounded by the water lapping at her feet, she found more memories that would help her.

Grace's memories had always appeared to her as though she were watching someone else's life, but she felt every emotion. She saw herself as a young girl sat at a table eating a dried piece of bread, dunking it into warm milk to soften it; the girl glanced at her drunk foster mother sat opposite, hoping that for once there would be some connection, but there was none.

"What are you looking at, girl?" she snapped as she caught Grace looking at her.

Grace already knew in the brief time that she had been with her it was not a good idea to answer her when she had been drinking. Lowering her head, she investigated her cup, wishing that she was somewhere, anywhere else.

"Answer me!" she shouted, causing Grace to jump, look up, and make eye contact.

Before she could answer her, a fist hit her in the face. Grace fell off her chair into a heap on the floor. Her head spinning with the pain, she bit hard on her lip and tried her best not to cry, but her face hurt so much.

As she watched herself, she remembered exactly how small and vulnerable she felt then, and the anger boiled over. That rage sparked the power inside her once more. A huge energy blast erupted out from her chest, forcing her head back. Her eyes focused on the ceiling, and her arms instinctively outstretched. Grace's power filled the room, bouncing off each of the stone walls, the ceiling, and the floor. Grace had lost control and stood at the centre of the destruction.

"Help me!" she shouted, hoping that Helen could still hear her.

"Tell me what is happening, Grace," she replied.

Grace tried her best to explain.

"You are in control here. The energy is yours. You need to focus on what you want it to do."

Grace was not sure she could, but she took a deep breath and focused. The door needed to be destroyed if she was ever going to get away. The energy blast was weakening as she dithered, but it was still quite strong. Helen told her to concentrate on what she needed the power to do. She told her to take hold of it in her mind, to harness the power and direct it at the door.

Grace slowed her breathing and then tried to picture in her mind what she needed it to do. She imagined it as a battering ram that would free her from her prison. The energy swirled around her; it felt like a small tornado, and she was at the centre. Grace opened her hands flat, feeling the force surrounding her and cascading over her palms. Gently, she moved her hands together, trapping the energy between them; as it solidified in her hands, she pushed it with all her might towards the door.

A splintering sound filled the air, and once she could focus her eyes without the energy distorting her vision, Grace saw the remnants of the door strewn across the floor.

"I did it!" she exclaimed to Helen as much as to herself.

"Well done, Grace. Now we just need to get you to where we can rescue you. Are you ready?"

"I am," Grace replied.

She walked towards the opening where the door used to be, unsure of what she would meet next, but she felt more confident in herself than she had been moments earlier.

"She is free of the chains, and she has destroyed the door keeping her in," Helen told Adred.

It pleased Adred to see the progress Helen had achieved so far with Grace, but that was just the first step. The hardest part for them would be to get her back to Elysium, back to them and relative safety.

"We are not exactly sure where she is, so we need to be incredibly careful. Keep with her, Helen. Let us get her home," Adred said.

"Of course, I will not abandon her again," she replied with an edge to her tone.

Adred understood her meaning and regretted that he had stood in the way of Helen raising Grace; he knew that if anything happened to her, he would always regret it.

"Grace, it is time to get you home. Now let us see exactly where you are, shall we?" Helen asked.

Grace stepped out of the room. She was standing in a rock lined passageway. Water trickled down from the ceiling and pooled on the floor. It had a cold and damp feel to it, just like the room she had come from, and Grace shivered with the low temperature. There were lit torches on the walls, the orange and white flames flickered and danced as she walked forward.

"Tell me what you see, Grace."

Grace described what she saw as she continued to walk slowly away from her room. The passageway stretched out in front of her, and it appeared to go on forever. The flames of the torches flickered every now and again as a breeze whipped through, causing Grace to stop and listen for anyone coming towards her. Every noise and every flicker caused her heart to skip a beat, her nerves building more with each step she took.

Eventually, the passageway gave way to an opening, a cavern with four other passages leading from it.

"What do I do now?" Grace asked once she had described the view in front of her.

Helen took a deep breath and asked if there was any light coming from the other passages. Three of them were lit up, and one was in complete darkness.

"I cannot tell you which one to pick, Grace. Choose, go with your instincts," Helen told her.

Grace stood for a few moments, listening to see if there was any noise in any of the tunnels. She could hear talking in two of them, but one of the lit passageways was silent and so was the one in complete darkness. Grace chose the dark one.

"What if the one I choose leads me directly to him?" she asked.

"It is a chance that you must take, Grace. We need to get you away from there, but while you are deep in their base, we cannot get you out. Now choose. I will be with you," Helen said, trying to reassure Grace.

Grace walked into the dark tunnel and instantly regretted her choice.

Chapter twenty-eight

"**A**re you really that fucking stupid? Did you really think that we would not know that you had escaped from your chains, Grace?" The effect Berran's disjointed voice had on her was as strong as if he had walked out of the darkness himself and slapped her across the face.

Cali stepped out of the darkness of the tunnel. It surprised her that it was not Berran that she was face to face with. She also noted the six Fallen who were with him, each holding a weapon of some sort in their hands.

"Do you not understand who you are dealing with here, dear sister?" he mocked, "Father knew exactly what you were doing, every movement you made he was aware of."

Grace knew exactly who she was dealing with; a snivelling boy who wanted his father's approval. It did not help to know that, and it did not stop her from panicking. She tried to tell Helen what was happening. There was no response, and no matter how hard she kept calling, her cries remained unanswered. The connection had been severed, and Grace did not know how to repair it.

"Is my dear sister scared?" Cali did not need to ask; he saw it on her face. He took his pleasure in taunting her.

Grace stood firm and silent, hoping that her emotions would not give away just how scared she was. Inside, she was in turmoil and panic threatened to overcome her.

"Take her to Berran. He can decide what to do with her, personally I would finish her here," he ordered the other Fallen.

"Helen!!! What do I do? I am outnumbered, and they are going to take me to Berran," she pleaded, hoping that Helen could still connect to her.

Those few seconds of silence felt like a lifetime to Grace as she watched the six Fallen heading towards her. Her heart was beating so hard and fast. No sooner had she focused on steadying her breathing and composing herself than Helen was back with her.

"That is good Grace, keep taking deep breaths, use your emotions again, this time direct them at The Fallen, make them feel what you felt, no fire, no energy, just hopelessness, and then take control of their minds when they crumble in that emotional pain. You can do this," Helen replied.

"I can control people using my emotions?"

"Grace, you are capable of so much, and you can use that for good or bad but now is not the time to go into all the details, for now we need you to use it to escape, it may not be pleasant, but it is necessary. Now concentrate and get yourself out of there."

Two of The Fallen had almost reached Grace. She smiled at them, a false smile because she was not as confident as she was projecting, but she knew that giving in was not an option. Grace dug deep into her memories again. The emotions ran through her body, emotions that Cali or the other Fallen would never understand. She understood now that the loneliness she felt throughout her childhood could now fuel her power. This time there was no fire, no energy, as Helen told her, but as she stared at the two men walking towards her, she let her emotions free. Grace aimed those emotions towards them both. Loneliness struck deep within both of their hearts at the same time; a feeling of complete and utter abandonment hit them hard, causing them both to die inside. As she saw hope leave them and the emptiness fill the void, she reached out and offered them peace and comfort, which they welcomed. Grace was their master now and they would do her bidding.

The two Fallen stopped in front of Grace, bowed their heads, and turned around and took up defensive position against Cali and the others.

"What the fuck are you doing???" Cali shouted.

They stayed mute and unmoving, observing their adversaries intently. Cali ordered the other four to detain Grace. As they moved towards her, she dug deep and did to them exactly what she had done to the others. Within moments, all six of The Fallen were protecting Grace. They stood by her side. Grace fully unfurled her wings, which almost filled the tunnel, and stood staring defiantly at her brother, who now seemed to have lost all his confidence. Cali turned and ran from the tunnel like a wounded animal. Grace laughed. She liked how strong she felt. Possibly just a little too much.

"Grace, are you okay?" Helen asked her.

"Yes, Helen. I am more than okay. I now have six of The Fallen protecting me," she replied.

"Tell them to get you out of there. They need to get you into an open space above ground so that we can get you home, Grace," Helen ordered.

When Grace heard the word home, it jarred for a moment. Home did not exist for her. The one place that was her home was gone. Charlie was gone. Home was a myth for Grace, one she felt she would never experience. She pulled herself together and ordered her bodyguards to get her to open ground as Helen told her.

The Fallen moved slowly through the tunnels, inching their way forwards when a noise caught their attention. Grace had folded her wings away and followed them, while keeping her senses in tune with her surroundings. She did not want to be taken by surprise.

Noises in a distance caught their attention, shouting and thudding sounds were getting louder and louder. It did not take long for Cali and another group of The Fallen to reach them, this time though, accompanied by Berran. Hiding in the shadows behind him was Cayla. Grace spotted her, but nobody else had.

"Grace, you will stop this!" Berran bellowed.

"And exactly how are you going to stop me?" she responded.

"I will destroy every inch of you if you do not surrender to me. Do not doubt me, girl."

Grace contemplated her options for a moment. She had just been told that she could do anything so surely. She could destroy Berran easily, couldn't she?

"Destruction of Berran is not an option Grace, you must be smart. There needs to be a balance, and unfortunately, that means you cannot kill your father," Helen whispered in her head.

"Then how will the war ever be over?" she asked.

"That is for The Peacekeeper to achieve. It is not your battle to fight. Now just do enough to get out of there, Grace," Helen told her.

Grace took a deep breath. She could not argue with Helen. She did not know enough about The Celestials and The Fallen to get in the middle of them both, not yet.

"Can I transport myself out of here, away from them all?" she asked.

"No, Grace. There is a protection barrier around Berran's home. While you are inside that barrier, even you cannot escape using your powers. Well, not until you master them. Somehow, we must get you outside," Helen told her.

Unsure of what she could do, the first thing Grace did was to unfurl her wings again. She knew it annoyed Berran; she wanted to appear imposing in front of The Fallen accompanying him and she wanted to come across like that in front of her snivelling twin brother.

"Don't you realise how powerful I am? How do you think you will stop me from leaving?" she taunted.

With an effortless swish of his arm, a black light flew from his hand. It curled around in the air and formed a rope like shape which instantly wrapped around Grace's wings. The light tightened and gripped around her body completely and she was bound with no way to escape. Air forced from her lungs; she was immobilised as she struggled to breathe. The Fallen guarding her turned and tried to break the ties that bound her, but nothing they did could loosen them.

Lights danced in her eyes as the lack of oxygen threatened to rob her of her consciousness. She fell to the ground, she knew that she had failed.

In the distance, Grace heard screaming. She did not know whether it was her own voice or someone else's.

"Let her go! You are killing her!!! Father, please?" Cayla rushed over to her sister.

Berran did not flinch. He continued to put pressure on his eldest daughter, determined that she learnt her place.

As the young woman continued to plead for her sister's life, she could see the delight on her father's face as he continued the torture. Eventually, he loosened the bindings just enough so that Grace could breathe, though not enough for a deep breath. He needed to keep her subdued.

"Take her away! Then sort out those disappointments," he ordered, pointing at The Fallen that were no longer under Grace's control.

A group of The Fallen picked her up, her wings dragging along the wet stone floor as they carried her from the tunnel. Those following closely behind, standing on them, ripping, and damaging her wings as they walked. Cayla followed at a distance as blood dripped from the wounds.

Helen had lost contact with Grace. She did not know what was happening, but what she knew was that whatever was happening, it had to be bad.

"I think Berran has recaptured her. I do not know how we are going to get to her Adred. It is hopeless," Helen said.

"Nothing is completely hopeless; it is just going to take a lot of work and reliance on Marcus. We will get her away from him, Helen. It is just going to take longer than we hoped, but we will get there," he replied, trying to reassure her, but not fooling himself with his words.

Grace was soon back in the prison that she had escaped from, but this time it was empty apart from a thin dirty mattress and a bucket. This time chained to the wall by the same black light that her father had bound her with. Defeated, she lay in a ball with her damaged wings wrapped around her for warmth; her arm the only part of her not covered by her wings. She felt alone and extremely sorry for herself.

Darkness engulfed Grace, taking away all of her hopes and dreams. She closed her eyes and gave up; there was nothing left for her to fight for, there was nobody left alive that she loved. Grace's spirit broken.

Chapter twenty-nine

"It is imperative that Marcus get up to speed. There is no way that we can leave Grace there any longer than necessary. Helen, you, and I both know that if Berran breaks her spirit, then we have lost." Adred was worried, and it was not a sight that Helen had seen many times before.

"You must keep trying to contact her, Helen. I will speak to Marcus; I will tell him exactly what Grace is dealing with."

"Of course. You go; I will not give up, Adred. I promise," she replied.

Adred left reluctantly, but he understood he could not just sit around hoping that Grace could escape. His heart ached for the lost Celestials, and the fear of losing more was overriding any semblance of hope for the future. The war had to be stopped, but Adred was retreating into his own grief. Before he realised where he was, he looked shocked to see Marcus stood in front of him.

"Adred, I realise that I have a fight ahead, and that I have been all over the place, you must be frustrated with me. I want to do all I can to help put an end to this war, but I need to understand Celestial and Fallen history before I can step into the middle of all of this. I can promise that I will try my best to bring this all to an end," he said.

Adred felt a great weight lifted. He had been extremely concerned with the way that Marcus said he was ready, only to have something else question his decision. Hope filtered through the fog of despair that he had been feeling.

"Thank you, Marcus. May I ask what helped you come to this decision?"

"Losing Stephen and the life we had. That you put your trust in me and gave me back the man I love. I owe you all."

"But why now? You've both been here for a while."

"I just needed time to get my head around things. I can be stubborn when I am taken out of my comfort zone. Sorry that it has taken me this long to realise the gravity of what we are facing. Please forgive me."

"No forgiveness needed. Thank you, Marcus. Please follow me. I know just where to start."

Adred led Marcus to a room that he had not been in before. As the door opened, he was stunned to see an extensive library with some solid wood tables in the middle, all piled high with books. Dust particles danced in the gloomy light filling the room. The tables each had a small lamp in the centre of it, which cast enough light to illuminate whichever book was being studied; but there were no windows allowing daylight to enter the room. It felt oppressive to Marcus. Everywhere that he looked was full to bursting with leather-bound books. It made sense that he would start his study of Celestial history here, but he had envisioned something a little more physical today. More combat training, perhaps.

"A library?" he asked.

THE DIVINEXUS

"This room has the history of Humankind, The Celestials and, of course, Berran and his Fallen. Every event in history recorded, the life of every being written here, so this is where you will find the answers to all your questions," Adred told him.

"Every being? Surely this is not big enough for the millions of humans, let alone anyone else," Marcus questioned.

"This room is big enough. It is a special room, and our librarian, Astrum, maintains it. He will help you with anything you need to know. Let me introduce you."

Adred called out into the room, and from nowhere an impressive Celestial appeared carrying a pristine-looking book in his hands.

"Astrum, meet Marcus. Can you answer his questions, please?"

"Of course, Adred, leave him with me," he answered, bowing his head.

Adred returned the bow and then turned and left the room, saying nothing else, leaving Marcus and Astrum staring after him. Astrum handed Marcus the book that he was carrying.

"Thank you, but what is this?" he asked.

"This is your family history, the place for you to begin, I think. If you disagree, then I will get you the information you need," he answered.

"How did you know?"

Astrum just looked at Marcus and smiled without answering his question. He was not about to give up his own secrets to The Peacekeeper. He would share them later, but not right now. Astrum cleared one table and directed Marcus to it. As he sat down, he turned to thank Astrum, but the keeper of the library was gone. He just disappeared without a sound.

A little disconcerted, Marcus shrugged and then opened the book. The pages caught his attention immediately. He skimmed through them until he found his father, then he started reading. Marcus discovered his father knew who he was from childhood, which opened the question of why he was never told about everything when he was young himself. He read about his father's training, his life with The Celestials and The Fallen. It shocked Marcus that he knew nothing about his father's secret life. Marcus felt like he never knew his father. There had been too much kept from him. His discoveries left him disappointed and angry.

The hours passed as he sat in the library, learning all that he could about his father and their ancestors before him. Finally, he arrived at the last few pages, unprepared for what he read there. Marcus had been told that his father had died in a plane crash on his way back from a business trip. Now he read that Berran had been responsible for his death. Every detail about how his father died there for him to see. He forced himself to read it all. Tears fell as he discovered how Berran had stripped his father's soul from his tortured body and destroyed it so that he could not pass on in peace to the next life, denying him his reward for keeping the balance between them all.

Marcus was raging. An uncontrollable anger gripped him, and all he wanted was to destroy Berran, not to keep the peace.

Astrum appeared by his side. He understood the anger he saw etched across The Peacekeeper's face. Simon had been such a close friend of his, and Astrum mourned for him every day.

"Your father was a wonderful Peacekeeper, Marcus. Please do not let your anger stop you from becoming the same," he said as he gauged the young man in front of him, "We can never know why he didn't tell you about your destiny, but he must have had his reasons."

"You know, Berran tortured him and then destroyed his soul. How am I supposed to react to that? I want to destroy every part of him!" he replied.

"I knew your father very well, Marcus. He was a gentle and kind man, but you already know that. You are very much like him in a lot of ways," he began. "He would be immensely proud of you; please stay true to yourself and not act out your immediate need for revenge. Take a little time before you do anything to avenge your father's death."

"Why did he never tell me that this was my future too, especially if he knew his fate from an early age?" Marcus asked.

"I do not understand his reasons for not telling you. I can only surmise that he thought he was protecting you so that you could have a relatively normal life for as long as possible."

"He left me completely unprepared. I want to talk to him about what he did and ask him what I am supposed to do. This would be so different if I could just have his advice. I will not ever have that, will I?"

"No, unfortunately you will not, but I will help all I can, and so will the others here. We will try our best to support you as we did your father."

"Ask me whatever questions you have, Marcus. I have as much time as you need."

"How am I supposed to keep the peace between everyone when Berran is determined to rule over everything?" Marcus asked.

"That is a question pondered by many Peacekeepers, Marcus, and each of them had their own way of dealing with him. Your father made a friend of him, he gained his trust until he did not have it."

"Do you know what happened between them?"

"From what I know, one day he went to visit Berran, just to remind him of the agreement in place between The Fallen and The Celestials and to have their usual catch up. When he got there, Berran was in a furious mood. Simon asked him what had happened," Astrum told him.

"Berran had discovered that your father knew where Grace was. It was the ultimate betrayal for him. He had been searching and getting nowhere since her mother died."

"She must have still been young; my father died a long time ago now."

"Yes, she was. The Elders entrusted Simon with the secret of her whereabouts from the day she arrived on the Earth. He swore he would never divulge the information to anyone, and nor did he. Simon died because he would not tell Berran where Grace was. I do not know the detail of how he died. I never wanted to know. What I know is that his wonderful gentle soul left us that day, and we have no way to retrieve it," he explained, with tears forming in his eyes.

"How did Berran find out that my father knew where Grace was?"

"I am sorry, Marcus. I do not know the answer to that. We tried to find out, but we could not understand what happened."

"How am I supposed to make peace with the evil that killed my father?"

"That is the question that only you can answer, Marcus. Only you can find that path," Astrum answered.

Torn between his anger and the expectations of everyone in Elysium, Marcus knew he had to bury his feelings and embrace his destiny as The Peacekeeper, but it would not be a straightforward thing for him to do. There were too many unanswered questions.

"I will leave you alone with the book for a bit, Marcus, and let you digest what you have been told. Please take your time."

Astrum put a supportive hand on Marcus's shoulder, then turned and left. A tormented Marcus spent the next few hours reading more about the previous Peacekeepers and their dealings with Berran. Eventually, tiredness overtook him. He closed the book and went to find Stephen. He needed to sleep.

Chapter thirty

Marcus opened the door to the room he shared with Stephen and the dogs. It was empty; they were nowhere to be seen. Marcus panicked and was about to leave the room again to look for them when all three strolled through the door looking like they did not have a care in the world.

"Where were you? I was worried when the room was empty."

"There were a few things that I wanted to discuss with Adred, and I thought I would take the boys with me; we didn't know how long you would be," Stephen answered.

"What did you have to discuss?" he asked, puzzled.

"I want to understand more of what is expected of you, so I thought Adred was the person to ask. Do not forget this is new to us both and I want to be as prepared as I can be with the expectations they have of both of us."

"Did speaking to Adred help?"

"Not really. He said that you would tell me when you understood yourself, which was infuriating." He answered, rolling his eyes.

"I have been reading about The Peacekeepers that went before, and about my father's death. I am not sure how I can move beyond that, but it is something I will have to do if I am going to be of any help here," Marcus replied.

"Do you want to tell me about it? Maybe I could help?"

Marcus shook his head and told Stephen that it was bad enough that he had the image of his father being tortured and murdered. He did not want that for him.

"I know you never met him, but you should not have to deal with the images that I have in my head. Stephen, let me protect you from that."

Stephen nodded. He understood where Marcus was coming from; he knew he would always try his best to protect him from the awful things that happened in the world, even if he did not always agree with him.

"I can deal with it, Marcus; honestly, you know I am stronger than you give me credit for, so if you change your mind, then I will listen. It is time for you to let me be your rock. You do not have to be strong for me all the time. Let me be there for you," he told his troubled husband.

Marcus listened to Stephen. He nodded at his words, even though he was certain that he would never share his visions with him.

"I am tired. I need to get some rest. Can we talk about this more when I have slept?" Marcus asked.

Stephen agreed. He felt a little dismissed by Marcus, but he made allowances for his husband. He was dealing with a lot and Stephen knew how overwhelmed he was. Stephen only wished that he could help his husband more.

Marcus undressed and got into bed; Stephen sensed he wanted to be alone, so he sat in a chair near the window stroking the dogs. He watched on as Marcus slept. At first, he slept with little movement, but suddenly Marcus was thrashing about in the bed. Stephen knew he should not, but he could not help himself; he moved closer to Marcus, put his hand on his shoulder, and closed his eyes.

Stephen was at once transported into Marcus's nightmare. Adred had shown him how to enter dreams and nightmares should he ever need to protect Marcus. In that moment, he felt like he needed to do just that. He did not see it as invading his husband's thoughts and betraying his trust.

As he looked around, Stephen saw him standing in a stone-built room, more of a cave. Water was running down the walls and a damp and musty smell filled his senses. In the middle of the room was a chair, sat on that chair was a man that looked just like Marcus. It was Marcus' father, Simon; but somehow it was not, and he did not know why.

Berran was standing behind the chair, his eyes red with rage, and he had a weapon in his hand that Stephen had never seen before.

"Tell me where she is and I will let you go back to your family, Simon!" Berran demanded.

"You know I can never divulge that to you, Berran. I must remain impartial, as I always have."

"How are you being impartial by keeping this a secret? You have let the role of Peacekeeper down; you are a disgrace!" Berran replied.

"The only way to keep the peace, Berran, is for you to not know where she is. Humankind and The Celestials are better protected if you do not know," Simon explained.

"Then you give me no alternative, my dear friend. She is my daughter, and you have no right to keep her from me. I would apologise for what I am about to do, but what would be the point?" Berran sneered.

He walked around the front of the chair and scrutinised Simon. For a few moments, Berran just stared, contemplating how to begin. Eventually, once he had decided on his course of action, Berran lifted one of Simon's hands, inspecting the nails closely. Simon tried to prepare himself for the pain that he knew was coming. One at a time, Berran pulled each nail from its nail bed, blood flowed from each finger, and Simon silently screamed within. With each pull, Berran asked where his daughter was, and when he got no answers to his questions, Berran turned his attention to the other hand. Tears pricked Simon's eyes, but he did not let them fall.

With steely determination, Simon looked directly at Berran; he would never to let him see the pain that he was in.

"You are stubborn, my friend, but you *will* tell me what I want to know. Eventually, you will break. Now let me see how you react as I take each finger from your hands," Berran laughed, "and I will continue removing body parts until you tell me exactly what I want to know."

Over the next few hours, slowly and with tremendous delight, Berran removed Simon's fingers; the sound of the flesh being cut and torn and bones breaking filled the room. Eventually, Simon only had the thumb on each hand remaining.

Still no information about Grace's whereabouts was forthcoming and so Berran moved onto removing all of Simon's toes. Then his ears. Stephen watched on in horror as

Berran moved onto slicing the nose from Simon's face. Still, he sat in silence despite being in excruciating pain.

Simon was a disfigured shell of a man by the time that Berran finally realised that his torture would not work. Berran released Simon from the bindings that had kept him seated in the chair. He told him to stand, but Simon did not move; he just sat expressionless on the chair, goading Berran with his silence. With a single movement, Berran thrust the weapon deep into Simon's stomach. He fell forward onto the floor and watched his own blood flow from his body as the sound of Berran's laughter echoed about the room.

"You will die here; you will not move onto the promised next life. Your soul will always be mine!" he told Simon gleefully.

Simon looked up at Berran as he pierced his chest with a long, sharp claw that had appeared on his hand. The claw ripped open the skin on Simon's chest and Berran forced his hand into his body and ripped out his heart, leaving an empty cavity where it had once been. Simon died instantly, and just as his soul left his body, Berran sliced it into tiny pieces before collecting each one and destroying them. Simon was gone, and Stephen had witnessed everything.

Marcus woke up, his body drenched in sweat, shaking uncontrollably. The sound of sobbing filled the room. Stephen lifted his husband to his chest and held him as he cried.

"I am so sorry, Marcus," he said tenderly.

"What are you sorry for, Stephen? Invading my dreams when I told you I would not tell you about my father," he snapped.

"You knew I was there?"

"Of course I did! You were in my mind. I felt you were there," he replied angrily.

"Marcus, I am sorry. I should not have done that, but you were struggling. I just wanted to help you."

"We are married, and I love you with all my heart, but you should never have invaded my dreams. How could you betray my trust like that?"

Stephen regretted what he had done instantly. He felt an immediate shift in their relationship.

"Please, just leave me alone. I need time to think," Marcus cried.

With no argument, Stephen kissed Marcus on the top of the head and walked out of the room, taking the dogs with him.

Marcus continued to shake as his mind made him relive every moment of his nightmare. He knew he could never forget. He had felt the excruciating pain, the fear, and the emptiness that his father had felt. Marcus's father died alone, but true to his principals and destiny, he did not once consider telling Berran where Grace was. Marcus admired him for that, and he hoped he could live up to the strength and determination that he had shown. He was proud to be his son. Now it was time for him to show the same fortitude that his father had.

Marcus dressed and went to look for Adred with a newfound sense of determination and purpose. He was ready to fight for the peace that was desperately needed.

Chapter thirty-one

Grace could not make out if the images dancing through her mind were memories or just dreams; everything felt disjointed, and her sleep was fitful. She did not know how long she had slept when she heard the door open. As Grace woke from her visions, she stayed encompassed in her wings. Grace did not want to see anyone or deal with anymore of her father's demands. She did not have the strength to fight. In fact, more than anything, Grace wanted to die. She felt she had nothing left to live for.

"Grace?" she heard a voice she recognised whisper gently.

"Are you okay?"

Grace sat up, her wings retracted, and she looked at her half-sister stood in front of her.

"What are you doing here?" she asked Cayla.

"I want to help you get out of here, Grace," she answered.

"How? From what I have seen so far, you have no powers to help me."

"That is the whole point Grace, I am invisible here. Nobody pays any attention to me, so I have walked freely throughout the underworld my whole life. I know of places here that nobody else does. I can get you out of here, I promise."

A shocked Grace was relieved that her sister wanted to help her, though she did not fully understand why Cayla would want to risk the wrath of their father?

"Why would you risk helping me, Cayla?"

"You are my sister, and I want to get to know you. Our brother tortures me, our father ignores me, and I want to get away from here. Grace, *you* are my way out. I hope we can become friends, even proper sisters one day, in more than just a title?"

Cayla's honesty struck Grace; she had already worked out that her sister was unloved. Nor was she respected. She had noticed that when she first saw how Cali had spoken to her. Grace knew what that felt like. She stood up, stepped forward, and embraced Cayla.

"How did you get in here?" she asked her.

"I told them I had some food for you," she gestured with the plate of food in her hand. "The guards had to let me in. Here you are, you must be starving."

Cayla was not wrong; she was starving. It did not take long for her to devour the food and drink.

"How do we get out of here?" she asked Cayla.

"I can't go into it now. I will be back later with some more food, then I will tell you some of what you are capable of and how we can escape. For now, though, I want you to concentrate on repairing your wings," she told her.

"How do I do that?" she asked.

"You have a healing ability. Your touch will heal them. You just need to want that, but you must try to keep out of sight of the door, as the guards will spot what you are doing."

"How do you know I can heal?" she asked.

"I have studied everything about a Divinexus. Trust me, I know all about your powers and I promise I will tell you more once we get out of here," she explained.

"I am chained by Berran's dark magic. How can I get out of sight of them?"

Cayla moved forward and gestured for Grace to hold her hand.

"Grace, put you hand on the dark light with me, let your energy free into that light. Focus on disrupting it," Cayla told her.

Grace did as Cayla told her. She focused on the light that chained her to the wall. Eventually, she closed her eyes, and an energy seemed to run throughout her body and into her hand. A dim white light entwined with the dark light, it grew brighter and brighter, dimming the dark light until it extinguished. Grace was free.

"How did I you know that I could do that?" she asked in shock.

"Do you have powers too, Cayla?"

"I have some powers. They come from my father, but nobody knows about them, especially him. My mother discovered them. She warned me from an early age that I was to never show them to anyone, but I trust you Grace," she explained.

"I am honoured that you have shared that secret with me. Where is your mother?" Grace asked.

"She died a long time ago; our father's doing. I was incredibly young," she told Grace with tears in her eyes.

"Your mother was a human, wasn't she? How did she know you had powers?"

"Who told you she was human?" Cayla demanded, ignoring the rest of the question.

"Cali did. He said that you were from a dalliance with a human woman."

"Cali was right. I miss her very much."

"I am so sorry about your mother, Cayla." She moved to embrace her sister, the similarities in their histories forging a closeness between the two.

"I must go. I have been here long enough. The guards will get suspicious. I will be back a bit later. Be ready and make sure you repair your wings."

With that, Cayla walked towards the door. She looked back and smiled at Grace. The loneliness and despair that Grace had been feeling was now slowly receding into the darkness, and a little hope filled the space that it was leaving.

Cayla closed the door, and Grace heard it lock. The guards looked through a small grill in the door to check on her. She drew her wings around her body and sat down, turning her back to the door to obscure their view completely. Grace could not let them know she was free.

Grace heard their footsteps as they walked away from the door. She heard their laughter and talking gradually diminish as they got further away from her. She stayed exactly where she was until she was completely sure that there was not anyone outside her room.

Eventually, she decided that she could risk moving out of sight of the door. Grace stood up and walked towards the corner of the room, the furthest point from the door and into the darkest part of it.

Cayla had told her she could heal using her hands, so she reached down to one of the more damaged parts of her wing and did as she was told. She imagined them healing, imagined the bones knitting back together. She was not sure what else to do.

Nothing happened, which frustrated Grace. She decided Cayla must be wrong. She could heal nothing. Reluctantly, though, she tried again, and she closed her eyes. This time she imagined a warmth going through her hands like she had seen in films where there were healers. She knew it was fiction, but she thought it could not hurt to try.

As Grace imagined the warmth spreading through her hands, she felt a tingle in her fingers. She moved her hands through the softness of the feathers, deeper into her wings. Gently moving her hands over the painful and damaged areas, she felt the tingling spread to her wings. The pain gradually eased. Grace continued until the pain had receded completely. She opened her eyes; her wings were perfect, not a sign of damage remained.

Grace quietly moved back to the chains; her wings wrapped around her again. It was her only way to keep warm. Noises caught her attention and periodically she could hear the guards walking towards the door and looking at her. Time was dragging. She just wanted Cayla to come back. She hoped she was trusting the right person, but she had no other choice.

While she was waiting, she kept trying to contact Helen, without success. With her nervousness about the situation, it was not long before her stomach fought against the food that she had eaten. Grace could no longer avoid using the bucket. She listened to make sure that nobody would see her and picked a time when everything was silent. Her dignity left her as she gave into the stomach cramps, and she squatted over the bucket. At least she could use her wings for some semblance of privacy.

Grace waited and waited, but Cayla was taking a lot longer that she had hoped. She finally fell asleep on the floor.

As she slept, Grace dreamt of her life with Charlie. Wonderful memories flooded her dreams; memories of the day Charlie proposed to her.

Charlie had collected Grace from her flat. His battered and extremely noisy car announced his arrival before he parked in front of the block of flats that she lived in. As soon as she heard his car approaching, Grace ran down the stairs to meet him. She was excited about their day out by the river.

Charlie met her with a smile that melted Grace's heart every time she saw it. She loved him.

"Are you ready for our day out?" he asked.

"Of course! I cannot wait, and the weather is beautiful!" Grace responded.

Grace and Charlie chatted on the journey, both sharing stories and laughing at each other's jokes. The drive to the river passed in no time at all. There was a small car park by the track down to the waterside. Luckily for them both, there was a space left. Charlie parked the car and took a picnic basket out of the boot, which surprised Grace. She was just expecting a walk but loved the idea of a picnic. The two of them held hands as they walked towards the bank of the river. It was a familiar walk, which they both loved.

There was a family of swans following along beside them in the water; two adults and two cygnets. Grace watched them as they swam alongside the riverbank.

"I bet they want some of our picnic!" Charlie said, laughing.

"I bet they do!"

They arrived at an area that was quite secluded, a small clearing in some woodlands that bordered the river. It was the perfect spot for the picnic. Charlie unpacked a blanket and set out an array of food on it. All of Grace's favourites were there, and Charlie's efforts touched her.

The two of them sat, ate, drank, and then lay down, looking up at the calm blue sky above them. Charlie went quiet, and suddenly he sat bolt upright, which made her jump.

"What's the matter, Charlie?" she asked as she sat up.

Charlie fumbled about in his pocket, a nervous expression carved on his face and Grace was worried, but before she knew it, Charlie was on one knee looking lovingly at her.

"Grace, are you ready?" she heard as she was being shaken awake, pulling her away from her wonderful dream.

Chapter thirty-two

Reluctantly, Grace sat up, her sadness showing on her face. It took a few moments for her blurry eyes to focus on Cayla. Grace was pleased to see her, but sad that she had to leave the comfort and happiness of her memories.

"You slept, that is good. I can see that you repaired your wings. Do they feel better?" she asked.

"Yes, the sleep and my wings repaired has certainly helped how I am feeling."

"Are you ready to get out of here?"

Grace was eager to leave and nodded her response.

"Follow me," Cayla instructed.

"What about the guards?"

"Well, that is down to you. From what I heard from our father, you had some under your spell, so you need to do that again. Do you think you can?"

Grace did not want the ability to have control over other's actions. She had found it hard to reconcile how she felt when she had used it on The Fallen earlier; but if it was the only way to escape, then she would do what was necessary.

"As soon as I open the door, the guards will be there. You are going to have to act fast, so get ready," Cayla told Grace.

Grace extracted herself from her wonderful memories, making it easy for her to connect with the familiar feelings of loss and loneliness. She was ready to aim them at the guards.

Cayla opened the door; Grace stood directly behind her. The guards took a moment or two to realise that she was no longer bound. Cayla stepped sideways as the guards marched towards them both.

"Now Grace!" Cayla shouted.

Grace dug deep and looked directly at the guards. The emotions flowing freely from her, directed straight at them. She watched as all their hope left them. She saw every bit of light that they had inside of them die. The two guards looked like lost puppies as the darkness overtook them. Grace then reached out to them again, this time offering them comfort, which they eagerly grabbed onto. She had them in her power. Cayla smiled. She was relieved that Grace had been able once again to use her power to control the guards.

"You two will stay here and not let anyone into the cell. As far as anyone knows, Grace is still being held prisoner in there," Cayla ordered.

"Won't they revert to themselves when I leave them?"

"No, only you or our father can break that. They will do as ordered. Now follow me," she replied.

For a moment Grace regretted taking control of the guards, she knew Berran would castigate them when he found out that they had failed him. Grace followed her half-sister out of the room, Cayla closed the door behind them, and the guards stood firm in front of it. The two women walked away.

"Keep close, the tunnels here are vast and I don't want you to get lost."

Grace followed close behind Cayla and moved as quietly as she could. Cayla had understated the vastness of the place; the tunnels were long, and branches broke off in so many directions.

"How are you not getting lost in here?" she asked.

"I have travelled these tunnels my whole life," she replied.

It was cold and damp, not at all how Grace had imagined the underworld. The damp seemed to reach into her bones, she shivered. Grace would have given anything for some of that fire and brimstone she had always heard about.

The two women walked and walked, crouching down when the rock above them lowered and finally looking up in awe when the tunnels opened into a huge, stalactite filled cavern. At its centre, a crystal-clear lake. Grace had seen nothing anywhere near as beautiful before, and she wondered how anything so beautiful could exist in a place that was full of evil.

"How much further?" Grace whispered.

"We are here," Cayla replied.

Grace was happy, but also surprised that they had met no one on their journey. She found it odd. Where were all the other Fallen? She buried her questions and continued to follow Cayla.

"But we are in a cavern. I cannot see a way out of it. How are we going to escape from here?" she asked.

"Can you swim?" Cayla replied.

"Yes," Grace tentatively answered.

"We need to go into the lake and head over that way," Cayla told her, pointing to the solid rock wall in front of them. Grace looked at her, completely confused.

"Below the surface of the water is an opening, with a tunnel that leads up to the surface and out of here. You will need to hold your breath for a little while. There is an air pocket halfway through it. We will be able to rest there and catch our breath," she explained to Grace.

Grace was nervous. She could swim, but she had never done any underwater swimming. She was not sure she could do what Cayla was asking.

"I know you are nervous, but you can do this. It sounds much worse than it is, trust me," she said, trying to reassure Grace.

"Are you ok? Ready to do this?" she asked.

Grace nodded. Cayla stepped forward and gave her a hug, which she eagerly accepted.

"How are you so confident?" Grace asked. Cayla did not answer. She just shrugged her shoulders.

Cayla stepped into the water and beckoned Grace to follow. As she stepped in, the warmth of the water shocked Grace; she had expected ice cold. The underworld was a complete contradiction for Grace, cold when it should be warm, warm when it should be cold, but she was extremely glad that the water was warm.

As they made their way further into the lake, the water steadily got deeper, but not deep enough that they had to swim. As they got closer to the rock wall in front of them, the water never went above chest height. When Grace mentioned this, Cayla told her the swimming part would come when they got to the submerged tunnel.

As they reached the rock wall, Cayla stopped and turned. She told Grace it was time to swim, pointing to a barely visible opening below the water. Nerves gripped Grace, her stomach was in knots, and she felt herself spiralling emotionally. Cayla took hold of her hand.

"Do this, Grace, or you will never get out of here. Please trust in me, I will get you through this," Cayla tried her best to reassure her, but she was not sure it would be enough.

Grace's head spun; whisked back to her childhood; and locked in a dark place with no room to move. She could barely breathe. The silence was deafening. She would strain her ears to hear if anyone was coming. Sometimes she wondered if being locked up was better than the alternative. Ultimately, she suffered more in the cupboard with her imagination than she did at the hands of her drunk foster mother.

"Grace, where did you go?" Cayla asked, concerned by her sister's demeanour.

"Nowhere, sorry, I just needed a minute. I am as ready as I will ever be. Let's go," Grace replied, not wanting to share her fears.

"Take a deep breath and follow me, and if you get into trouble, just tap my foot, but I am sure you will be fine."

As they both took a deep breath, they heard a noise behind them. They turned to look and saw Cali standing at the edge of the water, surrounded by guards.

"Stop there!" he shouted as some guards jumped into the lake.

Immediately, both Grace and Cayla took another breath and then submerged themselves in the water and began swimming quickly towards the tunnel opening to escape from their brother and the guards.

Grace did her best to hold her breath. She struggled but kept going as fast as she could. Suddenly, a hand grabbed her foot. It was pulling her backwards towards the opening into the cavern. Taken by surprise, Grace instinctively let out a scream. All the air she had in her lungs erupted into bubbles in the water. She choked. Grace flailed around in the water. She felt like she was drowning and did not know what to do. Panic set in and she kicked out at the hand holding her.

Grace was about to black out. She was giving up. Hopelessness and fear gripped her; every cell in her body was screaming with the pain from the lack of oxygen. As she took her last breath, she felt her lungs fill with the water surrounding her. Every sense failed, and her body went limp as she slipped into a dark and soulless place. Death was not what she expected. She was not ready to accept it; a rush of anger engulfed her; Grace was not giving up. She had so much left to do. Time seemed to stand still; the anger built within her until her emotions erupted.

An immense power took over from the fear that Grace felt. The very cells that were screaming in pain were filling with a force she did not recognise; the power building in her body exploded. A loud thunderous noise deafened her, her ear drums vibrated, she recoiled, holding her hands over them. The water cascaded and flowed from her; the tunnel emptied within seconds; a hand holding Grace forced to let go and its owner disappeared with the water back into the cavern. Grace spluttered and took in a large gulp of air. She struggled, but eventually she stood up in the empty tunnel. Cayla looked at her, their eyes locked, both shocked by what had happened.

"Run!" Cayla shouted. "We don't have long to get away."

Grace did not need to be told; she was already preparing to run. They ran for their lives, expecting at any second that the guards would catch them up. Cayla and Grace stopped when they heard a low rumbling noise, gradually getting louder, signalling that the water was returning to the tunnel.

Grace could just about make out a light in front of them and she heard Cayla shouting at her to run faster. Breathless and struggling on the slippery surface of the tunnel, they finally reached the opening just as the water cascaded towards them, knocking them both off their feet with the force of a tsunami.

When the water settled, the women stood up and supported each other as they walked out of the tunnel. They were physically exhausted and soaked to the skin, but they were free.

"Now what?" Grace asked.

"Now we get you somewhere safe away from everyone that wants to use your powers for their own plans, especially our father," Cayla replied.

"No, I am not hiding. We need to go to Elysium," Grace told her sister.

"The Celestials will not welcome me. I am a Fallen, and worse than that, I am the offspring of Berran. Trust me, they will not want me anywhere near."

"It will be okay. I will tell them you helped me. That will reassure them," Grace said, trying to convince herself as well as her sister that The Celestials would accept her.

"We need to move; the guards will soon be through the tunnel. Where can we stay until you can get us to Elysium?"

"Follow me," Grace answered as they walked away from the tunnel entrance.

Chapter thirty-three

Marcus found Adred in the hall, slumped forward with his head in his hands. He appeared frail and broken. It did not take Marcus long to realise that Adred was crying; he guessed he was recounting the loss of his fellow spiritual beings. Without saying a word, he took a seat beside Adred.

Adred lifted his head and looked at Marcus. They each nodded their acknowledgement of one another before Adred lowered his head again. The atmosphere in the hall, combined with Adred's silent sobs, brought tears to Marcus' own eyes as he reflected upon everything that had happened, and everything they still faced. The men sat there, side by side for quite a while, silently mourning the senseless and violent deaths that they had both seen.

Eventually, Adred sat up straight and turned to face Marcus, who was drying his eyes.

"You know how your father died now, don't you?" he asked.

Marcus nodded. Adred could see the distress in the eyes of the young man sat next to him.

"I am so sorry Marcus, it was a horrible way to die, and then for Berran to destroy his soul was just evil. There is no justification for what he did. Berran could never accept that

The Peacekeeper was a necessary part of our worlds. Is there anything that I can do for you?"

Marcus shook his head and took a deep breath before responding, trying his best to compose himself.

"It was such a brutal death. How can I be a Peacekeeper when all I want to do is to destroy the evil that killed my father? I do not see a way forward. How do I do this when all I can feel is anger?" Marcus responded.

"Marcus, it is only natural to feel that way about him when he took away you father. I cannot lie to you. I am also filled with that anger and despair; he slaughtered my fellow Celestials. All I know is that the only way forward for us, The Fallen, and Humankind is peace. As painful as the process will be to get there, we must try."

Adred studied Marcus. He hoped his words would help him move forward with his role, but he was worried. Berran had dealt a severe blow to them all, and he was not sure that they could find their way through the pain.

"Marcus, there is nobody else. Please do not let this knowledge destroy your resolve to help. Think about how you might move forward." He paused before asking, "is there anything else troubling you?"

Marcus was not used to discussing his personal relationships with anyone, but he did not know what else he could do. He had never been in this situation before, and there would not be many people who would understand, so Marcus decided he would confide in Adred.

"Stephen invaded my dreams. He watched as my father died. I had already told him I did not want to discuss what had happened. I am so disappointed in him. He betrayed my trust, Adred. I wanted to protect him from that horror, and he ignored my wishes. What do I do now?" Marcus said.

"Marcus, please forgive me. I told Stephen how to do that, but it was only if he thought you were in danger and needed protecting. I will reprimand him. That goes against everything we stand for. Please let me deal with it," Adred replied. "You need to remember he is new to all of this as well. He will make mistakes. Stephen loves you and he probably thought it was okay to stand by your side when you were struggling in your dreams. It does not excuse it but try to give him a bit of slack. I am sure he is bitterly regretting his actions."

After a bit of thought, Marcus calmed down and told Adred that he would try. He knew he was right. Stephen had been through so much as well. He stood up and shook Adred's hand and turned to leave. As Marcus walked towards the door, it burst open. Helen looked flustered, her face almost scarlet, and her breath was quick, as though she had been running.

"Please do not leave, Marcus. You need to hear this as well. Adred, there is something happening. We believe Grace has escaped from Berran. We are not completely sure, but we think she is out of the underworld," Helen blurted out.

"How do you know?" Marcus asked.

"We can feel her. She is not alone though, unfortunately there is a Fallen with her."

"Do we know who?" Adred asked.

"No, we do not, but I am trying my best to find out. I would like to contact Grace again if that is alright with you.

My reluctance, though, is that I do not know how safe it is for her if she has Fallen is with her."

Adred thought for a few moments, pondering his choices. He knew it would be a risk to Grace if The Fallen was one of Berran's minions tasked with keeping her away from Elysium and The Celestials.

"We need more information, Helen; do you know where they are?" Adred asked.

"Not exactly, but we are trying to get a location. We know they are on the move. If I may not connect with her, once we know where she is, could I go down and try to follow at a distance to see what is happening?"

"You have a target on you Helen, you betrayed The Fallen when you were undercover. They will not forgive you for that, and I cannot willingly put you in that danger. Please ask Orin to come here. He can go with two Celestial Guards to track Grace."

"But Grace does not know them. She would trust me if I got close to her. I could persuade her to come home and hopefully counteract any lies that Berran has told her. Adred, let me go with Orin, please," Helen pleaded.

Adred took a deep breath. He was not happy about sending Helen anywhere near The Fallen. He knew exactly what they were capable of, and she was too dear to him to risk her life. Helen looked at him. She could see the conflict within Adred. Helen knew that what she was asking was dangerous, but she would not give up. Helen needed to find and protect Grace, and she was not prepared to take no for an answer this time.

"Adred, I am sorry, but I am not really asking you. I will go with or without your blessing. I cannot back down this time. Please do not make me go against you."

Adred knew all too well that Helen still harboured a great deal of resentment after not being allowed to raise Grace when her mother died. He understood that nothing he said would change her mind and so, reluctantly, Adred nodded.

"You will not go alone, though. I must insist that you take Orin and some guards with you, and you will not put yourself in danger! Helen, you must promise to stay at a distance until Orin says it is safe for you to contact Grace," Adred responded. "Now bring Orin to me so that we can discuss this further.

Helen thanked Adred and left the room to find Orin. She was eager to get to Grace as soon as she could.

"What can I do to help?" Marcus asked when she had left the room.

"Nothing just yet, Marcus. The best thing for you to do is to reconnect with Stephen, resolve your issues, and then continue your training with the Celestial Guards. We need you fully prepared for when you must face Berran. Can you do that?" Adred replied.

"I hope so. I will certainly try my best. Thank you for your words of wisdom, Adred. I will leave you to sort this out and I will be with Stephen."

Marcus left Adred alone once more. This time, Adred felt more hopeful. Grace would soon be home; he was certain that Helen would do her best, but what he was unsure about was how everything else would work out.

Berran had gone further than he had ever gone before. A lasting peace with The Fallen would be hard to achieve with the losses that The Celestials had suffered at his hand. There was still so much anger in Elysium, and Adred could not help but worry. Earlier conflicts played in Adred's head; Berran had been his best friend when they were younger. They had done everything together. The two friends should have been the caretakers of Elysium. Berran's betrayal of The Celestials had left deep wounds that had never healed. It had been many years since he left, but for Adred, it only felt like yesterday. He never understood what went wrong with Berran and did not think he ever would, and deep regret was an emotion he constantly lived with.

Humankind had always been aware of good and evil, but Adred remembered a time when there it was just The Celestials and Humankind. Things had changed so quickly when Berran destroyed everything, and he longed for the simple days before the constant battle. The Fallen should not exist. Berran had orchestrated their formation, and they had thrived upon human weakness and their propensity for violence. Their complete lack of regard for the consequences of their own actions only fuelled The Fallen further.

Adred knew that something had to shift. He just did not know how to change the innate characteristics of Humankind. There were many that only wanted the best for everyone on Earth, and that gave him hope. But there were others who had been so influenced by The Fallen that change would be almost impossible. Still, he knew they had to try.

Chapter thirty-four

Grace was not completely sure that she wanted to go back to the place of her childhood memories, but they needed a safe place to stay where Berran could not find them. Her last foster home seemed to her the only place that they could hide. Grace just hoped that he was not aware of where she had lived. She did not think he could have known, otherwise he would have taken her then.

The house that she lived in had burnt down long ago, but she had a secret hiding place that nobody, but Charlie knew about; where she could escape whenever she needed time by herself, time to calm down.

Adam and Julia were her last foster parents. They were so nice when she moved into their home. Grace was their first foster child. At thirteen, she was already quite streetwise because of her earlier experiences in care. Grace had faced many things that no child should ever face. The first few months went well, and trust was built between them all. For once, Grace felt settled. She was happy.

She had not needed to change schools when she moved homes, so she continued to attend the same one as Charlie. There was a gentle rhythm in her life for once. Grace felt comfortable for the first time; she excelled at school, which

Adam and Julia were pleased about. They had been worried that Grace would be behind her peers, but it was not the case. Charlie was by her side; they spent every moment that they could together.

Grace knew little about what Adam did, just that he worked long hours, Julia was an artist, and she spent her days painting in her studio. She liked them both and was gradually letting her barriers down with them, gently encouraged by Charlie. She was happy. The months turned into a couple of years, and Grace loved how her life was turning out. She was grateful that Adam and Julia had taken a chance on her and given her a home.

One day, when Grace got home from school, she intuitively knew that her life was about to be turned upside down again. Her heart sank. Adam and Julia were screaming at each other. Grace could not make out what they were fighting about, but she could tell that Julia was drunk. She could not mistake the venom in her voice. Julia was throwing things at Adam as he tried to calm things. Grace had never seen them behave like that before. She ran from the house, her flight mode activated as soon as she saw the scene at home. Her mind was racing; she could not go through another foster family disaster, but she did not know how to stop it.

Grace had built a den deep in the woods that surrounded their house not long after moving in. She needed a place to be alone in, or with Charlie. It was a place to call her own. The den was full of things that she had accrued from home, stuff no longer needed or missed. She walked through the opening and collapsed in a heap. Grace had hoped that this would be her forever home, her family, but in an instant, all of that had changed for her. She stayed in the den for a couple of hours, trying to figure out what she could do. Eventually hunger got the better of her though and she risked going home.

As she walked through the woods towards home, she could smell an overwhelming odour of burning wood, and as she got to the tree line, she saw where it was coming from. Flames engulfed the house. The entire building was on fire. The crackling sound of burning wood filled the air. Grace struggled with the sight in front of her. The intensity of the flames shocked Grace. She had seen nothing like it. She shook with fear and hoped that Adam and Julia were not inside. Moments later she heard sirens coming up the track to her home, and it was not long before fire engines surrounded the house and water jets were directed at the flames. Grace stood motionless in shock, watching on as people that she did not know tried to save her home and family.

Grace remembered little more about that day, just that she was told that Adam and Julia did not make it. She was told that it was likely that they had died instantly. The fire chief explained to the police that were on scene that the fire was likely caused by a gas explosion, but they were not one hundred percent sure. He told Grace that there would be an investigation. The rest of the day was a bit of a blur. People fussed about her while she sat motionless in the same social services office she had sat in many times before. Someone came and told her they had found her a spot in a group home.

Over the coming days, she asked many times for news about how the fire had happened, but nobody seemed to know. Despite the constant questions, she was told nothing else about it. The group home was in the same town, so Grace often went back and spent time in the den when she needed time alone.

"Grace, where are we going?" Cayla asked, forcing Grace out of her memories.

"We are going to one of my foster homes, but I do not know where we are, so I am not sure how to get there. Do you know exactly where we are?" Grace asked.

"Honestly, no, I just know that we are in some woods. I have never been further than this. I have always stayed in the Underworld."

At that point, Grace was unsure exactly how to proceed or how much more help Cayla could be, but she knew she could not give up.

"Well, let's get walking, shall we, and find out where we are?" She told Cayla.

The two of them walked through the trees, each of them hoping that they were heading in the right direction but unsure of what they were going to do next.

Adred did not have long to wait. Helen was soon walking back into the hall, accompanied by Orin.

"Helen has filled me in about Grace. We can leave immediately but I think to remain inconspicuous, it should just be the two of us. We can blend in better than if there is a group of us," Orin told Adred.

"I do not agree. We do not know who she is with. If it is a high ranking Fallen, you could both be in trouble," Adred replied.

"Adred, really? As the most senior Celestial Guard, I have seen and been in battle before. I think I can take care of us both, don't you?" he replied, offended by Adred's doubt.

"I know you have. You are a formidable warrior, Orin, but you were not there when they attacked, when they mutilated us and killed our friends. If you had been here, it might have been a different story."

"I wish I had been there, but I was not, and I cannot change that, but I can do this Adred, stop being so stubborn, old friend. It is time to delegate; you cannot continue to take on everything."

Orin's response shocked Adred. He had never spoken to him like that before, but he knew he was right. It was just that he was not prepared to lose anyone else, let alone Helen and Orin.

"Adred, we cannot leave this too long. We need to get down there and see what is happening with Grace," Helen added.

Adred turned away from them both. He stood with his back to them, looking upwards as if waiting for a sign. A few moments passed before he turned around and nodded.

"We can go?" Helen asked, noticing the fear etched across his face.

"You can, but you must keep your distance until you gauge exactly who she is with. I want you both and Grace back here safe. Do not take any risks!"

"Thank you Adred. I promise we will be careful," Helen replied.

Orin nodded at Adred. He did not need to speak, there were no words needed. He would do as asked and protect Helen.

"Where do you think she is? How accurately can you pinpoint her location?" Adred asked.

"I believe she is in a woodland somewhere near a cave system in Wales, that is as close as I can get, unfortunately. Once we are on the ground, though, I should be able to narrow that down," Helen replied.

"Ok, stay connected with me, and good luck to you both. Remember no risks!" Adred reminded them both unnecessarily.

"I will be back in a few minutes Helen, I just need to get my sword and knives just in case," said Orin.

Orin left Helen and Adred alone. Adred took Helen by the hands and looked deep into her eyes; his fear and concern were still plain to see.

"I almost lost you once before. Please do not risk yourself. We can find another way to get Grace if we need to," Adred said, pulling Helen close to him.

"I will be careful; I promise, my love. It is pointless telling you not to worry, but trust that I heard what you said. I will bring Grace home," Helen replied, trying to reassure him.

Adred had been against Helen going undercover with The Fallen, but she insisted she could do it, and ultimately, she had rescued Grace. He hoped she would be successful again without putting herself in danger.

The relationship between Adred and Helen had been a secret for a long time. They could not risk Berran finding out and using Helen as a weapon against him. Adred pulled her even closer and kissed her tenderly, not wanting to let her go, but he knew her well enough to know that when she wanted something these days, she would not give up. He knew how much he hurt her when Grace left. Adred would not make that mistake again. He loved her and thankfully she had forgiven him, though there were times lately that she reminded him and that struck at his heart.

Helen broke away from Adred, stepped back, and smiled at him just as the door creaked open. Orin had returned, and it was time for them both to go.

"Are you ready, Helen?" He asked.

"I am. Let's get down there and find Grace. I will keep in contact, Adred. Please try not to worry too much."

The two of them vanished from the room. Adred stood alone once more; he was not good at waiting for anything. Patience was not one of his virtues.

Helen and Orin arrived in the woodlands that they believed Grace could be in.

"Which way?" Orin asked.

Helen stood silently, listening to her senses. Moments went by, but eventually, she answered Orin.

"Follow me," she replied.

Both walked deeper into the woodlands, treading quietly as they went. Orin inspected the woodland floor for clues that Grace had been there; there was the odd footprint, and broken bracken, but he could not be sure it was her. They made their way slowly and steadily through the trees, hoping to find some evidence that she was near.

"Can you feel her at all?" Orin asked.

"I can feel a spiritual being, but there is a darkness too. I hope she is okay and not corrupted by Berran already," she replied.

Helen was usually quite the optimist, but nervousness gripped her; she knew that she and Orin needed to find Grace quickly. Everything depended on it. They continued to walk towards the beacon of spirituality that Helen could feel.

Chapter thirty-five

After Marcus walked out of the room, leaving Adred alone, he felt deflated. He understood some of the reasoning behind Adred's decision, but he was there to help. The talk about Stephen had helped to calm Marcus's anger at what he had done, but now the anger he had felt before was replaced by other emotions, and he did not like the way he felt. A frustrated Marcus was used to being in control. He did not like to be left on the side-lines.

Opening the door to their room, their two dogs greeted Marcus, bounding around, and jumping up at him. Marcus could not help but smile at their excitement. He knelt on the floor and fussed over them both, before turning his attention towards his husband.

Stephen was sitting on the bed, the look on his face revealing that his guilt weighed heavily on him.

"I am so sorry Marcus, I will never do that again, I promise," he said.

Marcus stood up and crossed the room. Holding his hand out, he gestured for Stephen to stand up. Stephen took Marcus's hand and pulled his husband close, wrapping his arms around him, holding him tight. Initially, Marcus resisted the embrace. By the time they parted, any lingering anger was gone. He was happy that he had Stephen's support; he knew he would always need that.

Stepping back, Marcus's heart filled with love and gratitude that somehow, despite all that had happened, he still had his husband. Everything else was insignificant at that moment.

"Stephen, I know you are. I am sorry too. I should never have reacted that way; it has always been you and me against the world. Let's make sure that never changes," he responded.

Stephen let out a huge sigh, relieved that he had not ruined the trust that Marcus had in him. He knew that if he ever broke his trust, he could not live with himself.

"You were so angry. What changed?" Stephen asked.

"I spoke to Adred. He reminded me that you are still very new to your abilities, and that you were acting in my best interests, protecting me as you always do. But just so you are aware, I think you might be in a bit of trouble with him."

"I will take whatever he throws at me. Boundaries are important, and I should have known that if you said you did not want to tell me about your father, it was for a reason. I know you were trying to protect me," Stephen said, "but now I know, please do not hide how it made you feel. I want you to talk about it. Should you need?"

"It was a shock reading about how he died. I needed to process it, and I just was not ready to share it, and of course, I wanted to protect you. When I visually saw what happened in my dream, it shook me to the core and then I realised you were there. I could not deal with my own emotions, then factor in what you were feeling as well. I was so overwhelmed by it all. It does not excuse how I acted towards you. I should have given you the chance to explain why you were there, and I am so sorry that I did not."

"Let's try to put it behind us. Never forget that I love you."

"I love you too, and I wouldn't have it any other way," Marcus replied.

The two of them held each other close again, both relieved that they had cleared the air. As they hugged, the dogs jumped up, wanting their attention. It was playtime, as far as they were concerned. Their dads were soon on the floor with them, playing with their toys until they had tired them out and the dogs eventually flopped into their beds.

"Is there any news about Grace yet?" Stephen asked.

"Helen and Orin are somewhere in Wales looking for her," Marcus replied. "They think she has a Fallen with her."

"Why aren't you with them?"

"Apparently, I am not ready yet and need more battle training, according to Adred. I will be honest. I am miffed. Aren't I here to help?"

Stephen took a deep breath and then reminded Marcus that he was also new to everything in Elysium and the world of The Celestials and The Fallen.

"I know you are used to leading things. It is what you do, but here you are not the one doing that. Adred is, and I also know that it will eat you up inside. My advice to you is that you need to step back, train, and when you are ready, they will know, and you will do what you do so well."

"I know you are right, it's just so frustrating, I just want to get this over with so that we can go back home, back to our lives," Marcus responded.

"Marcus, you realise that there is no going back to our previous life. This is it for us now. Surely, you understand that?" Stephen questioned.

"But I want our life back, so no, I am not ready to accept that we will not get back to it. How can you give up on it so easily?"

"It is difficult, but I am a Celestial now. I will never be human again and like you, I have different responsibilities, and I cannot change that; I cannot go back Marcus, I died. Do you want to know what frightens me now, though?" He asked.

Marcus knew Stephen was right. He just could not let go of his hope just yet.

"Of course, I want to know everything about how you are feeling."

"Marcus, one day you will die. I am now immortal, so there will be a time when I am without you. How do I deal with that? What am I supposed to do with the thoughts of that? It can never go back to the way it was before. It is impossible. You and I both know that if I was not here, then I would be dead. There are things we cannot change and so we must live the life we have while we have it," he tearfully replied.

Neither man wanted to contemplate life without the other. Marcus had not even thought about the fact that Stephen was now immortal and that he himself would age and die, but Stephen would not. As Stephen's words permeated into his mind, the realisation hit him like a bolt of lightning. Stephen watched as Marcus slumped back onto the bed. He looked beaten and lost, which was exactly what he was feeling himself.

"I cannot and will not accept this. If they want me to help restore peace, then there must be something they can do for us. Surely, they owe us that, don't they?" Marcus asked.

"Marcus, they made me into a Celestial for us, otherwise you would be on your own now. I am not sure we can ask more than what they have done already," Stephen replied.

"Well, I am not fucking accepting that! If they want my help, sorry, our help, then they need to bloody do something so that you do not end up alone. I will not have it!"

"Perhaps it's something we could broach with them once everything settles down, but now is definitely not that time. Maybe we talk to Adred once we restore the peace, but for now, I think we just have to help them," Stephen replied.

"You are right; I am just so frustrated. It feels like not only have we lost our lives together, but you have a fucking awful life to look forward to. I do not want you to be alone, Stephen."

"Marcus, I know, but you find that inner strength you have always had, otherwise you cannot bring about the peace that is desperately needed. You must stop focusing on the negatives, just the positives, and the best one is that you and I are together now."

"I will try. Please, I do not want you to worry. I guess I am just wrestling with how I am supposed to bring peace when all I want to do is to destroy Berran because of what he did to my dad," Marcus said.

"I understand, but I know you will find a way through those feelings. It will not be easy for you, but you will get to the point of acceptance because, Marcus, you need to protect everyone. Trying to destroy Berran will only make things much worse."

Marcus nodded. He knew Stephen was right; he was always right and trying to destroy Berran would escalate everything, and it was bad enough already. Marcus knew he had to bury the images he had of his father's death, and he had to do it soon if he was to be of any use in the unfolding conflict.

Marcus went to find one of the Celestial guards to see if he could do some combat training. He told Stephen that he needed to release some of his pent-up emotions, and training seemed to be the solution for that.

"Can I come? I would like to watch you and see how you are getting on."

"If you want to, but it could be brutal," Marcus replied, "and you must promise not to laugh. I will end up on my arse a lot."

"Now you know I cannot promise that, Marcus!" he replied, laughing already.

The two of them left their room and headed towards the hall where Marcus had trained with the Celestial Guards. As they approached the room, they could hear grunting noises and the clanging of metal on metal. Marcus took a deep breath, opened the door, and stepped into the room, followed by Stephen.

Chapter thirty-six

"Helen, we are going around in circles. I am sure we have been this way before. That tree looks familiar," Orin said.

"Orin, I know. I do not know what is going on. I just cannot seem to find Grace. I am not sure why."

A noise caught Orin's attention; he heard breaking of twigs off to the right of them. He told Helen to stay where she was and to stay silent. Orin moved towards the area where he heard the noises, every step slow and deliberate. As he progressed, Helen did not hear any noise from him, but she heard other noises coming closer to them.

Suddenly Orin stopped; he could hear voices and gestured for Helen to hide. She looked around and saw a clump of bracken and slipped silently into the middle of it. Orin disappeared from her view. He was an expert in disguise, and she was not surprised that she could not see him any longer. As Helen waited, she saw four men walk through the trees; One of them she recognised was Cali, accompanied by three Fallen. He seemed flustered and was ordering the others to search every inch of the woods. The four of them were getting closer and closer to her. Her heart was pounding. She held her breath as long as she could and she kept as still as possible, hoping that they would walk straight past her.

Cali stopped and suddenly seemed to look at her. She did not know whether he had seen her, or if he was just looking at the area that she was in. It did not take long for her to find out. Cali lurched forward and grabbed her by the hair, dragging her from her hiding place. Helen screamed in pain and struggled in vain to free herself from his grip, but he was too strong. A few moments later, he let go of her; she fell momentarily to her knees, before two of The Fallen dragged her to her feet, each gripping an arm.

"Helen, so nice to see you again," Cali said sarcastically, "my father will be so pleased that I found you; I believe he has some plans for you."

Helen stood up straight. She was not frightened of Cali. He was just a lackey for his father. He had no power to speak of, and he knew she knew that.

"I wish I could say the same, but we both know that he has a bounty on me, dead or alive, so just get on with it," she replied.

"And which would you prefer? I am open to both choices."

"Honestly Cali, do you really think that you have the power to take me, alive or dead?"

"I may not, but these three are more than a match against a pitiful Celestial like you. I will leave them to decide whether you live or die."

Cali ordered The Fallen to take care of her, but Helen was not about to make that easy for them. Unfurling her recently restored wings, she broke free from their grasp.

Instantly, The Fallen had their weapons drawn and were pointing them at her. She flapped her wings and rose above them all. One of The Fallen drew an arrow and placed it in a bow. He took aim at Helen and was about to fire when Orin flew at him out of the tree canopy, knife in hand, ready for battle. The Fallen did not stand a chance, he did not see him coming. Orin's knife penetrated his chest and tore through his body as he landed on the ground. Orin then used his dagger to sever the spirit of The Fallen from his body. Dark light rose and dispersed into the air, disappearing almost at once. He would never return from that.

Meanwhile, the two other Fallen had grabbed hold of Helen again and they were trying their best to control her. She was not making it straightforward for them. Cali moved forward to help them, but Orin was standing in between him and the others. He stood firm and looked directly at Cali, who had a sword drawn and ready to use.

"You think you can take me down with that pitiful little knife, Celestial?" Cali shouted.

Orin smiled. He knew of Cali and how insignificant he was. He stepped forward with his knife ready and he drew his own sword. With both weapons in hand, he was ready to take another Fallen soul.

"Do you really want to take me on? You know who I am?" he shouted to Orin.

"I know exactly who you are, and I really think you should think about what you do next," Orin replied.

Cali smirked and goaded Orin some more. The two other Fallen looked at each other. They knew of Orin's reputation, so they let go of Helen and moved towards Cali.

"So, the three of you think you can win this?" he asked, knowing that they thought they could.

All three of them charged at Orin, each with a weapon in their hand. He was ready for them. Swords clashed, Orin moved lightly on his feet, fending off each of their attacks. Lunge after lunge, the sound of metal on metal reverberated around the woods. Orin was a formidable swordsman, but so were the two Fallen with Cali. He twisted and turned to avoid the blades. The Fallen matched Orin's every move. Helen decided that even with no training, she had to help an outnumbered Orin. She shouted at Orin to throw her a weapon, distracting him for just long enough for one of The Fallen to plunge their sword into his side.

Orin stumbled and fell to his knees. Celestial blood flowed from the wound; delicate golden light beams floated above him. His soul was leaving his body, he was dying. The Fallen that inflicted the wound smirked. He had brought down the head of the Celestial Guard. He moved closer, readying his sword to kill Orin.

As Helen screamed at Orin to get up, he weakly pulled himself back into a standing position. Blood was flowing freely, draining his strength. The light surrounded him. He did not have long left. Helen knew he was in a bad way and that she had to get to him. She ran over to him and picked up a knife. She stood with her wings shielding Orin from The Fallen.

The Fallen lunged at her, the sword tip pierced her clothing, and she could feel it break the skin on her stomach. She waited for the pain, but it did not come. She waited for death, but that did not come either. Everything around her stopped, frozen where she stood. Her eyes fixed, she could not understand what was happening.

"Did you hear that, Cayla?" Grace asked.

"Hear what?"

"The noises over there, it sounds like someone is fighting. We need to see if anyone needs our help."

"We need to get out of her Grace. I am sure whatever it is, does not need or concern us," Cayla replied.

"We can't just walk away; Cayla, we need to see if we can do anything."

The noise was close by, and Grace would not leave until she had found out whether she could help. Cayla reluctantly followed her sister towards the commotion. As they got closer, they saw Helen with a sword penetrating her stomach. Her wings drooped behind her, and they saw another person with a golden light beam surrounding him. It drained his life; he looked so weak.

Grace stepped forward, the horror at what she was seeing permeated her mind, anger rose through her body, she raised her hands in front of her and shouted "STOP!" and as she did the whole area froze, nothing moved, she was the only being able to.

Grace ran over to Helen. She gently removed the sword tip from her body. The wound looked small, just a graze from what she could see, but she could not be sure. She pushed The Fallen away from Helen. As Grace touched him, he violently exploded into a cloud of ash, which floated into the surrounding air. Shocked by what had happened, Grace stopped dead. Guilt quickly took hold. She had just killed someone, and she did not know how. As she contemplated what had happened, everyone else moved. Snapped back to reality, she saw the second Fallen running towards her. Grace did not want to be responsible for another death, so she concentrated on his eyes. She soon overwhelmed his emotions, as she had done with the other Fallen before. Moments later, he was under her control. Without uttering a word Grace had The Fallen turn and walk towards Cali, outnumbered, he realised he was in trouble. Cali looked over at his younger sister and for or a split second they locked eyes and then he disappeared.

Helen and Orin were both lying on the ground, blood visible from their wounds. Grace knelt by Helen, who told her to see to Orin first.

"He is in a bad way; he needs your help first, Grace."

Grace nodded and moved over to Orin; quickly finding the wound and placing her hands on it. She closed her eyes, gently directing all her energy through her body and into both of her hands. Grace felt the heat generating in them. That energy spread through them and into the wound in Orin's stomach. The golden light beams surrounding him moved towards his wound. It looked like a tidal wave, a rush of the light violently entered his body and disappeared. Orin slowly sat up. The blood had stopped flowing and his soul was intact.

Grace kept her hands on him. She did not see the wonder of his soul returning to his body. Her eyes stayed closed until she felt him move. His hand touched hers, and when she opened her eyes, she could see Orin's gratitude towards her.

"Heal Helen now. I am okay, thank you, Grace," he said.

Grace got to her feet and walked over to Helen, who was bleeding more than Grace realised. She was worried, but hopeful that she could heal her like she had Orin.

"Your turn Helen, I will have you better in no time," Grace said reassuringly.

"Grace, I will not make it. This is not the first injury I have had like this. I have a fractured soul. I can feel it dying," she said, struggling with every word.

"I can do this Helen, let me try."

Helen nodded her agreement. As she did, Grace placed her hands on the slight wound. As soon as she touched Helen, a bolt of energy sparked and forced Grace back, pain and a tingling sensation causing her to stop. She was confused but tried again. The same thing happened.

"Grace, you cannot heal me. The Fallen have healed me before. I am not pure anymore and that means you cannot help me," she said.

Grace was distraught. Helen could not die.

"Cayla, can you help Helen? Please tell me you can?" Grace pleaded.

Cayla took a deep breath and moved over to where they both were.

"Tell me you can help Helen, please?"

"Only Berran can help her, but he will not, because Helen is a traitor. She fooled him, and he will never forget that. I am sorry, Grace, but there is nothing that can be done," Cayla told her.

"Why can't I heal her? I have Fallen and Celestial blood running through my veins, I should be able to do this!" she screamed.

As the emotion rose in her body, the air became still. The woods were silent. Grace stood up, inconsolable about her lack of ability to help Helen. Fear, frustration, and anger were the only emotions that she could feel. She buried everything else deep within her.

Grace stood up, looking down at Helen dying in front of her. She looked up to the sky as if she was trying to find answers, but there were none. She screamed; an ear-piercing sound of heartbreak reverberated around the area.

The sky darkened, black clouds filled the sky, and day felt like night. The sun had disappeared. With Grace still screaming, a lightning bolt shot down and hit Helen directly in her chest, the full force of it piercing through her body and disappearing into the ground. Orin, Cayla, and The Fallen froze where they stood, none of them able to believe what they were seeing.

Oblivious to what had just happened, Grace fell to her knees, tears of failure falling from her tightly closed eyes. She could not bear to see Helen dead.

Chapter thirty-seven

Time stood still for a few moments. Grace did not move. Kneeling on the ground with her shoulders slumped and her head down, she felt like a complete failure. Helen needed her, and she could not help. The silence broken with voices; they were shouting at her, but she could not take in what she was hearing. Trying to bury her fears, Grace slowed her breathing and heard what was being said. She slowly opened her eyes.

"How did you do that?" Orin shouted at her.

"Do what?" Grace was confused.

"How did you summon a lightning bolt to heal Helen? I have never seen anything like it."

Grace looked up; she saw Helen stood in front of her. Not a speck of blood was visible, no injury either. She certainly was not dead. There was a small scorch mark on her clothing and an even bigger one on the ground where Helen had laid. Helen saw the confusion in Grace's eyes. She walked forward and put her arms around her.

"Thank you," she whispered in Grace's ear.

"How?" was the only thing that Grace replied.

Helen pulled away from the frightened young woman, looked deep into her eyes, and shrugged.

"Grace, I do not know, but we will find out. Let's go home, shall we?"

Grace nodded, drained of all her strength, and exhausted by her own emotions. She looked broken to both Orin and Helen. Grace looked around. The Fallen that had been under her control was nowhere to be seen.

"Where is the other Fallen? Did I kill him?" she nervously asked.

"No Grace, he ran off. The hold you had on him broke when the lightning hit," Orin replied.

Holding onto Grace, Helen turned towards Cayla and with a steely gaze asked her why she was there.

"She helped me to escape, and more than that, she is my sister," Grace answered before Cayla did.

"I know who she is Grace, we have met before. She is the other daughter of Berran. I do not understand why she would help you," Helen responded curtly.

"Cayla helped me because she needs to be free of Berran, just like I do. It is disgusting how he behaves towards her. I saw how she they treated her. She just wants a different life. She wants to be with me, and I want to get to know her," Grace replied.

"That is out of the question. She cannot come to Elysium. The Fallen are not welcome under any circumstance. Grace she is a banished soul, and there are no exceptions," Orin explained.

"But she helped me to escape, she protected me, surely that means something doesn't it?"

"I am sorry Grace, we can't."

"Grace, you need to say goodbye. We need to leave now; we must get you back to Elysium. I am sorry Cayla, but you cannot come with us even if you helped Grace," Helen said.

Cayla stood motionless, looking at Grace. She did not say a word, but everything she felt was clear to see in her expression.

"I will not go with you if Cayla cannot come with us. She is not safe now because she has helped me. Can't you see that?"

"Grace, I am not the one that makes our laws. I cannot say yes to this," Helen replied.

"Then who is? Let me talk to them!" Grace snapped back.

"Adred would need to contact The Elders and see what they say, but I am sure it would be no from them. Grace, the laws are in place for a reason."

"I will not leave Cayla, not after I have just found out that I have a sister. She is my family."

Helen could tell from her demeanour that there would be no persuading Grace. She was determined to help Cayla.

"OK. I will contact Adred, but first we need to find a safer place than this to hide. Where were you heading?" Helen asked.

Grace explained about the den at her last foster parents' house. She told Helen that they were on their way to it, but that they were not sure where they were or what direction to go.

"Grace, you are a Divinexus. You can transport us there. If you can picture where you want to be, then you can go anywhere in an instant. We desperately need to tell you all about the powers that you have, sooner rather than later."

It shocked Grace that she had powers that could do that. She was very curious about what else she could do. So far, she could heal, summon lightning, and take control of others.

"Can you show me exactly how I get us to safety, please, Helen?" She asked.

"The safest way would be for me to get us there until you have had some practice. It is a power we Celestials also have. Take hold of my hand Grace, close your eyes and picture where you want to be, and I will see it too."

Grace did as Helen asked. She gripped her hand and closed her eyes. Grace could sense that Helen was with her as she pictured the den and the surrounding area. She hoped it would be enough for Helen to take them all there to safety.

"That is plenty of detail. You can open your eyes again, Grace."

"Do we have to do anything for you to get us there, Helen?"

"Just hold on to me, and I will do the rest."

Orin, Grace, and Cayla held onto Helen. Instantly, all four of them arrived at the woodland that Grace knew so well. Feeling a little disorientated, Grace did a double take. She could not believe that she felt nothing as they relocated, though she should not have been so surprised as, after all, she had already travelled from the earth to Elysium.

"Are you okay Cayla?" Grace asked, "have you travelled like that before?"

"I am fine, and no, it was my first time traveling like that. I have travelled nowhere before, as you know, but it was amazing!" She replied.

Helen looked suspiciously at Cayla; she was not as eager as Grace to trust the young woman stood with them. Trust was not synonymous with The Fallen. In all her experiences with them they had proven how self-serving that they were, however, Cayla had helped Grace and that was unexpected. Cayla returned the look, giving nothing away to Helen. She was also uneasy being with The Celestials.

"We need to get out of view. Can you take us to the den, Grace, please?" Orin asked, feeling the tension building between Helen and Cayla.

Grace gestured for the three of them to follow her through the trees. It was only a matter of minutes before Grace stopped walking and turned to them. None of them could see the heavily camouflaged entrance of the den.

"The den is just there," she told them.

Even though Grace was pointing it out to them, they could still not see it. Leading the way, she walked towards the entrance and the others followed behind her. Pushing through the branches covering the entrance, they all stepped into the pitch blackness of the den. Grace told them to stay where they were as she walked around lighting lamps that were spread throughout the den. As the light banished the darkness, the sight surprised each of them. As they took in the view, they saw that Grace's den was a cave filled with furniture, blankets, rugs, and lamps. It was cosy and inviting. Helen could see why Grace went there to hide when things got tough for her, or if she just needed some space of her own.

Grace immediately felt safer within the walls of the cave. She slumped down in a chair and took a deep breath. Helen knelt in front of her, looking up at the exhausted woman staring back at her. As she studied her, Helen saw how alone Grace really was. She saw it in her expression and the sadness in her eyes. Helen realised she had to persuade Adred that he should allow Cayla to be with Grace. It was essential for Grace to have someone of her own bloodline by her side, even if it was a Fallen.

"Grace, for now you need to rest. Please try to get some sleep. I will go to Adred and see what I can do. Orin you and Cayla stay here with Grace, look after her. I will be back soon," Helen said.

Grace nodded, and Orin reassured Helen that he would make sure that she stayed safe. Helen stood back up, nodded at Orin, and then disappeared.

Helen appeared in front of Adred in his chambers. He was a little surprised, but happy to see that she was safe, though the scorch mark on her clothing worried him a lot. Adred stepped forward and kissed her. He placed his hand over the scorch mark. He was relieved to find that there was no other evidence of injury. She returned the kiss and then stepped back a few steps.

"We have a problem, Adred," she told him flatly.

"Are you okay? Is Grace okay? Did you find her?"

"One question at a time. Yes, I am okay, and yes, Grace is safe. However, when we found her, she was with Cayla, Berran's other daughter. Apparently, she helped Grace escape," she began. "Grace will not leave Cayla and is insisting that she come to Elysium with her."

"You know the law, no Fallen can be here, and after the attack, I can guarantee The Celestials will not welcome Cayla to Elysium," Adred replied.

"I know, Adred, but she needs Cayla with her. She needs someone of her own, someone that is her family. It goes against everything that we believe about The Fallen, but maybe, just maybe, Cayla will prove us wrong. I think you must discuss it with the Elders. At least then I can go back and tell her you tried every avenue to make it happen if we have to say no."

Adred nodded. He was reluctant to have any Fallen in Elysium. Despite this, he knew he had no choice but to do as Helen asked. He asked Helen to wait in his room as he grudgingly left to contact The Elders. Helen sat down, she nervously waited for what seemed like an age; expecting that it would be a futile request. She knew they could not lie to Grace and say that they had asked. They had to be completely truthful with her if they wanted her to trust them.

Eventually Adred returned; flustered, Helen could tell that the conversation with The Elders must have been fraught.

"What did they say? Or do I really need to ask?" She asked.

"Honestly, Helen, it was me arguing against letting that Fallen into our sanctuary. Shockingly, The Elders thought she should come. They told me that if it is the only way Grace will come here, then it is a sacrifice we must make. I am not at all happy with this, and I made that abundantly clear."

"How did they take that?" she asked, a little surprised by Adred's confession.

"Their exact words were, *if you won't allow this, then another could lead here in Elysium*. The Elders gave me an ultimatum; accept The Fallen into our fold or move out of the way. It was not what I was expecting at all," he said flatly.

"Did you agree to their ultimatum?"

"What choice did I have? I told them we would have them both here today. Helen, I am totally against this. I hope it will not be a decision that we come to regret. The Elders may rue the day that they let Cayla into Elysium. I just hope that I am wrong."

Adred sighed. Helen could tell that he was struggling with the situation. She understood why, but Grace needed Cayla despite their opposition. They could not allow themselves to trust a Fallen.

"Put some safeguards in place, limit her movements, assign guards to her. Adred, we will just have to be on top of things from the moment she gets here," Helen replied.

"I will get things ready here. You go back to them and brief Orin before coming back here but be discreet about the restrictions that will be in place. Grace and Cayla will be told about them when we get them back here," Adred told her.

Helen nodded, kissed Adred, and left him to sort everything out.

Adred left his chambers and headed towards Marcus's room. He knocked on the door and waited for an answer.

Chapter thirty-eight

"Come in," came the response from within. Adred opened the door. Both Stephen and Marcus were in the room playing with their dogs. He was glad that they were both there. He needed to talk to them together.

"You look troubled. Is everything okay?" Stephen asked. Marcus always marvelled at his husband's perceptiveness; he saw nothing in Adred's demeanour to suggest that there was an issue.

"We have found Grace. She is safe, but there is a rather large issue that we must deal with if we want to get her to come back to Elysium, and I need you both to help," Adred replied.

"Whatever we can do to help, Adred," Stephen replied before Marcus could open his mouth.

Adred told both men about Cayla and that Grace would not leave her behind. He explained he was against her setting one foot inside Elysium after the attack but that The Elders had overruled him. Adred looked crestfallen and a little less formidable than when they had first met.

"Adred, what do you need us to do?" Marcus asked.

"There will be an enormous amount of opposition to Cayla being here. There is so much sadness and anger here; we lost so many in the attack. I need you to become The Peacekeeper you are destined to be," Adred replied, "And I need you to start sooner than I expected."

Marcus nodded. He understood why he needed to start without completing his training with the Celestial Guards.

"I should be able to keep a young woman safe and out of trouble. It will not differ from being a member of law enforcement and dealing with all that goes with that job. We need her to keep a low profile and have her isolated until things settle?"

"She will have limited movements here, and someone will be accompany her at all times, and Stephen, I want you to be the one that does that please?"

"Why me? Surely a guard would be better off doing that. I am still learning what it means to be a Celestial, and I do not want to be the one that lets you down."

"A Celestial Guard would be too antagonistic right now, but they will remain close. You are a Celestial and new to Elysium, so you have that in common, and hopefully she will trust you because of that," Adred answered, "You also appear to be a soul that radiates empathy, so I believe you will put her at ease here."

Stephen pondered his answer for a few moments and then agreed that he would do as Adred was asking.

"Helen has gone back to bring them home; they should be here soon. Please be ready for me to call you and can you bring the dogs with you, Stephen? They will be a good icebreaker, after all, they are the cutest beings here." Adred said, as he was patting them both on their heads. The stress on his face seemed to lessen.

"Marcus, you will be with the guards. I would like you to arrange round-the-clock security, please?"

Marcus nodded. He could do that.

"We will be ready and waiting for your call," Stephen assured him.

"I will arrange a meeting with my fellow Celestials now to let them know Cayla is coming. This is a discussion I never thought that I would have with them, and it will not be a straightforward task persuading them that Cayla must be here. I am not convinced myself, so I am not sure I will convince the others, but it is out of my hands."

"Do you want us there with you for some moral support?" Stephen asked.

"No, I can handle this. You wait here. It should not take too long, I hope," Adred responded.

Both men nodded, and Adred turned and left the room. The men turned to look at each other; they knew it was going to be a challenging time with a Fallen in Elysium.

"How do you feel about being her guard, Stephen?" Marcus asked.

Stephen told him that Adred would not have asked him if he did not consider it necessary, but that he was not overjoyed about being in the company of a Fallen. After all, it was a Fallen that had destroyed their old life.

Adred arranged for as many of The Celestials as he could contact to meet him in the great hall. He was not looking forward to telling them what was about to happen.

Slowly, the hall filled up with his fellow Celestials, many of them looking concerned at being summoned. It was not usual for Adred to call a meeting with such urgency.

Eventually the vast room was full, many seated and others standing all looking at Adred to hear what was happening. Adred took a deep breath.

"First, thank you for coming, I have some news," he began, "We have found Grace. The good news is that she is safe and Berran has not corrupted her." Adred began.

The room erupted in applause. The Celestials were relieved that The Divinexus was not in the hands of The Fallen any longer. Smiles replaced the haunting looks of loss on many of the faces. Adred was reluctant to carry on. He felt their happiness, too. It engulfed him and warmed his own battered and bruised soul. However, the news he had was a double-edged sword.

"Grace will be back here soon; Helen and Orin are with her now. We know Berran will be livid that she is not under his control any longer and we must prepare Elysium for further attacks. This time, we will be ready for him."

A collective "yes" echoed around the room. The feeling of defiance filled the room. All the attendees were eager to protect Grace and Elysium.

"I have one further bit of news," Adred continued.

The room fell silent. A palpable feeling of unease quickly replaced the eagerness to protect. Every eye in the room focused in on Adred.

"When Grace escaped the clutches of Berran, a Fallen helped her. That Fallen is her half-sister Cayla; another child of Berran. Grace is not willing to leave Cayla to the mercy of The Fallen or her father. The Elders agree Cayla will come here with Grace and that we will protect her."

The entire room erupted; the joyous voices of just a few moments ago raised in anger. He stood waiting for the furore to calm. Eventually, the noise and shouting abated, and he could talk again.

"I can understand how you feel. We lost so many souls in the attack. The Elders have decided that it is a necessary compromise for Grace to come back here."

"How can Grace ask this of us?" One of The Celestials asked.

"She feels protective towards the young woman, and she is her half-sister. Her own compassion will not let her leave her at Berran's mercy, for that we must applaud her."

"Can't we hide this Fallen somewhere else like we did with Grace when was a child? Does she really have to be here?" Another Celestial asked from deep within the room.

"Grace knows about her lineage now. Her powers are growing by the day. We need her here so that we can offer guidance. If we refuse her request, we will not have the opportunity to do that. Cayla will come here, and you all need to accept that," Adred replied.

A group grumble reverberated around the room. Adred continued to reassure his fellow Celestials that measures would be in place to make sure that Cayla cannot cause any issues.

"We do not doubt the restrictions she will have, Adred, but they destroyed many souls. We are grieving for those that we have lost and you, sorry The Elders, expect us to welcome her here?" One of the Celestials asked.

"I know, I know, and I feel that too, but I cannot do anything about the decision. I must ask you to curtail your anger. If you do not welcome Cayla, we will lose Grace, and we cannot risk that."

Arguments broke out, the mood of the room was extremely tense, nobody wanted Cayla to be allowed into Elysium and they made their feelings clear to Adred.

As well as the objections, there were many questions to be answered. Some Adred could answer and others that he could not, but eventually, the mood settled. The Celestials reluctantly agreed that they would hide their displeasure and anger. Grace was the one that needed their help, protection, and guidance. If it meant putting on a united front and accepting Cayla, then that is what they needed to do. Even if they did not like the decision, they accepted it.

Adred watched as his fellow Celestials left the room. He was aware of the hostility that they all felt. He knew they would carry that for many years. Losing souls in the brutal way that they had would impact Elysium for eternity. Adred grieved the loss of them and the peace that disappeared the day that Berran attacked. He hoped that Marcus and Grace could restore some sort of calm, and soon, but he was not convinced that they could.

Adred sat down, despair about the situation that he was putting everyone in overwhelming him. He knew that he would have to tread carefully with Grace and keep his opinion in check. He hoped that his fellow Celestials could do as he had asked, but he was uncertain that they all would be able to. There was the unmistakable feeling of betrayal in the room, but there was nothing more he could say to them.

Chapter thirty-nine

Helen arrived back at Grace's den. She stood outside for a few moments, pondering what was about to happen, torn between happiness that Grace would go back to Elysium, and her sceptical and untrusting feelings of Cayla. Helen knew what it would mean having Cayla in Elysium. She was fighting with her own feelings about the decision made by The Elders. She understood what it meant to Grace, but she also knew how angry and hurt every single Celestial would feel when they were told about Cayla.

As Helen stood in contemplation, Orin stepped out of the den and took her hand. Her demeanour suggested to him that whatever was decided did not sit well with her.

"Helen, what happened?" he asked her.

Helen took a deep breath and looked at Orin. Mixed emotions ran through her, but she knew she must do as The Elders had instructed.

"We are to take them both back to Elysium. Cayla is to be accompanied, and safeguards are being put in place by Adred," she told Orin.

"Seriously, do we have to take that girl with us? The offspring of Berran, the one responsible for murdering our friends? How can they agree to that?"

"Grace needs to be in Elysium, and if it is the only way to get her there, then they will take that risk. I do not agree with it and nor does Adred, but Orin, right now, we have no choice."

Disappointed with The Elders' decision, Orin had no choice, he was not in charge, and he had to obey orders without question or recourse, but it did not sit right with him, and he did not agree with it. Helen knew Orin would not go against The Elders.

"There will always be one of my guards with her. I will make sure of that," he told Helen.

"I know you will do everything you can to protect us. Let us just hope she is sincere, and that Grace is right to give her that trust. We have no choice but to take her back with us," Helen said.

Orin nodded, and they both walked back into the den, ready to agree to what Grace had requested of The Celestials.

It surprised Helen to see both Grace and Cayla asleep on an old and battered sofa when she stepped inside. They were completely unaware that she had arrived back at the den. Orin whispered to Helen, asking her if he should wake them.

"No, let them sleep. It will give Adred time to get everything in place. It gives us a bit of breathing space to prepare," Helen whispered so she did not wake them.

Helen sat down in a chair opposite the two young women, struck by how much alike they looked. As she watched them, memories of Grace's mother filled her mind. Her heart ached for the friend she lost, even after the passing of many years. Helen grieved the loss of the mother that

Grace should have known. She hoped she could help her get to know her a little by sharing her memories of her.

"You were miles away Helen, are you okay?" Orin asked.

"I am good. I was just thinking about how much Grace lost when her mother died," she replied.

"She has all of us. We loved Athena too, and we can share our stories of her before Berran destroyed her. Grace will know what her mother was like, Helen," he said, trying to reassure her by taking her hand in his and squeezing it gently.

The hours passed by, eventually both women woke up. As Grace opened her eyes, it surprised her to see that Helen was back. Helen noticed how much better Grace looked. The exhausted young woman that she left a few hours ago was now looking refreshed and radiant, though she still looked very troubled.

"Hello Grace, do you feel better after your sleep?" Helen asked.

"Yes, I feel much better, thank you. What did The Celestials say about Cayla? Can she come to Elysium with me?" she asked impatiently.

"Yes Grace, Cayla can come with you, but I have to warn you she will not be free to come and go as she pleases," Helen told her.

As they were talking, Cayla stirred and woke up. She sat bolt upright when she saw Helen was back.

"Can I come to Elysium?" she asked.

"Yes, Cayla, you can, but you will need to abide by the rules that are set out for you," she said.

Cayla looked directly at Helen. She said that she would do whatever was asked of her; but there was something that

Helen could not pinpoint that heightened her distrust of her.

"I know it will take time for you all to trust me, but I just want to be with my sister. Thank you for giving me that opportunity," she answered, as if she could read Helen's mind.

Grace was overjoyed with the decision, happy that they would be together. She had never had a family of her own and she needed someone by her side. For so long that had been Charlie, but he was gone. She hoped Cayla would be that for her.

"Thank you, Helen. You do not know how much this means to me," Grace said.

Grace and Cayla hugged each other, huge smiles spread across their faces. Helen could not help but feel the happiness that they were both radiating, but that nagging feeling of distrust would not go away. Helen caught Cayla's eye as the women pulled away from each other. It was a harsh and unfeeling stare that sent shivers down her spine, reinforcing everything that she felt. The smile on Cayla's face could not hide the coldness of her soul for Helen. She would always remain a Fallen as far as she was concerned.

"When do we leave, Helen?" Cayla asked.

"We will go soon. I just need to check that everything is ready for your arrival at Elysium," she answered.

Helen left them both in the den and walked outside, followed by Orin.

"I do not trust her one bit, Orin. She is a Fallen. Did you see the way she looked at me when she was hugging

Grace? Cayla cannot truly hide her darkness and that makes me extremely uncomfortable."

"I saw the look she gave you Helen, I do not and will not trust her either. Do not worry too much; we will keep her confined and she will not be able to do anything in Elysium," Orin replied.

"We do not know what powers she has, or if she even has any, but we know she has one. She has fooled Grace into believing her, and that is a big problem," Helen said, voicing her concerns.

"We have no choice but to do as asked, but I promise you, we will not let her out of our sight. Now you see if Adred is ready for us and what room he wants us in, I will go back into the den and wait with them both," Orin said.

Helen nodded and watched as Orin walked back towards the den entrance and disappeared inside. Helen vanished from the woodland and was soon standing in the great hall with Adred. She could tell at once that the decision The Elders had made still troubled him. Taking his hand in hers, she gently squeezed it.

"Adred, we are ready to bring them both here. Where do you want them both?" she asked.

"Thank you, Helen. Here in the hall will be best to start with. I have arranged for Stephen to be her constant companion when she is not with Grace, while we gauge her intentions," he replied.

"Stephen?" she questioned. "He has no experience in our ways yet. Stephen has only been a Celestial for a brief time. How can he assess her?"

"Stephen is the perfect person to assess her. He has not been with us long enough to have all the baggage that we have. He does not have the history that we have," Adred answered.

"But The Fallen killed him, he lost his life because of them. How can he deal with her when she is a Fallen?"

"If Stephen spends time with her, assesses her and can get over his own experiences with The Fallen, then for me, that will be a good gauge of what we are dealing with. Who here is better placed than a human that has lost his life at their hands to do that?" he replied.

"She will have guards as well, won't she?" Helen asked.

"Of course, they will be always close. I have the first ones ready for the task. They are waiting outside the door. I have sent for Stephen; he will be here momentarily. Now bring Grace home."

Helen nodded, kissed Adred, and vanished from the great hall. Standing in front of the entrance to the den, she was nervous about the protections that were now in place. She was uneasy about entrusting Stephen with Cayla, but it was not a decision that she could overturn. Taking a deep breath, she stepped into the den and told them all that it was time to go.

"Follow me outside," she told them.

All three did as Helen asked. They walked out of the den and back into the dense woodland.

"Take my hand, Grace, Cayla, you take Orin's, and we will be ready to go."

The women did as they asked. Instantly, they were all standing in the great hall in Elysium. Three of them had not seen who was watching them in the woods as they disappeared. Cayla was aware of who it was.

"Grace, I am so pleased that you are back with us unharmed, Cayla. I am Adred, and I am in charge here. Welcome."

"Thank you Adred for letting me come here. I know it must be disconcerting for you all to have me here, but I said to Grace that I just want to be with her. She is my family," Cayla answered.

"Yes, thank you Adred. You do not know how much this means to me. I promise you will not regret letting her come here with me," Grace added.

Adred nodded at both women, unable to articulate his words, anger burning up inside. His wounds throbbed where a Fallen had ripped his wings from him. His head was pounding, he could hear his heart beating quickly in his chest. Just the proximity of Cayla made him furious, but he knew he could not show it. Stephen stepped forward with his hand outstretched.

"Hello Cayla, it is nice to meet you. My name is Stephen, and I will chaperone you during your time here in Elysium." He said as both of his dogs stood by his side.

Cayla shook Stephen's hand; she knew exactly who he was, and it shocked her to see him stood in front of her. Cayla had been told that he was dead. She bent down to stroke the dogs. Both recoiled slightly, though she did not notice.

"Nice to meet you Stephen, and these two beautiful creatures," she replied, standing back up and looking him directly in the eyes.

Stephen stepped back. He felt a coldness from Cayla. Beau and Henry were not comfortable with her, either.

"Cayla, when you are not with Grace, Stephen will be with you, and always you will have guards close by. This is for your safety as well as ours," Adred told her.

"I understand. I hope it will not be like that for long and that I can earn your trust and the trust of your fellow Celestials," she replied.

"Well, let's just see how things go, shall we?" Adred answered sharply.

Adred asked Stephen to show Cayla to her room and get her settled and comfortable in Elysium. Grace looked put out, but did not voice her displeasure.

"Follow me Cayla," Stephen said.

Both Cayla and Stephen left the great hall, leaving Helen, Orin, Grace, and Adred watching as they left.

Chapter forty

Two guards went with them as they left the room. Cayla followed Stephen along a corridor lined with many doors. The guards followed closely behind them. She was not happy with the restrictions, nor about having to leave Grace, but she knew she could not make waves in Elysium if she wanted to stay there.

"I know who you are, Stephen. What I do not understand is how you are here. There were rumours that my father had you murdered," she commented as they walked together.

"I will not be discussing that with you. My task is to look after you and that is what I will do. Your room is this way," he answered flatly, gesturing towards the end of the corridor.

Beau and Henry walked behind their master and Cayla, both with their tails hanging limply, their usual exuberance curtailed by the uneasiness they felt. Stephen noticed that immediately when they met her. There was no jumping up with excitement, no tail wagging, or friendly barking. They had stood still and looked up at Stephen for reassurance. He decided they would not be near Cayla again.

There were a further two guards waiting by a door leading to what Cayla assumed was her room. Stephen reached around her and opened the door, gesturing to her to make her way into the well-furnished room. The dogs did not follow them in, instead they remained patiently at the threshold, waiting for their master to come back out. Stephen felt his strength draining, his head was spinning, and his limbs felt heavy and weak. He did not know why, but he had the urgent feeling that he needed to get away from Cayla.

"I will let you get settled. If you need anything, just ask the guards. I will be back soon and give you a tour of the areas where you may go," he told her and then turned and walked out of the room as quickly as he could without giving Cayla a chance to say anything in return.

The door closed behind him; the dogs looked at their dad as he collapsed to his knees in the hallway. Stephen was exhausted. All his energy had disappeared, his head filled with the images of his death. The dogs snuggled up to Stephen, sensing his fear. Two of the guards helped him back to his feet. He stood with his back against the wall for support while his energy levels recovered a little. Eventually he recovered his composure, and he thanked the guards for their help, then he strolled back towards his room. He needed Marcus to hold him. Stephen needed his husband's strength to help him deal with what was being asked of him.

As soon as Marcus saw Stephen, he knew there was an issue. He was pale and scared. Marcus could see the distress in his eyes. He reached his arms out to hold his husband. Stephen happily accepted Marcus's arms. They both stood together, locked in each other's embrace for a few minutes.

The dogs sat by their feet, waiting for the attention to turn back to them.

Marcus settled the dogs and then walked over to join Stephen, who had collapsed on their bed.

"What happened? Who or what did this to you?" he asked.

"Nothing happened, really. Adred introduced me to Grace's sister, and I took her to her room. She is just so cold; I can feel that she is evil," he replied. "All of my energy seemed to drain from me. It was as if my Celestial life force was under attack. I do not know how she did it, but I saw my death, and felt it all over again," Stephen sobbed.

Marcus could feel the anger building up inside himself. He hated seeing Stephen in pain, and the images of him dead still burned into his own brain. He could only imagine how terrifying it must have been for Stephen to have to relive it again.

"You should not have to do this; I am going to Adred. I do not want you to do this, Stephen!"

"It is okay Marcus; today was just the first time I have been around a Fallen. I am more prepared now. I can bury these feelings and do as Adred has asked me," he replied.

Marcus was not about to accept that. He wanted to protect Stephen and was about to argue his point with him when a knock on the door stopped him.

"Stephen, Adred has asked that you come back to the great hall, and can you come as well please Marcus?" a guard asked them both.

"Yes, of course," Stephen answered before Marcus could say anything, knowing that his husband had plenty more to say.

Marcus looked at him, rolling his eyes. He knew that arguing with Stephen then would be utterly pointless. Once his husband had decided on something, he was as stubborn as him. He watched Stephen as he composed himself, and then they both left their room and walked to the great hall, leaving the dogs asleep in their beds.

Adred looked at Grace as Stephen left the hall with Cayla. He could see the joy in her eyes. He was extremely relieved that she was back in Elysium, even if it was with a Fallen by her side.

"Grace, I am sorry that there are so many restrictions on Cayla, but they are for her safety and the safety of everyone here," he told her.

"Effectively, she is a prisoner here, isn't she? There is no other way you could describe it!" she snapped.

"No Grace, she has some freedom to move about areas of Elysium, but she must be accompanied. We need to be sure of her intentions. Surely you must understand?" he replied.

"She is my sister. I trust her. She helped me escape at significant risk to herself."

"Grace, she is a Fallen. You were there when they attacked us. You saw their viciousness. I find it strange that you do not understand our reservations." Helen replied, trying to conceal her own frustrations.

"But how can you hold her responsible for what our father organised?"

"We know Berran was behind the attack and that you believe Cayla when she says she wants to be by your side, but the distrust between us and The Fallen goes back many centuries. There is a history that you do not fully understand and because of that, we cannot and will not risk any more Celestial souls. Grace, I am sorry, but this is the way it must be for now. There will be no relaxation of the restrictions until we are convinced of Cayla's intentions," Adred told her flatly.

"Then I will leave here with Cayla. We will go somewhere else away from all of you where we can be free!" she snapped.

"Grace, calm down, please. You trust me, don't you?" Helen asked. Grace nodded. She did trust Helen.

"You know your powers are showing themselves, and you also know that you need help to control them. Elysium is the safest place for that, we can help you learn everything you need to know," Helen continued, "We will look after Cayla too, she will get any help that she needs and hopefully it won't be too long before she has gained our trust as well as yours."

Grace took a deep breath and calmed down a bit. She understood what was being said to her, but she did not want Cayla to feel trapped or invisible any longer. She knew what that felt like from her own childhood. Reluctantly, she nodded in agreement.

There was a knock on the door. Adred bellowed for whoever it was to come in. A nervous-looking guard walked in and asked Adred if he could talk to him privately. Adred excused himself from the others. Both stepped out of the room into the empty corridor, where the guard told Adred what the issue was. Once the guard had finished, a displeased Adred asked him to get Stephen and Marcus and to bring them to the great hall. The guard bowed his head in agreement as Adred turned and stormed back into the hall.

"Helen, will you take Grace to her room and let her rest for a while, please?" Adred snapped.

Helen knew that something was wrong. She also sensed that Grace was about to argue with him. She placed a gentle hand on her arm to stop her.

"Just rest a little Grace, let everyone get used to the idea that Cayla is here. Patience is what we all need just now," Helen advised.

Grace saw the look on Adred's face and thought better than to start an argument. She did not agree with him, but she knew Helen was right. Adred paced up and down the hall as he waited for Stephen and Marcus to arrive, his anger building by the minute. Finally, the door opened, and they both walked in.

"Stephen, did I not clarify that you should be with Cayla at all times when Grace is not with her?" Adred bellowed as soon as the door closed behind them.

Taken aback by Adred's tone, Stephen became flustered. He took a breath.

"Hang on Adred! Do not attack him as soon as he walks into the room. You did not see the state Stephen was in a little while ago," Marcus snapped back before Stephen could answer.

"It's okay Marcus, let me answer him please?"

"Sorry Stephen, I did not mean to come across so aggressively," Adred said, calming down a little.

"I took Cayla to her room and got her settled; once there, I immediately felt weak. It is hard to explain what happened, but I knew that needed to get away from her. When I left the room, I collapsed in the corridor. All my energy was gone, and visions of my death filled my head. I needed to compose myself and get the dogs back to our room," Stephen explained.

"You lost all your energy? We do not have energy like humans, our souls are our energy. Do you think that your soul was being attacked?" Orin asked.

"I do not know. I just know that I felt so weak that I collapsed to my knees."

Both Adred and Orin were extremely concerned.

"Is Cayla doing this? Can a Fallen attack a Celestial soul?" Marcus asked.

"No, the only way to destroy our souls is how Berran destroyed your fathers. Even if our bodies die, our souls move on and join with The Elders. We do not know what powers Cayla has, if any at all. It would be prudent to assume that she does. I do not know how, but it is possible that what happened to you could be down to her." Adred replied.

"So how am I supposed to be around her if she can do that to me?" Stephen asked.

"I will come to her room with you, and we will ask her outright if she has powers and see if she will answer us. It would be a good idea if we asked Grace to come as well. I hope she will not lie to her," Adred said.

"But for now, the guards are at her door. She is not going anywhere, so regain your strength and we will meet up a bit later, and I am terribly sorry for my attitude, Stephen. I forget that you and Marcus are new to all of this. Please forgive me?"

"We understand. Adred, there is nothing to forgive," Stephen replied. Marcus, who was not as accepting of Adred's apology, did not respond.

Chapter forty-one

Grace did not realise how much the last few days had taken out of her. She felt weak and mentally exhausted. Her heart was heavy with the grief at losing Charlie and his parents hit her in waves. They weighed heavily on her mind. She missed them so much. On top of her grief, she was struggling to process the fact that she had siblings also sent her emotions spiralling.

Lying down on her bed, she looked up at the ceiling, trying to get things straight in her head. She found it hard to contemplate that she was the daughter of the most evil being in existence. It was not something she could ever have imagined. Grace thought that her childhood was the worst thing that could have happened to her, but now she had to contend with this.

Although she now knew that she had family, Grace still felt alone. She was the only Divinexus in existence and she wondered how she would cope with the pressure of that. How could she ever have a normal life? Only a brief time ago, she was due to marry the man that had been by her side through all the dark days. The man who had her heart, and whom she loved more than any other. Now she was alone.

Tears filled her eyes, her heart ached with the pain of a life lost, sobs wracked her body, finally the exhaustion won, and Grace fell asleep.

"Grace, you are not alone. We are here for you," she heard someone whisper in her ear.

Out of the darkness of her dream stepped a man. He was tall with hair the same ebony colour as her own. The colour of his eyes matched hers perfectly. Dressed all in black, the man had outstretched wings of the darkest, inky black. The man smiled at her, and all her pain disappeared. Her doubts about her life left her. Grace felt immediate comfort. Even more, Grace felt safe.

"Who are you?" she tentatively asked.

"My name is Eli."

"Why are you in my dreams?"

"I am here because you need me to be here, Grace. We can feel your pain, your loss, and your loneliness," Eli replied.

"Who are you, and how are you in my dreams?"

"The first thing you need to know is that you are not alone; I am a Divinexus, like you."

"There are no other Divinexus. I am the only surviving one. I was told that all the others before me had died," Grace responded.

"You are not the only one Grace, we are not dead, we are just not here anymore. I know that this must be a great deal for you to take in. You have had a very traumatic time. I will not stay in your dreams. I only came to tell you that you are not alone, but if you need me, then just call my name," Eli told her before he disappeared as suddenly as he had appeared.

Grace woke up confused, but for the first time in a while, she did not feel alone. It puzzled her. If the dream was to be believed, she was not the only Divinexus in existence. Why had The Celestials lied about it? Was it just a dream? Had her subconscious created another Divinexus as a way of coping with all that had happened to her since the wedding? More confused than ever, she got up, walked over to the window, and looked out at Elysium.

A knock on the door made Grace jump. She opened the door to find Adred, Stephen, and Marcus standing in the hallway.

"Come in," she told them.

As the men walked into her room, she sensed they were nervous and wondered why.

"Grace, will you come with us to talk to Cayla? We have some questions, and you should be there with her," Adred asked.

"Of course, I am sure that there are many things that you need answers to, and I am also sure that she will be eager to help you in any way that she can," Grace answered.

Grace was unsettled about her dream, but she put it to the back of her mind for the time being. She resolved that after the chat with Cayla, she would ask Helen about the history of the Divinexus. She followed the three of them out into the corridor towards Cayla's room.

"Please be gentle with Cayla. My father and brother treated her badly from what I saw. She needs your patience and understanding, Adred," Grace said.

"I will be gentle with her Grace. We do not want problems here either, so the best thing for all of us is to be open and honest, isn't it?"

Grace was relieved that Adred felt that way, and she hoped they would all eventually accept Cayla into Elysium. The guards were on either side of the door to Cayla's room, and both bowed their heads when Adred approached. Adred responded by bowing his head before knocking on the door.

Cayla opened the door. It shocked her to see a group in the corridor. She opened the door fully to let all four of them in.

"How are you settling in, Cayla? Is your room comfortable enough for you?" Adred asked.

"Yes, thank you. It is the nicest room I have ever had," she replied.

"Can we ask you a few questions?"

"Ask away," Cayla replied, looking at each of them. She had not met Marcus before, but she knew who he was.

"You are a Fallen, and as such, I must ask what powers you have?"

"I have no powers. My mother was human, and I took on her traits and not those of my father," Cayla replied.

Grace was confused. That was not what Cayla had told her. She looked at her sister suspiciously before joining in the conversation.

"Didn't you tell me you had powers, but that nobody knew about them apart from your mother?" she questioned.

"I wanted to make you feel safe and believe that I could help you if I needed to when we escaped. I am sorry that I lied to you," she responded.

"Cayla, I have had many people in my life lie to me. I cannot accept someone else into my life who does that. Be honest with us if you want our help," Grace replied.

Cayla looked sheepishly at the group in her room. She sat silently for a few moments, but eventually she nodded and said that she would be completely honest with them.

"Stephen's energy was drained when he was around you earlier. Can you explain that?" Adred asked.

"I cannot. I did nothing to him," Cayla answered.

Stephen was sceptical, but he kept quiet and listened to the conversation, as did Marcus. Cayla denied many times that she had any powers, and eventually, Adred had nothing more to ask.

"I am certain that your father will try to get you back and Grace. Cayla, do you have any insight into how he might do that?" Marcus asked.

"Sorry Cayla, I should have introduced you. This is Marcus, and he is The Peacekeeper. Please answer his questions as well," Adred said.

"My father will not want me. I am no use to him. He will only want Grace, and he will stop at nothing to get her back. I can guarantee that he will attack again and that many, many more Celestials will die at his hand," she began. "Grace is the only thing that he wants. He has made that clear to me my whole life. He wants her power, and then he wants to destroy you all."

"We are prepared for him this time. We will be ready, but my job is to make peace between The Fallen and The Celestials, and I would like to know if you have any insight into how we could do that?" Marcus asked.

"You can never make peace between him and The Celestials. He does not care about any of that! My father wants ultimate control and power over everything and everyone. He will not stop. Just remember what he did last time. That was a minor attack."

"And how does he intend to achieve ultimate control? Have you seen any plans or heard anything that could help us prepare?" Adred asked.

"I have never been involved in any attack plans. I have told you; Grace knows I was invisible as far as my father and brother were concerned. I was an inconvenience to everyone," she replied sadly. "They left me alone most of the time. I cannot tell you how happy I was to meet Grace and to get away from them."

Everyone in the room felt the sadness in Cayla. Grace, most of all; she understood that feeling completely.

"Grace is his priority. He will take her by force again. You cannot stop him. My father will destroy anyone who gets in his way. Including me," she reiterated.

"Cayla, you are welcome here. We will protect you as best we can. For now, though, you must always remain accompanied when you leave this room, for your safety and for ours too. I hope you understand that?" Adred explained.

"Adred, I will do whatever is necessary," Cayla replied.

Marcus sensed an ambiguity in how Cayla had replied. Her answers did not convince him, and he decided he would keep a close eye on her. Grace was more relaxed. She understood why Cayla had lied and could forgive her for that.

"Thank you, Cayla. We will leave you with Grace for a little while. Please let the guards know if you need anything," Adred said. With that, the three men left the sisters alone.

Grace sat down in a chair by the window in Cayla's room, her attention drawn to the garden outside. She saw a movement at the edge of the woods that surrounded the beautiful gardens, but as she tried to focus on it, the movement stopped. She could not see anyone and brushed it off as her mind playing tricks on her.

"Cayla, what do you know about the earlier Divinexus? What happened to the others?" she asked.

"You are the only one, Grace. I have not heard of any others before you, but I have never been told any history or taught anything, so I cannot help you," she replied.

The two women sat silently for a while, neither sure what to say to each other, awkwardness had replaced the need to escape Berran. Both women were relieved when a guard knocked on the door to see if there was anything that they needed.

"No thank you," Grace replied to the guard, then she turned to Cayla, "I must see Helen. I will ask Stephen to come and keep you company and give you that tour he promised."

"There is no need. I will stay here for now. I am not ready to meet other Celestials just yet. Will I see you later?" Cayla asked.

"You will. I will be back soon."

Grace left her sister alone and went in search of Helen, hoping that she could provide answers to her many questions.

Chapter forty-two

Adred, Marcus, and Stephen walked along the corridor from Cayla's room in silence, each of them digesting their conversation with the young woman.

"We need to discuss Cayla further. I would like your thoughts," Adred said. "The weapons room should be empty. We can talk privately there."

They entered the room, and Adred closed the door behind them.

"Well? What are your impressions of Cayla, Marcus?"

"There is something not quite right; she lied to Grace, and she was very non-committal with some of her answers," he began. "Her comment about doing whatever is necessary was odd and possible not meant in the way we think."

"Agreed. I got the sense that she admitted to lying to Grace to gain our trust. I am not at all impressed by her, nor am I taken in by what she is telling us. We need to keep her at arm's length. I think that there may be ulterior motives at play here," Stephen commented.

"Thank you. I also got the impression that she was giving us a little to gain trust but hiding her actual intentions. We could be wrong, but for now, we must trust our initial instincts. I will inform The Elders of the current situation," Adred responded.

"What about Grace? How do we deal with her feelings about this?" Stephen asked.

"We follow her lead. We must keep our suspicions to ourselves and be there for her if they come to fruition. Grace will need our support should Cayla betray her," Adred advised.

"One thing that we can be sure of, what Cayla said about Berran not giving up on getting Grace back, is absolutely true. We can expect there to be another battle," he continued.

"Life here is going to be hard for everyone; the threat of attack will make for an unpleasant atmosphere. Stephen and I will do all we can to help," Marcus replied. "We may be new to all of this, but we will do our best."

"Thank you both, for now though, Marcus. Can you catch up with Orin? Get your swords skills perfected. You will need them in battle. The attack is imminent, and it saddens me that it has come to this. Stephen, can you go back and take Cayla on that tour? Try to show her you trust her. I know you do not, but she needs to think that you do. I will check in with you both later. Thank you. I am glad that you are both here with us."

All three of them went their separate ways, each of them with jobs to do.

Grace knocked on Helen's door and waited nervously for an answer. She knocked again, but there was no answer. Grace did not know Elysium well enough to guess where she might be, so she strolled away, not knowing where she was going herself.

Grace's mind replayed her dream of Eli and what he had said about The Divinexus. In her absent-mindedness, Grace soon found herself at the door out of the building. She opened it and stepped out into the sunshine that was beaming down on the beautiful gardens. Scanning the edge of the woods surrounding the flower beds, she looked to see if there was anyone in them. She had not forgotten the feeling that she had seen someone there. Grace walked alongside the flower beds towards the trees. There was nobody around and she decided that her mind had just been playing tricks on her. As she was about to turn around and go back to her room, a slight movement caught her eye.

"Are you looking for me, Grace? If you are, then just take a few more steps. I am in the trees." She heard whispered in the breeze.

Grace looked around to see if anyone else was there, but she saw nobody. Drawn in by his soft voice, she stepped forward into the trees. Eli walked out from behind a huge oak, a smile spreading across his face. Their eyes met. Grace felt an instant bond with him, a spark like no other. Her faced flushed as he stared back at her.

"How are you here? You were in my dreams and now you are standing in front of me."

"Because you called for me," Eli replied.

"No, I did not. I didn't believe that you even existed," Grace replied, confused by Eli's answer.

"But I was in your thoughts; you were wondering if I was real. That summoned me here. Now you know that I am not a figment of your imagination. "

"That makes no sense at all! How can me wondering if something is real summon that something?"

"You know what you are, don't you, Grace?"

"I am a Divinexus, the offspring of a Fallen and a Celestial. According to you, I am not the only one, but others have told me I am. Please explain that to me," Grace responded.

"There were many Divinexus, Grace. Good always attracts evil, and evil attracts good. That is the way of the world. The way it has been for all of time. As a result, many offspring were born. The difference is that you are the only one born of Berran and a Celestial; aside from that useless twin of yours, of course, he should never have been born," said Eli.

"So where are all the others, then? And why have you not contacted me before now? Why have you let me suffer through the life that I have had?" Grace snapped back.

"Even The Divinexus could not help you. Your life was pre-planned; your experiences will be what makes you the best of us all Grace," Eli told her.

"We Divinexus are everywhere. We can appear wherever we want, we can blend in with our surroundings, we can live the lives that we want, or we could until now."

"What changed? Why are you here?" Grace asked.

"You, Grace. You are more powerful than all of us. The balance has shifted. People will fight a war over you. You can see that already, can't you?"

Grace nodded. She knew she was in the centre of everything that has been happening, and she wished she wasn't.

"The moment that you set fire to the church on your wedding day was the day that everything changed, it was the day that Berran noticed you again, the day that we did too, and now there is a choice for you to make," he replied.

"I did not set fire to the church. I do not know what happened, but it was not me," she told him.

Eli took a moment and then told Grace that the different factions inside her mind were battling on the day of her wedding. The Fallen part of her was not willing to let her marry a Celestial, even if she knew nothing about her lineage.

"You cannot be bound to a Fallen or a Celestial no matter how much you love them, Grace, it is impossible. You can only join with another Divinexus," he explained.

All that she was hearing confused Grace. Was she there talking to Eli, or was she dreaming again?

"I am real. Grace, you are not dreaming," Eli announced.

"How do you know what I was thinking?"

"As Divinexus, we are all connected. An invisible but unbreakable bond has formed since I met you in your dreams. You are at one with us all now," Eli replied with a smile on his face. A smile that made every cell in Grace's body come alive. She brushed the feeling away.

"You are welcome to find love with another, Grace, but I can guarantee that you will not find it within The Fallen or The Celestials. One day, you will come to accept that your love will be bound only to a Divinexus. No matter how long that takes. For now, I must leave, and you must follow the path laid out for you."

Anger and guilt about her body's responses to Eli rose throughout Grace. She would not be told by anyone who she should love. Grace loved Charlie and no one else.

"I will see you soon," Grace heard whispered in the breeze.

Grace found herself alone in the woods once again. She walked for a while, thinking about what she had been told. Grace thought about the way Eli had made her feel; she brushed it off as nonsense and walked back towards the building. She would concentrate her efforts on finding Helen, so that she might get some questions answered. The list seemed to get longer by the minute.

"You must keep me secret, Gracie. You must let no one know we exist," were the last words she heard as she opened the door to the building and stepped back inside.

"My name is Grace, not Gracie," she said aloud to nobody, but somehow, she knew Eli had heard her. She could feel it, she could feel him.

"Grace, are you feeling okay?" she heard from behind her, making her jump.

She turned and saw Helen standing in the doorway to a room in the corridor. She looked concerned. Grace hoped that she had not heard her.

"I know that the past few weeks have been difficult for you. There has been so much for you to deal with. Can I do anything to help settle you here?" she asked.

"Can I ask you some questions, please, Helen?"

"Yes, of course you can. Shall we go to your room? Would you be more comfortable there?" Helen asked.

Grace nodded and walked back to her room with Helen following closely behind, passing Stephen as they did.

Chapter forty-three

Grace and Helen said hello to Stephen. The three of them chatted for a moment or two before they parted and continued towards Grace's room. He watched as they went in and then turned and knocked on the door to Cayla's room. Stephen was apprehensive and not looking forward to spending time with her. He did not trust her at all. Every single one of his senses pointed to her being more trouble than they could deal with, but Adred had asked him to bury his mistrust and show her around. So that is what he was about to do.

Cayla opened the door, she smiled at Stephen, it was a forced smile; it did not reach her eyes, and it confirmed what he felt towards her.

"Are you ready for the tour that we promised?" he asked.

"I am. It will be nice to leave this room and see what Elysium is like," she replied.

"Shall we start outside? We have some gorgeous gardens and a beautiful woodland full of wildlife. Does that interest you?"

"I suppose so. I have not been out very much in my life. There were no trips outside with my father, that is for sure."

Already bored with Cayla's company, Stephen gestured for her to follow him. The atmosphere between the two of them was frosty, and they walked in silence as they made their way through the building and out into the gardens.

The sun beamed down, and Stephen felt the warmth on his cheeks. He closed his eyes and took it all in. When he opened them, he looked at Cayla, who had a fixed expression on her face. As they stood in the garden, her face softened as the sun warmed it. The warmth of the sun seemed to break through that hard, frozen expression. He watched as she closed her eyes and soaked up the heat touching her cheeks.

"Are you okay?" he asked, a little surprised that the sun could break through her tough exterior.

"The sun is so warm, I didn't realise that it would be," Cayla replied. "Contrary to widely held belief, my home is cold and damp, and not the fire and flames that everyone believes. Warmth is a new feeling for me."

"Can I take it you did not get out to see it very often when you were growing up?"

"No, I rarely left home. My father insisted that my place was in the Underworld and nowhere else."

The two of them continued with the tour. Stephen watched as Cayla studied the beautiful gardens. She picked some flowers as they walked, sniffing them as they went. Stephen encouraged her to look around and he stood and watched her for a little while. Cayla was just like a small child to him, experiencing everything for the first time. For a moment, he forgot himself and felt sad that she had experienced little in her life.

"Would you like to have a walk through the woods? We can see what wildlife is around in there," Stephen asked.

Cayla told him she would love to. She seemed enthusiastic. He relaxed a little in her company, trying to think of her as just a young girl who had had no life experience instead of a Fallen. He hoped it would make the tour easier to deal with.

The pair of them walked into the woods, leaving the gardens behind them. Stephen momentarily saw movement in front of them, but as he tried to focus on where it was, everything became still again. He thought he must have imagined it, and they continued to move further into the woods.

A rabbit hopped in front of them, sat up on its back legs, it looked at the two of them curiously, tilted its head and hopped off through the bluebells carpeting the woodland floor. Cayla seemed engrossed in the surroundings. The two of them did not talk. They slowly walked, watching out for any wildlife they could see.

"Stephen, can we stop for a moment, please?" Cayla asked, taking him by surprise.

Stephen did as asked. He turned to look at Cayla to see why she wanted to stop. She laid the flowers in her hands on a tree trunk that was rotting in the woods. She sat down and looked at him, saying nothing.

"Is there a problem? Do you need something?" he asked.

"There is no problem for me, you however, have a big one," came the answer.

Cayla's face lit up. Stephen was confused, his senses heightened. Something was seriously wrong, and every cell in his body told him to run, but his feet would not move, frozen to the spot. As fear rose through him, he looked at Cayla, who was smirking at him. An evil and frightening stare drained every ounce of his energy. At that moment, Stephen's mistrust of Cayla resurfaced. His eyes darted around to see if there was anyone that could help him when he spotted someone stepping out from behind the trees. A man walked towards Cayla and stood by her side.

"You have done well, little sister. Now let's get on with this, shall we?"

Cayla nodded, stood up and took a knife from her brother. Stephen was powerless to react. He felt a sense of déjà vu; he knew he was going to die, and this time he did not think there would be any way back. All his energy and Celestial powers were gone. Stephen could not even protect himself with his wings. As much as he tried, they stayed firmly tucked away.

Cayla walked towards him and swiftly plunged the knife deep into Stephen's chest. The weapon stopped his heart instantly, just the one wound took his life. This time, there was no pain. Lights danced around in the woodland as his Celestial soul left his body. Stephen's thoughts filled with images of his husband and beloved dogs, before his consciousness faded into black and his soulless body fell to the floor.

Cayla saw the instant that Stephen's soul left his body, and with swift movements of her knife, she deftly sliced it to pieces. She stood proudly, looking down at the body on the ground. She smiled at what she had done, taking a great deal of delight in her actions. Cayla knew her father would be proud of her.

"Quickly, time is short, and you need to take his form before anyone comes. Cali, you must be exact in this. Nobody can know that you are here or that he is dead. We cannot let father down. The entire plan rests on you being able to fool these imbecilic Celestials. The hardest task, however, will be to fool his husband, but father has faith that you can do that, me not so much," she told her brother.

"Father has made sure that nobody, not even The Elders, will know that I am here. I am completely undetectable. I hope you did not doubt him. After all, he has not failed in his plan yet. And you do not have to remind me what I must do. Just remember your place, dear sister," he spat back.

Cali knelt and grudgingly touched Stephen's dead body. As he did, he changed his form. Within seconds he was standing in front of Cayla, looking identical to The Celestial she had just murdered.

"What about the wings? Do you have them?" she asked.

"I do," he replied as he unfurled them.

"Cali, they are not brilliant white, they have a light grey tinge to them, the colour is just slightly off. Let's hope they do not notice. Keep them hidden as much as you can," Cayla told him.

"I told you; nobody will tell that I am here, not even The Peacekeeper! It feels disgusting having wings at all. I will not be getting these out very often, that is for sure," he replied to her with a look of absolute disdain on his face.

"I do not blame you. The Celestials are abominations, the lot of them; flaunting their superior attitude every time they unfurl them. I hate them, but they will all pay for how they have treated us soon," she responded.

"Let's get rid of this body. We cannot risk it being found. We will not have long, but we need to hide it well," Cali told his sister.

Cayla nodded, and they both dragged the lifeless body of Stephen deeper into the woods. Abandoned and alone, covered in branches and leaves, they left him deep within the woodlands, his death not witnessed or mourned by anyone. He died alone.

Pleased with the ease that they had destroyed a Celestial, Cali and Cayla walked back into the gardens as the sun set in Elysium, both satisfied that their father's plan was well under way.

"I will follow you back to your room. You can point out where Stephen's room is on the way back. We cannot risk being found out just yet," Cali said.

Cayla agreed. They both knew most of Elysium well thanks to the maps and directions from The Fallen that had lived there before banishment. They did not know who lived in the individual rooms though.

The two of them walked back into the building, Cayla pointing out various rooms as they went along the corridor. She pointed out to him where Grace's room was, and then she showed him where Stephen and Marcus stayed. Cayla warned him about the dogs to prevent him from being taken by surprise. It did not impress Cali that he had to deal with them. He hated dogs, in fact, he hated animals of any kind.

As they got to the door of Cayla's room, two Celestials appeared ready to guard the door once Stephen had left.

Cayla rolled her eyes as she walked into her room. Her brother felt her disdain for them. He nodded at them both as he followed his sister into her room.

"I am a prisoner; I am guarded or with someone all the time. Thankfully, you are here now Cali, that at least enables us to get to places that we would not have been able to reach had it just been me here."

"Time for me to leave you. I am sure his husband will wonder where he is. They are a sickly and loving couple, I believe, not something I am going to enjoy acting out. See you tomorrow," Cali replied with an evil twinkle in his eye and a monstrous smirk on his face.

Cayla knew her brother would enjoy every moment. He took pleasure in tormenting others, and he would relish playing the part of Marcus's husband and everything that went with that. Marcus was a dead man, but not before Cali had some fun of his own with him.

Chapter forty-four

"Please have a seat Helen, are you sure you don't mind me asking you some questions?" Grace asked.

Helen sat down and assured Grace that she was happy to answer the questions she had. She told her she may not answer them all, but she would certainly try.

"Why was the decision made to not bring me here to Elysium when my mother killed herself? Why was I abandoned to the foster system on earth?"

"Grace, you were a pawn. If you had come here to grow up, you would have been in danger your whole life. You would have been a magnet for all The Fallen. Attacks would have been relentless here," Helen began, "but you have already been told that it was for your safety."

"I know that, but surely there was a better place to hide me than in a badly run foster system where the people who cared for me were only after the money paid to them. Wasn't there?" she asked.

"You had a wonderful family for some of that time. I know many of your homes were not ideal, but you felt love from some of them, didn't you?"

"One couple in my entire childhood seemed to care for me. Just one! I felt at home with them until they died, and then I moved around so much, and my only anchor was Charlie and his family. They became my family. Now, though, I know they were only there to watch me. I thought Charlie loved me, I thought they loved me, and it turns out it was just a job for them."

"Don't you ever think that Charlie did not love you? He adored you. Lying to you broke his heart, and his parents' too. You were a daughter in their eyes. Please do not let your anger take that away from you Grace, hold on to that love for your own sake," Helen replied, trying to reassure Grace.

"Helen, deceit has followed me my whole life. How am I supposed to trust anything that I feel or that I am told?"

Helen could feel the pain radiating from Grace. She felt so guilty that she had not been there for her as she had wanted to be.

"I understand, Grace. I would feel exactly like you do now, but please let us in, let us help you. Let me help you. I know that your mother would have wanted that. She would never have wanted you to feel so alone and unloved. She loved you so very much," Helen responded.

Grace did not know how to respond to Helen. She sat quietly for a little while, gathering her thoughts. Helen watched the young woman that she already loved and admired as she struggled with her feelings.

"Do you think that the other Celestials will accept Cayla? Will you be able to?"

"In time, and if she proves herself trustworthy, we will accept her here. Wounds are very raw now; it will take some of us a long while to get over what happened. I will be honest with you, Grace. I am having trouble knowing that there is a Fallen here, but she is your sister and eventually I will also accept that. You must be patient and try to understand our mistrust for now." Helen replied.

Grace nodded. She understood their feelings, but not the root cause; she had not been told the full extent of the history between The Fallen and The Celestials. Grace could, however, feel the same resentment and loathing she felt for The Celestials in the Underworld.

"I was told that there have been Divinexus before me, but that I was the only surviving one. Can you tell me what happened to those that came before?" Grace asked.

"That is painful for us all to remember Grace, I really do not want to go into details just yet, but when you are stronger and when this tension between us and The Fallen subsides, I promise you I will take you and show you where each of them perished. I will tell you their stories."

Grace was not happy with that; she was eager to know about the others, but what she garnered from Helen was that as far as The Celestials were concerned, she was the only surviving Divinexus.

"Will I die like they did?" Grace asked.

"Honestly Grace I can't answer that, but what I can say is that you have been alive longer than the others were, they were very young and so I have hope that you will not die in the same way that they did," Helen answered.

"Helen, will you tell me more about my mother?" she asked finally.

"Can we do that tomorrow? I will prepare some things that I have of hers, things that I can now pass onto you. Would you like that?"

Grace told Helen that she would, pleased that Helen had kept some of her mother's belongings and she was eager to see them.

"Shall we leave it there for today? I am sure you will want to spend a bit more time with Cayla. She will need your support as much as you need hers. You are both here in a very unfamiliar environment, and you both need to settle. I need to see Adred, too. He will want to know how things are going with you both."

As Helen stood up, Grace walked over to her and hugged her. She thanked her for her support before Helen turned to leave Grace alone in her room.

Cali opened the door to the room that Stephen shared with his husband. It was empty apart from the two dogs, who were asleep in beds by the window. They heard the door and jumped up and ran over to him. Just as they got to him, though, they stopped dead, both looking up at the man standing in front of them. Their tails dropped, and they turned away from him. Whimpering, they walked back to their beds and sat down, staring at Cali. Beau and Henry knew he was not their dad, they felt the difference. They snarled at him, but did not move from their beds.

"Shut the fuck up, you mangy animals!" he shouted at them, raising a fist. Both dogs cowered and then lay down in their beds. Not another sound came from them.

Cali looked around the room for clues about Stephen, things that would help him fool Marcus, but he could not find any personal items that could give him an advantage over The Peacekeeper. He sat down and waited for Marcus to come back to the room. He did not have to wait long.

Taken aback by the sight of The Peacekeeper, he was not expecting such a handsome man. Cali was ready to have some fun, and he knew he would relish in every moment. Marcus was oblivious that the man in his room was not his husband, and he did not know what was coming.

"I did not expect you to be waiting here for me. I thought you would still be with Cayla," he said.

"Oh, I gave her a tour of the gardens, but honestly, it is so hard to be around her. She makes me uncomfortable," Cali replied, not lying, as he hated his sister.

"I know, looking at her and reconciling what happened to you must be impossible to deal with. I am so proud that you are doing as Adred asked, even though it is hard for you."

Cali looked closely at Marcus. He saw the sweat glistening on his forehead and dark patches on his top.

"You are looking very handsome today. I do like the ragged look from your physical activity, Marcus."

"Really Stephen, you hate it when I am all sweaty, you always have! Has becoming a Celestial changed that?" he replied with a laugh.

Cali could not keep his eyes from The Peacekeeper. He had an aura about him he found mesmerising. Cali had not expected to feel anything for him. He was going to enjoy his time with Marcus, savouring every second before he satisfied his blood lust and killed him.

"Come here, let me show you how handsome I think you are,"

"No, let me shower first. I stink, and I know you do not like that."

Cali stepped forwards; he grabbed hold of Marcus's hand as he turned away from him. He pulled Marcus closer to him, clasping his hand, resolute in his actions. Cali did not let go. It took Marcus by surprise. Stephen was not usually so forceful, but he did not pull away and looked deep into Cali's eyes. He saw that something was different. Flames danced in them, a fire that he had not seen before, one that mesmerised him, one that he did not want to pull away from.

Cali aggressively kissed Marcus, passion rising in his body. He had not expected to feel a connection to The Peacekeeper, but he did, and his animal instincts took over. Marcus had not seen this side of his husband before, and his body responded to the passion. He ripped the clothes from him and removed his own. The room immediately filled with the sounds of their physicality, the air thick with their passion. For hours, they explored every inch of each other's bodies, overwhelmed by the intensity of the reactions. They revelled in them. Eventually, they both lay satisfied and exhausted on the bed.

Cali had not experienced that level of intensity before, his lust satisfied for the first time in his life. He resolved to repeat the experience a few times before he took the life of The Peacekeeper. Marcus slept soundly by his side, completely unaware that the man next to him was an imposter and that his husband was dead.

Chapter forty-five

Cayla was bored. She wanted to get out of the room and put into action more of the plan to destroy Elysium. Patience was not one of her virtues. She opened the door to the long corridor. The guards stood on either side of it. They had not moved since she got back.

"Can you please arrange for Grace to come and see me?" she asked one of them.

"I am sorry, neither of us may leave our post. There will be more guards here soon, but until then, we cannot do as you ask," one replied.

Cayla slammed the door shut, rattling the frame with the force. She stormed over to the window, determined to find a way out of the room. Cayla tried to open the large window that dominated the room, but the catch would not move. She could not even get some fresh air in, frustrated she sat on the edge of the bed. Unable to use any of her powers for fear of being discovered, she waited impatiently for Grace to come to see her. A couple of hours passed by, and she paced the floor.

Eventually, there was a knock on her door. She opened it to find Adred standing there. Cayla opened the door fully and invited him in.

"Hi Cayla, I just came to check that you have everything that you need, and to make sure that you are comfortable," he said.

"Yes, I am comfortable, and grateful that you have let me come here. I am not used to being caged, though, and unable to move around," she replied.

"Stephen has been with you for a while, has he not?" Adred asked.

"Yes, he took me on a tour of the grounds. The gardens are exceptionally beautiful, but what young woman wants to look at flowers all day? I want to help you and The Celestials with the problems my father is causing. I cannot do that trapped in here."

"You must be patient. We must get to know you, trust you, and then you can help us, hopefully," Adred replied.

Cayla looked at Adred, trying her best to hide her true feelings. She knew the plan needed to be actioned, and it seemed like the ideal opportunity to ask Adred for something.

"I can fight. I watched my father's men. Can I train with the Celestial Guards? What trouble could I get up to with them watching me as I train?" she asked. "Surely Orin would be okay with that, wouldn't he?"

"I understand how hard this must be for you, but you must also understand how difficult it is for us. Please give me a little time to think about your request and to discuss it with the others," Adred replied.

Cayla seethed with anger. She was not used to being told what to do by lower beings such as The Celestials. Trying her best to hide her frustration, she agreed to what Adred had said. He asked her if there was anything she needed; she told him that there was not. Adred excused himself and opened the door to leave. Standing in the opening was a surprised Grace, her hand raised as she was about to knock on the door. Adred and Grace exchanged warm smiles and nodded.

"Grace, I am so glad to see you. I am so bored!" she blurted out as they closed behind Adred.

"Stephen took you out for a tour, didn't he?" she asked.

Cayla told Grace exactly what she had told Adred. Flowers were not her thing; she did not mention going into the woods.

"I have asked Adred if I can train with the guards. Surely, I cannot cause an issue there?" she told Grace.

"Adred knows what is best. You know that there are many people who object to you being here. I would imagine that there may be guards amongst them," Grace told her. "If there are, then they could cause you harm if you are training with them. I do not want you getting hurt. Just be patient Cayla."

"I cannot just sit here all the time waiting for somebody to come and talk to me. Could you? I need to do something, Grace. Please, can you talk to Adred and see if you can sort something out for me?" she pleaded.

Cayla could see that she was getting her point across to Grace and with a few more tries, her sister agreed to talk to Adred for her. Everything was progressing as planned.

Grace spent a few hours talking to Cayla. They chatted about their childhoods, comparing notes, and consoling each other at the lack of love they felt as they were growing up. They seemed on the surface to have a lot in common.

"Tell me more about Charlie. Who was he and what was he like, Grace?" Cayla asked, guiding the conversation.

"Charlie was my best friend for as long as I can remember. I miss him so much," she replied sadly.

"We met at school, and the instant I set eyes on him, I knew we would be friends. He was my anchor whenever I had trouble at any of my foster homes; he dried my tears, he made me laugh, and I loved every bone in his body."

Grace continued to tell Cayla about him, telling stories of their life together. She avoided telling her what happened on the day that they were due to be married. The memories were still fresh; Grace was not ready to go into the details.

"I know he died, Grace. Our father took delight in telling us all the details of your wedding day. He said that Charlie perished in the fire at the church."

"How did he know?" Grace asked.

"Berran noticed you the moment the fire started. He felt your power, and it was not long before he knew everything that had happened. That was when he got you and kept you in his facility, away from everyone," Cayla told her.

"He was furious when he found out that Helen was a Celestial and that she helped you to escape. Berran has a huge bounty on her. He has told everyone that Helen is to be captured alive and taken to him. I know that he has an extremely specific punishment for her. I am not sure that she will survive him," Cayla continued. She knew exactly how her father would deal with the traitor. She relished in the idea of it.

Grace's blood ran cold. She knew very well what could happen to Helen. She had seen the results of Berran's evil in the cellar they kept her in.

"Charlie did not die in the fire, nor did his parents. They were Celestials and were here when I first arrived. The three of them were on earth to protect me. I was so angry at first that Charlie had lied to me, but I understand why. I just wish that I could talk to him more about it," Grace said sadly.

"Why can't you?" Cayla asked, even though she knew the answer.

"The Fallen killed him in the attack on Elysium. He died thinking that I was angry with him," she replied.

"I am sure that he knew you loved him Grace and would have forgiven and understood any anger you directed at him," Cayla said, trying to reassure her sister, but taking delight in her pain.

Grace nodded; sadness filling her face.

"You need to forgive yourself, Grace, otherwise you will never move on or be able to live the life that he would have wanted for you."

More time passed and Cayla gently wormed her way further into Grace's confidence, saying all the right things. By the time Grace was ready to leave her room, Cayla was certain that if her sister had any doubts about her, she had dispelled them.

"Thank you, I needed to talk, to get things straight in my head and I hope I helped you too?" Grace asked.

"I am so happy to have you as my sister Grace, I have never felt so wanted by anyone, you can count on me whenever you need a shoulder to cry on, or for anything else," she replied with a smile and a huge hug.

Cayla had done her job. Grace was well and truly sucked in. The two women said goodnight and Grace left Cayla alone.

Satisfied with her progress, Cayla waited for Cali to visit her. What she had achieved with Grace would please him. It was not long after her sister left when she heard a gentle tap on the door. Cali walked in without waiting for her to respond. As soon as he was in the safety of her room, Cali reverted to his own form.

From the self-satisfied look on her brother's face, Cayla could see that he had accomplished what he had set out to do. Just for a second, she felt sorry for Marcus, but it was fleeting. They had a job to do, and it did not matter who got hurt.

"How did you get on with Grace?" he asked.

"Grace trusts me, and I have spoken to Adred. I asked him if I could train with the Celestial Guards so that I can get close to Marcus. He is thinking about it. I am hopeful," Cayla replied.

"Now we wait, and I'll continue to have a bit of fun while we do," Cali said, revelling in the opportunity to repeat his earlier encounter with The Peacekeeper.

"Be careful. Do not let your mask slip, dear brother." Cayla was jealous that Cali was having fun. There was nobody in Elysium that she could use like he was using Marcus. For a moment, she thought about dragging a guard into her room, but one of them needed to stay focused on the task that their father had given them. Her own wants and needs would have to wait until she was back home, where she could have the pick of anyone.

She could wait, and it would be worth it.

Chapter forty-six

Days passed. Grace spent a great deal of time with Cayla, as well as learning as much about her mother as she could from Helen. The more she learnt about her life, the more she understood her mother's decision, though she wished it had been different. From time to time, she looked in the shadows, or at the edges of the woods, for a sighting of Eli. Each night she slept, she felt herself longing for him to appear in her dreams. He did not, and she woke each morning disappointed.

Cayla and Cali continued to play the roles required of them. Cali did not let his façade as Stephen drop for one moment. He spent time with Cayla as requested by Adred, using that time to fine tune the plans that their father had set them. Cali relished the evenings he spent with Marcus, continuing to fool him into believing that he was his husband. He took advantage of every moment that he spent with The Peacekeeper to satisfy his desires. Marcus did not disappoint. Cayla waited impatiently for Adred to decide on whether she could train with the guards. She became more frustrated by the day. The plan needed to move along. Berran was waiting for them to get everything in place.

After days of waiting, Adred requested Cayla joined him in the great hall. Accompanied by two of the Celestial Guards, she was soon standing in front of him. Helen was also in the room when she arrived. Grace, Marcus, Orin, and Stephen walked in moments later.

"Thank you for coming Cayla, I have been in contact with The Elders. They have agreed that you can do some limited training with Marcus and Orin," Adred told her.

"Thank you, thank you, thank you so much," Cayla gushed a little too eagerly. She caught her brother's eye, who scolded her without saying a word.

"There will be many rules in place until you have gained our trust. Orin will go through those with you."

"Can we start today? I am so bored and need to exercise," she asked.

"Okay, I do not see why not. Orin, will that be okay with you?" Adred asked.

"I suppose I can fit a little time in today when Marcus is training with me," he reluctantly replied.

Orin was deeply against letting Cayla near anyone else in Elysium, let alone agreeing to train her in combat. To him, that felt like they were inviting a fox into the henhouse.

"We will train in here. The weapons room where we usually meet is off limits to you," Orin told her.

"I understand Orin, I will not let you down or betray your trust."

Orin was not alone in his distrust of Cayla, all but Grace argued against the opportunity that she was being given, though it surprised him to find that Stephen had thawed his attitude to her and that he had spoken on her behalf when Adred had asked them all for their opinions.

"Can we begin now?" Cayla asked.

"Marcus, are you ready for some hand-to-hand combat training?" asked Orin.

Marcus told him he was. He was not a fan of hand-to-hand combat, but he needed the practice. He assumed Cayla would be an easier opponent than The Celestial Guards.

The others left the three of them alone in the great hall to begin their training.

"Have you done any combat before Cayla?" Orin asked once the room was empty.

"Nothing formal, just fighting with my idiot half-brother as we were growing up. He was a bully, and I had to defend myself," Cayla replied.

"Marcus has done police training, which contained some basic combat skills, but in my experience, they are not up to what we need to protect ourselves from The Fallen," he explained.

Marcus shifted uncomfortably on the spot; he did not need Orin to point out his failings. Orin told them to stand face to face and explained that they would start with a basic game.

"You will both take it in turns to hit the other across the face with a gentle slap. The other will try to deflect it, the one with most strikes wins. Now let's begin, shall we?" Orin said.

Standing across from Marcus, Cayla took a deep breath, it could be an easy exercise for her, she had trained with The Fallen, but she had to make out that she had not, so her first attempt to hit Marcus was weak and he easily deflected her. Marcus's first attempt landed directly on her cheek, harder than she expected, and at once, a red welt appeared where he had made contact. Anger spread across her face. She retaliated with a fist instead of a gentle slap, and as she made contact, it shocked Marcus. The force pushed him backwards, causing him to fall to the floor. Cayla smiled as she waited for him to get back up.

As soon as he was back in front of her, Marcus retaliated in kind. A fist hit her on the cheek, but Cayla was expecting it and did not move. As the game went on, the punches became harder and harder, both directing their anger at the other. Orin did not step in. He watched as they battered each other. Bruises formed on Marcus's face, but Cayla's face showed no marks at all. Being a Fallen had its advantages. Humans were weak and Cayla took great delight when a new bruise popped up on Marcus. She enjoyed every moment. Marcus's anger built to a crescendo. He was going to inflict some pain no matter how long it took.

Realising that things were getting out of hand; Orin stepped in and stopped the game. He nodded at them both and then announced that Marcus had landed the most contact. Cayla could not believe what he said. She knew she was the better fighter out of them both, but she swallowed her anger and stayed silent.

"A good start today, Cayla; Marcus, that is a definite improvement. Keep it up," said Orin. "Tomorrow we will start on some more physical exercises. Make sure you are both ready."

Cayla smiled at Marcus, her eyes antagonising him, provoking him even. They had their own war brewing and neither of them was going to back down.

"I look forward to tomorrow, Marcus. Bring your best with you," Cayla laughed as she left. Marcus saw two guards waiting outside the hall to go with her back to her room. Stephen was also there, waiting for him. Marcus tried to hide his face so that he did not see the bruises, but they were obvious. No amount of hiding would stop his husband from seeing what Cayla had done to him.

"You have never been a fighter, Marcus," Cali said as he took him by the hand and led him back to their room, slyly smiling as he did.

When they got to their room, Cali placed his hands on the bruises covering Marcus's face and healed them, his face was back to normal, with not a mark on it.

"How did you do that? You did not tell me you had the power to heal Stephen," a shocked Marcus asked.

"I didn't know that I could," Cali replied, trying to hide his slip up.

"I guess you are still learning all your powers. Thank you, my face feels much better. You may need you to do that for me more than once, judging by the strength that Cayla has," Marcus said sheepishly.

Cali was happy that Marcus had sustained injuries at Cayla's hands. He relished in being the one to repair the damage. He felt powerful watching The Peacekeeper doubt himself.

"Tomorrow is another day, Marcus. You will improve with more training," he said.

"I am perfect with The Sword of Berran. My sword skills shocked me. It feels so natural, but this does not. Maybe I can just fight with my sword and give this a miss. What do you think?"

"I am fairly sure that Orin will not see it that way. You need to do this Marcus, you have no choice," Cali answered.

"I need to sleep. I am exhausted. Getting punched takes it out of you. Do you mind?"

A disappointed Cali was not about to miss out on a night of fun with Marcus. He leant in and passionately kissed him, sparking the fire within Marcus, who could not resist his advances. Cali knew it would not be long before he would have to give up his passionate nights with Marcus and go back to his liaisons with random humans to satisfy himself. Not one previous encounter had come close to making him feel how Marcus had done.

Marcus fell asleep on the bed once Cali had fulfilled his passion. Quietly, he left him sleeping and walked out of the room, out of the building and into the woods, smirking as he went.

"How are things going in there?" a familiar voice asked.

"We will be ready soon. Cayla is now training with The Peacekeeper. She will be with him every day and we will have our opportunity soon, father," Cali replied.

"Good, I will wait, but do not make me wait for long. I want Grace back, and I have some things to discuss with Helen," Berran replied.

"I won't father, just a few more days should do it," he answered.

Berran stepped in front of Cali.

"Do not let me down, you know what the consequences will be if you do," he replied and then he vanished.

Cali took a moment, checking that nobody had seen his father and then he walked back into the building, and back to a sleeping Marcus. He gently stroked his head, causing Marcus to wake.

"Ready for a bit more fun, husband?" he teased.

Chapter forty-seven

Grace left Marcus and Cayla with Orin. She also excused herself from Helen and Adred. Overwhelmed by information and grief, she wanted to spend some time alone. She needed time to digest everything, some time to compose herself, and to work out what her life looked like. Now everything had changed. As she sat in her room, she stared out of the window towards the woods. She was looking, but she was not taking in the view in front of her. Deep in her own thoughts, Grace did not notice that darkness had fallen in Elysium. She did not see Stephen walking into the trees or see him leaving again a few minutes later.

Eventually, the present pulled her back, and she escaped the thoughts that were keeping her prisoner in her own head. Grace decided that it was time to bury her feelings of loss and abandonment and to live her own life her own way, no matter what that had in store for her. Her own misery had consumed Grace for her entire life, but she had a sister now, one that she was growing to love, and Helen was becoming more like a mother to her, and she was grateful for them both. It was time for a new chapter, and she was going to fully embrace it.

Like a caterpillar metamorphosing into a butterfly, Grace was changing. She was ready to accept that she was The Divinexus. A strength that she had never felt before flowed throughout her body. She did not know what was coming, but she was finally ready to find out.

"Grace, I can feel your acceptance," a voice appeared from nowhere.

Grace looked behind her. Eli was standing in the centre of the room smiling at her, a smile that lit up his chiselled handsome face. Her stomach somersaulted as he scrutinised her. The feelings that struck Grace shocked her, and she tried to bury them. Guilt would not let her embrace those feelings. Charlie was her love, and she was not ready to let anyone in or have anything more than friendship with another man, but her body was arguing with her mind. She blushed, Eli noticed the reddening of her cheeks and smiled again at her. He felt the connection with Grace from the first moment that he met her, but he would wait until she was ready. After all, they were immortal, and they had all the time in the world for love to grow.

"Grace, I felt the change in you, as did the others. Are you ready to join us?" he asked.

"Join you?" she questioned.

"Yes, come with me. Leave this senseless war behind you. Let them play out their silly little games," he responded.

"You think that leaving my father to destroy Humankind and The Celestials is something that I could do?"

"Why not? They know nothing of us. It is not our fight," Eli replied.

Grace was extremely angry with his attitude; how could he even suggest that she leave behind those that she was becoming close to?

"You attitude disappoints me. I hoped you would be more responsible than this. You better leave before I say or do something that you will regret," she snapped.

Eli disappeared without uttering another word. He left Grace flabbergasted, and she was soon pacing her room, angrily questioning her reactions. Eli was a self-centred and arrogant man. As far as she was concerned, he had no empathy for others, and she would never leave her family to go with him. The serenity that she had just embraced was in pieces on the floor. He had destroyed it and now she was angry once more and riddled with guilt. The feelings she had towards Eli made her feel like she was betraying Charlie.

Deciding that she would never speak to Eli again, Grace lay on her bed and soon drifted off to sleep. The night passed, and she was unaware of her surroundings.

Grace dreamt of her wedding day once more, walking down the aisle towards Charlie, but the aisle was getting longer and longer. Charlie was getting further and further away from her. Grace reached out to him, but he could not take her hand. Everything stopped. She stood looking at the man she loved, his eyes troubled but firm.

"Grace, you must let me go. I will always be in your heart, but you need to leave me there and not in your dreams. Goodbye my love," was the last thing that he would ever say to her.

Knowing that Charlie was right, Grace turned and walked out of the church, a warmth filling her heart. She would do as Charlie said. She would honour his wishes.

"Goodbye Charlie, I love you," she replied as she closed the large wooden church doors behind her.

Grace woke up. Her dream had confirmed her decision the night before. It was time to let things go, time to move on.

Grace's newfound acceptance meant that she was happier and more settled in the following days. Helen and Adred were relieved that she was settling in, assuming that Cayla was a big contributing factor in Grace's new attitude. Orin reported to Adred that Cayla was doing well in her combat training with Marcus. He relaxed a little with her, choosing to hope that she was not deceiving them all.

Both Orin and Helen were with Adred, discussing the progress being made by the new arrivals in Elysium.

"Adred, I am concerned about Marcus. He is becoming disillusioned in combat training. Cayla has a natural ability; honestly, I think she is holding back when sparring with him. Maybe it is time for him to concentrate solely on his sword skills," Orin said.

"I have been watching and agree with you. He is a born swordsman, but as you say, he is not natural in combat. See if one guard will train with Cayla instead of him," Adred replied.

"What about Cayla? Is it time for her to move on from combat training and try some weapons training?" Orin asked, hoping that Adred would say no, but he knew he had to ask the question.

"The Elders called me to speak to them. They have been watching her as well. She has been true to her word. She has done everything asked of her. Cayla can move onto weapons, but, and it is a big but, her weapons are not to be actual weapons. She is to use a wooden sword for now or a knife equivalent. Give her nothing that could inflict injury or death on anyone here," Adred replied.

"Do you agree with The Elders Adred?" Helen asked.

"It does not matter whether I agree. They have made their intentions clear, and I am not in the position to disagree with them. I have raised my concerns, and that is all I can do for now, Helen."

"Adred, I understand the reservations. I feel the same way. Wooden weaponry is a good idea and a way to mitigate any injuries. She can practice with a sword against the guards. We can move into the great hall. There is plenty of room, and she can learn some moves from Marcus."

"Before she starts Orin, you could arrange for a demonstration by the Celestial Guards and Marcus for the rest of us. I believe it would be good for everyone to see The Peacekeeper in action. He is very impressive with The Sword of Berran. I think that would reassure many," Adred suggested.

"Leave that with me. I will organise it for tomorrow. Will that be alright?"

"Perfect Orin, shall we say mid-afternoon in the great hall?"

Orin nodded and excused himself, leaving Adred with Helen in his room. He looked troubled, and Helen understood his reservations with Cayla. Although she had not put a foot wrong since her arrival in Elysium, Helen could not shake the feeling that there was an undercurrent working against them, and Cayla was who she felt it with.

"Helen, when Berran attacks, I want you out of the way. I want you to leave Elysium. We both know that he has a bounty on you. Cayla told us about it, and I cannot bear for you to be captured and tortured by him," Adred pleaded.

"I do not want to leave your side. You know that, Adred," she replied.

"You must. I am not giving you a choice on this. As soon as the demonstration is over tomorrow, you will leave here until it is safe for you to return."

"What about Grace? I cannot leave her alone; she has just accepted everything happening. I will not abandon her."

"She has Cayla, and I will look after her. You are my priority. You need to be safe. I will not lose you, Helen," he replied.

"Then let me take them both with me. Let me hide them while you deal with Berran. Adred please?"

Adred saw the emotion in Helen's eyes. His love for her clouded his judgement, and he soon agreed to her pleading.

"Okay, you can take Grace and Cayla, but you must keep your whereabouts a secret from us all. Nobody can know where you are going. I mean absolutely nobody, Helen."

Helen readily agreed. She knew where she and the others could go, a place that only she knew of. Helen was relieved to have Adred's agreement.

"You will not mention it to anyone. After the demonstration, you will take them both and leave," he told her.

Helen embraced him. It was a sacrifice for them both, but it was the right thing to do. Everyone in Elysium was in great danger. Getting Grace and Cayla away would take some of the reasons for that danger out of the equation. But Helen knew well that it would also mean that Berran would hunt them.

Chapter forty-eight

The great hall filled up with many Celestials eager to see how The Peacekeeper was progressing with his training. Rumours of his chosen weapon being the Sword of Berran had unsettled some of them. Feelings ran deep with many of those living in Elysium. Many needed reassurances that Marcus was a good man and that he would use the weapon wisely.

"There are a lot of Celestials here Orin, are you absolutely sure that I am ready to show them my abilities?" Marcus asked nervously.

"You are more than ready. We will start off with the guards showing off their skills and then you and I will step in and join them in the mock battle," Orin replied.

Stephen had joined them both. He squeezed Marcus's hand reassuringly and smiled at him. Something seemed off with him to Marcus, but he dismissed it as his own nerves playing tricks on his mind. He kissed Stephen, who left him and seated himself next to Cayla and Grace.

Once everyone sat down, the Celestial Guards put on an impressive display of physical combat, followed by their mock battle with their swords. The room echoed to the sounds of clattering metal, and the grunts of the guards giving everything they had. Orin nodded at Marcus when it was time for him to join in.

Marcus stepped forward into the middle of the room and raised the sword above his head for all to see. A collective gasp filled the hall. Not knowing whether it was a good sign, Marcus readied himself for his fight with Orin. The two men stood face to face with their swords raised, another nod and both lunged at each other and their swords clashed. The men danced around each other, and the battle had begun in earnest. Although it was a show battle between them both, it looked real to the audience, who gasped and clapped. For Marcus, the battle felt real. The strength in Orin's movements surprised him., he had expected him to go easy on him, but he was certainly not doing that. To begin, it took all his might to defend himself against Orin, but as he became increasingly confident and relaxed, he gained the upper hand, and his attacks were hitting the target. The demonstration lasted for about twenty minutes, and by the time it finished, Marcus was exhausted, but pleased with his performance, as was Adred. Finally, The Celestials had The Peacekeeper that they needed.

"Well done everyone!" Adred shouted as he made his way into the middle of the great hall.

The Celestial Guards, Orin, and Marcus all took a bow. Marcus was relieved and happy that it was over. He did not like to be the centre of attention at all.

The Celestials gathered around, congratulating Marcus on his performance. Many of them shook his hand, others told him they were more relaxed now that they had seen in him action, and Adred seemed pleased with the atmosphere in the hall.

Stephen and Cayla made their way over to Marcus, each of them smiling and clapping as they did. Marcus felt ten feet tall. His husband was proud, and that gave him a warm feeling, one like no other.

"Marcus, can I hold your sword, please? I would love to feel what it is like for you when you fight," Stephen asked.

"Yes, of course you can. Be careful, though it is extremely sharp," Marcus told him.

Stephen took the sword from Marcus and held it in both of his hands. He inspected the decoration on it and revelled in the feel. Marcus was not the keeper of the sword, that honour belonged to another.

"Can I have some quiet, please?" Stephen suddenly shouted.

Nobody was expecting it, and the room immediately became silent; all eyes were on Stephen with the sword in his hands. The symbols on the weapon lit up with a gentle glow, which was a surprise to everyone in the room. A wariness spread through the Celestials, and the imposter took a great deal of delight in that fact.

"Thank you everyone, firstly may I thank you all for coming, it will make our job so much easier now that you are all in one place," he began, "I sense you are a little confused by my statement though, am I right?"

Nobody replied. Each of The Celestials stood speechless, waiting for him to continue. Adred stepped forward.

"Do not move another step closer, Adred!" he bellowed, stopping Adred in his tracks.

"Well, let me explain for you. I am not who you think I am," he continued.

"What are you doing, Stephen?" Marcus questioned.

Without saying a word, Stephen moved closer to Marcus. As they stood face to face and their eyes locked together, the face of the man in front of Marcus changed. The eyes were different, the fire in them gone, the love in them gone. Hate and loathing filled the eyes, staring back at him. Marcus stepped back, suddenly able to see the man in front of him. A collective gasp filled the room.

"Who are you?" he asked. "Where is my husband?"

"I am Cali, son of Berran, twin of Grace and the man who has been entertaining myself with you for the past few days," he sneered. "Your husband, you ask? Well, he is rotting in the woodland, he was easy to kill. Just one stab with your knife, wasn't it, my dear sister?"

"Yes, just one simple stab to the heart and he fell," she sneered, "followed by the destruction of his soul. There is no way back for him this time, Marcus."

Marcus fell to his knees. For a second time, he had lost Stephen. Guilt filled his mind as he remembered the last few days, the joy he had taken from his evenings with him, only to find out that Cali had fooled him and that his husband was dead.

The entire room was in a state of shock. The guards sprang into action, drawing their swords, and quickly moved towards Cali. Cayla joined her brother, both basking in the thrill of having fooled everyone in Elysium.

"You have done well, my dear children!" a voice bellowed from the back of the room, stopping the guards in their tracks.

Everyone turned to see Berran standing tall. With a smug look on his face, he was triumphant. Seconds later, the room filled with more of The Fallen, a small group of them protecting him. Berran slowly walked to the centre of the room. The Celestials were in shock. The guards and Orin looked to Adred for guidance. He shook his head.

"What are you doing here again, Berran?" Adred asked.

"I am here for a few things, which will become clear soon Adred, but first things first, Cali, please pass me my sword?" he asked as he stopped by his son.

Cali did as Berran asked. He handed the Sword of Berran over to his father. The sword lit up even more than before. It glowed a light so bright that the room filled completely with a yellow glow. It was as if the sun had visited. He raised the sword above his head and the souls of The Celestials encased within set free. Instantly, The Fallen cut them to shreds so that not one of them survived.

"That is better. We cannot have them trying to control me or my sword, can we?" he laughed.

"Now for the first thing on my list," he said, "This should be quick."

Berran stepped forwards towards Marcus, he looked up at him, broken with tears falling down his face.

"What do you..." he began, but before he could finish his sentence, Berran moved, and in one smooth action removed The Peacekeeper's head. Marcus's body fell to the floor, his head landing just in front of Cayla, who was laughing maniacally.

Beau and Henry were sitting with one guard in the great hall. They ran over to Marcus's lifeless body, whimpering when he did not move. They nuzzled him and tried to wake him up. It was heart-breaking to watch. Grace stood up, sickened by what she had just seen, and she walked towards the defenceless animals, her wings unfurling as she went.

"Now!" Berran shouted.

The Fallen began a relentless attack on The Celestials, who had minimal weapons. Many of them fell and others put up a bit of a fight. They held off some of The Fallen, but the sheer number soon overwhelmed them. Confusion spread throughout the hall and in that confusion, one of The Fallen grabbed Helen and delivered her to Berran. Adred ran towards him, but Berran was ready. He lifted his sword. Adred could not stop, and moments later, his eyes were wide and lifeless, the sword buried deep in his torso. He died instantly; his soul destroyed by Cayla as it left his body. Helen screamed in pain, losing Adred too much for her to bear.

Grace got to the dogs, her wings wrapped around them, anger and sorrow rising through her body. A power spread through her, building in intensity. As the energy built, it erupted throughout the hall. Everyone thrown from where they stood, crashing into the walls, through the windows. Not one person escaped her wrath. The room was silent once more. The battle was over.

Grace stood up, the dogs by her side, scared and snuggling into her legs. As she took in the sight in front of her, Berran, Cali, Cayla, Helen, and most of The Fallen were nowhere to be seen, and everyone that remained was dead with no soul left to pass on. Death and destruction were all that she could see.

Grace froze, scanning the room for any sign of life. There was none. Adred and Orin's lifeless bodies were amongst the dead. She cried at the loss of her uncle and the guard that had given her some hope. Eventually, she walked through the room and the bodies strewn on the floor. Frantically, she searched for Helen, but she was gone. Grace knew that Berran must have Helen, and she could only imagine what torture she would endure. Betrayed again, this time by her sister, Grace fell to her knees and a mournful and heart-breaking sound erupted from her; her body wracked with sobs. The dogs whimpered by her side.

"Grace, I am here," a familiar voice said, breaking into her grief.

As she looked around, her face stained with tears; she saw Eli. He nodded at her and then knelt beside one body on the floor. Eli put his hand gently on Orin's head.

"Goodbye, father. I am sorry." He said and then turned back to Grace.

"Orin is you father?" she asked.

"It is time to go. There is nothing left for you here. Let us protect you now," he said, ignoring her question.

Grace nodded; she did not have the strength to ask questions or to argue with him. Eli stepped forward, his enormous black wings encircled both her and the two dogs. Grace managed one last look before they left. Elysium was now an empty tomb filled with the soulless bodies of all that had once lived there. The Celestials were no more.

About the author

First, a thank you to you, the reader of this story. I appreciate your support.

So, a bit about me, where do I start? It is so hard to write about myself, writing stories is much easier. My day job is in finance. I have done that for a long time; I have enjoyed my career, but these days writing has become my passion. I lose myself in it quickly when I am at my computer creating wonderful adventures or telling a poignant story.

I am a mother of two, and I have two grandchildren. I started writing because I wanted to create something that my grandchildren could read and lose themselves in, just like I did when I started reading as a young child. My own children experienced that feeling when they began reading Harry Potter by JK Rowling. As a family, we read those books together, chatting eagerly about the plots and what was happening to Harry and his friends. I have written a five-book series called Lottie Jones and the Magical Realms, under the author's name, H S Matthews, which is for the teen/young adult audience. It is a fantasy fiction series full of magic, mythical creatures and, of course, Dragons!

I have also written and released two short stories, and now this supernatural dark fantasy novel. The Divinexus is the first in the trilogy and I have started on the second book. After all, adults need fantasy novels too.

I live in the south of England with my husband and our two gorgeous dogs, Beau and Henry. We love to go walking in the countryside for long walks with our boys, come rain or shine we will be out!

I have two slightly different author names to keep the adult books separate from those aimed at a younger audience.

I hope you enjoyed this book and follow Grace's story in the following books. Thank you.

Hallie Matthews xx

Other Books Available

<u>Books by H S Matthews</u>

Lottie Jones and the Magical Realms: Dragoron

Lottie Jones and the Magical Realms: Veridian

Lottie Jones and the Magical Realms: Calithia

Lottie Jones and the Magical Realms: Imperium

Alfred's Story–a prequel in the Lottie Jones series

Tea For Two–a short paranormal love story

<u>Books by Hallie Matthews</u>

The Crate–a short psychological horror story

www.ingramcontent.com/pod-product-compliance
Lightning Source LLC
Chambersburg PA
CBHW051131030726
47504CB00004B/810